Stepping Down

A Novel by Michelle Stimpson

Acknowledgments

Thank You, Jesus, for living in me and enabling me to write what You put on my heart. I hear You, God. I hear You.

Several people allowed me to run the outline for this book past then and, in turn, gave advice on the plot: Chris Howell, Dr. Denise Strickland, my great Aunt TC, Vanessa Miller, Re Richardson, Colleen White, Glenyss, Lynell Logan, and April Barker—thank you! Kudos to my writing group for the insights into being a pastor's wife and what it means to oversee a church: Lynne Gentry, Janice Olson, Keisha Bass, Ann Boyles, Lyndie Blevins, and whoever else showed up the few times I was able to make it while writing this book! Love you girls!

Thanks to my editor, Karen Rodgers, for your editorial eye. I'm *always* nervous when I get edits back...but you always throw in a lump of sugar to help the medicine go down!

Thank you sooooooo much to those of you who have been reading my work over the years. Can you believe it's been almost 10 years since my first novel came out??? I believe God uses my hands to bless you. Thank you for your support. I pray that this book will be a blessing to you as well.

To God be the glory!

For my B-Kay.
The last one in the nest.

Chapter 1

Pastor Mark Wayne Carter, III cast his drooping eyes on the clock ticking away on the wall directly across from his desk. Last year his wife, Sharla, had lowered the clock so that it stared at him while he was sitting in his gold-studded leather executive chair.

"I know you're busy doing the Lord's work, but it *would* be nice to see you home before the sun goes down sometimes," she had nagged as she pounded a nail into the wall. She positioned the clock in its new location, then put both hands on her hips. "If you can see the clock, you might actually keep track of how much time you're spending here in your office."

Mark didn't like to fight with her about his devotion to New Vision Church. The church was his life's purpose, the reason he'd walked away from his short, but well-paying career as an insurance salesman. This church had given him a sense of accomplishment he'd never experienced in all his months as top-producer at StateWay Insurance.

More than anything, Mark hoped that New Vision Church would be the reason Jesus said, "Well done, my good and faithful servant," to him one day.

Late Saturday nights came with the territory, which was one reason he hired a very young man as his assistant and semi-mentee. At 38-eight years old, Mark was no old goat, but he wasn't bright-eyed and bushy-tailed, either. He needed an assistant to knock on the door every hour or so and make sure Mark hadn't fallen asleep at the computer.

A recent graduate of Southern Bible School, Jonathan Lawrence had come with stellar references and an excellent transcript. Mark wasn't too crazy about seminary kids.

Jonathan seemed eager, though, and he had been faithful to his previous mentor. Mark didn't mind showing a young minister the ropes, so long as he learned quickly and knew how to keep his mouth shut. Jonathan would do, unless he proved otherwise.

11:45. Mark did the math in his head. It would take him at least another half-hour to finish the outline. An hour to fill it out with scriptures and examples. Ten minutes to get home. In bed by 1:45, to be up again by six and back at the church for first service at 8:00.

If only the Jenkins' house dedication hadn't taken so long and the visit to Mother Morris in the hospital had gone as planned, he wouldn't be in this predicament. *Lord, I'll do better*, Mark prayed silently as he logged into SermonDepot.com to browse for a ready-made message. Briefly, he thought about the problems he'd encountered this week at the church.

He couldn't wrap his mind around anything in particular. In a church of almost 1500 in attendance weekly, the issues varied. Blessings, sin, healing, financial prosperity. Any of those topics would do.

Mark refined his search by checking the "60-minute" and "adult audience" boxes to decrease the number of results. "Lord, show me which one," he offered briefly, though he wondered if God would actually advise him about this shortcut. His eyes landed on a generic title: Seven Steps to Success, taken from the parable of the sower in Matthew 13.

Mark clicked on his "Used Sermons" folder to make sure he hadn't already preached this message. Six years ago, when he and Sharla founded New Vision, he wouldn't have dreamed of downloading a sermon from the internet. As he realized the growing number of lectures he'd copied from the web, it was hard to imagine how he'd gotten to that point.

He took a cleansing breath and reminded himself that he wasn't alone. There were, according to the site's banner, thousands of paying subscribers—other pastors and preachers, presumably—who utilized the sermons. *God's word is consistent and true. It doesn't change. No need to reinvent the wheel every Sunday,* Mark rationalized as he checked the "use" box and printed the accompanying four-page document.

His laser printer hummed softly as a display of lights signaled the connection between laptop and printer.

A soft rapping at the door gave Mark a second wind. He hoisted his smile into place and sat up straight in his chair. "Enter."

Jonathan poked his head in the office. "Pastor, you okay in here?"

"Yes," Mark said. "Leave if you need to."

Jonathan shook his head, "Oh no, sir. I'm in no hurry. I was thinking…you fell asleep in here last Saturday night, so…"

Mark could only laugh at himself. "Thank you, Jonathan. I'm good. I hit the gym this week. Got more energy." Mark swiveled his chair around and grabbed the papers from the printer. "About to wrap it up."

"Okay." Jonathan ducked out of the room.

Aside from sore muscles, the workout had given Mark a little more energy. Maybe, if he kept the exercise going and cut back on the fast food, he might actually feel like a 38-eight-year-old is supposed to feel. At six foot two and two hundred-twenty pounds, he'd been able to maintain a healthy weight, thanks mostly to good genes. His father had given him that much, if nothing else.

Despite the appearance of health, though, Mark was well aware that his cholesterol and blood pressure levels were higher every year. Or in his case, two years—which is about how long it took for him to actually show up at one of the appointments Sharla made for him with their general practitioner. Mark much preferred to leave his health in the hands of the Lord.

Quickly, Mark threw his parallel Bible and the pages of the next day's sermon into the front compartment of his rolling attaché. The laptop and charger fit perfectly into the second section. He gathered the rest of the papers on his desk and the surrounding counters into one stack. He still needed to review the notes, but he could finish it at home. If he made it there before midnight, he might actually get to spend time with Sharla before she drifted off to sleep.

How long has it been?

Another tap on the door. "Enter." With his back turned to the door, Mark switched off his printer and locked the overhead cabinets containing confidential church information. He heard the door open slightly, then close. He pivoted, expecting to find Jonathan standing there.

But this was definitely not Jonathan. *All that's good and perfect comes from God.* And He knew what He was doing when He made *that* woman. A form-fitting red silk blouse defining her full rack. White linen skirt so tight it bunched up across her hips. Legs that must have run track in high school, maybe even college. And a pair of heels that added a good five inches to her height, accentuating her lower half even more.

8

It only took seconds for Mark to process her body. His eyes made it up to her face in enough time to hide his intrigue. Hopefully. Respectfully, he stood. "How can I help you?"

"Pastor, I really need to talk to you." She sat down in the chair across from him, blocking his view of the clock.

"Um…well, if you want to set up an appointment—"

"This will only take a minute," she pushed past Mark's safeguards.

He sat.

"A long time ago, I made a big mistake. And now I need to fix it."

Her perfume wrapped around Mark's face. Sweet, but not overpowering. The whole scene reminded him of those cartoons where a bull's eye rotates around and around, hypnotizing an unsuspecting character.

She crossed one leg over the other, revealing a good six inches up the side of her thigh. Bare, taut skin. "I just don't know what to do. I was hoping you could help me."

Mark was no stranger to women's advances. Another thing he'd inherited from Mark Wayne Carter, II was good looks. Deep brown skin, a head full of short but wavy hair, and a sharp goatee could pull a woman from a mile away. But the one thing Mark could say he'd done right in his marriage was to remain faithful to his wife throughout their sixteen years together. He wasn't going to blow it on some misguided member who'd managed to outwit his new assistant.

Mark stood again. He'd played around with this fire long enough. "My sister, if you have accepted Christ as your savior, old things are passed away. It's late. I'm going to

9

have to ask again that you speak with Jonathan on your way out. He can put you in touch with the counseling ministry."

His abrupt end to their conversation obviously caught her off guard. "Um, b-but," she stammered for words. "But *you're* my pastor. Isn't this what you're *supposed* to do?"

Mark ripped the top sheet from the pad of sticky-notes on his desk. "The word of God is your counselor. Psalm one nineteen and twenty-four." He scribbled the reference on the note and handed it to the woman.

She snatched it from his hand, a scowl on her face. Mark noticed that one of her fake eyelashes slipped out of place. He had to hold in his laughter. "Meditate on His word. Have a good night, my sister."

Mark walked her to his office door, then past Jonathan and out to the door of the entire suite. "God bless you."

The woman didn't have a chance to respond before the weighted door shut behind her. With after-hours security on the church's campus, Mark was sure she'd make it back to her car safely.

Mark turned sharply to face Jonathan, who sat at his desk with a bewildered look on his face. "Sir, I-I, she said she was a frequent guest of yours."

Mark's eyes turned to slits as he tried to decide if Jonathan was deranged or just deceived. Since the boy was still in his 90-day probationary period, Mark would give him the benefit of the doubt. "With the exception of First Lady Carter, I don't allow women into my office alone, especially not women dressed like *her*, without one of the female ministers present. Do we understand each other?"

"Yes, Pastor. I'm sorry. It's just that my last supervisor had, you know, guests. I-it won't happen again."

10

"Jonathan, I don't know what kind of pastors or preachers you worked with before me, but I'm not *that* man."

Chapter 2

Mark was careful to watch the rear and side view mirrors as the garage lowered behind his 8-year-old Cadillac Escalade. Though his ride didn't turn heads anymore, he still made it a habit to survey his surroundings in case somebody wanted to try him. Maybe he'd slack up a bit once they moved out of their quaint 2500-square-foot home and into the mini-mansion behind security gates Sharla had her heart set on. Until then, he would remain on high alert.

A side effect of being raised in one of the roughest areas of Houston was a keen awareness of his environment. "If you get caught slippin', it's your own fault," his father had taught him during one of their rare free-world visits.

Mark had tried to teach his own son, Amani, how to look out for danger, but being raised in a fairly safe, middle-class world had distanced Amani from the lessons of living in survival mode. The boy had grown up in a world where kids left their bicycles on porches outside at night and people actually turned in lost wallets to the police.

Much to Mark's dismay, Amani hadn't been in a fight in all his thirteen years. Mark had been in at least ten brawls by the time he was Amani's age. He'd won some and lost some. Gave and took black eyes and busted lips with the best of 'em. No matter, he'd walked away each time knowing he could throw down when pushed to the brink.

This comfortable lifestyle Mark provided for his family had come at a cost.

Mark took his key from the ignition, clutched his bag from the passenger's seat and made his way around Sharla's bright red Benz toward the doorway of the laundry room.

The scent of fabric softener greeted him upon entrance. He wanted to be glad about the pleasant odor, but he couldn't. Sharla didn't do the laundry. She'd hired some older, foreign woman to do their cleaning and washing. The woman, whoever she was, did an excellent job. But Mark had to wonder exactly what Sharla did all day that warranted paying someone else to take care of the home he'd provided for them.

Sharla didn't work. She hadn't homeschooled Amani since he started junior high school. She'd delegated most of her previously held duties as First Lady to other women at the church, claiming that she needed to concentrate on home. Somehow, "concentrating on home" got translated to finding someone else to clean the house.

But Mark knew better than to question Sharla. The house was her jurisdiction. So long as she stayed within the family budget, he'd keep his mouth shut unless he wanted to handle the laundry himself.

"I'm home," he announced, not really expecting a response. Just seemed like something men on TV did.

He hung his keys on one of the hooks magnetically attached to the stainless steel refrigerator. He took off his tie and hung it on a bar chair, pried his shoes off and left them under the kitchen table.

Sharla would fuss. What else was new?

Mark traipsed through the family room and up the staircase to his home office to drop off the materials he'd comb through later. Down the hallway, he noticed the blue glow of the big screen television coming from under the door to the media room. He opened the door and found Amani stretched across the sectional sofa.

"'Mani, go to your bed," Mark ordered softly, shaking his son's shoulder.

Amani gave a loud snort, scratched his head a few times, stretched, and then obeyed his father's directive. "Night, Dad."

"Night, man."

As Amani brushed past, Mark noticed that they were nearly the same height. Another six months of this growth spurt and the youngest person would also be the tallest person in the house.

Mark grabbed the remote control and switched off the TV as his son trudged away to his own bedroom.

Back downstairs in his own space, Mark was surprised to find Sharla still up. She was seated in their bathroom, fooling with her hair.

Well, the hair that somebody put on her head. Granted, her style was always on point, but Mark couldn't remember the last time he'd seen his wife's *real* hair.

"Hey, babe," he said.

"Mmm," she moaned. To be fair, she did have several hairpins in her mouth. Apparently, the current style required her to position her mane a certain way before lying down on the satin pillowcases she dared not sleep without.

Mark stood in the bathroom's entry admiring his wife. He loved to see her like this—no makeup, hair swept off her face, a T-shirt and loose shorts. Her skin had always been a pool of caramel beckoning him to dive in when he studied her for more than a few minutes. Though she had gained some weight over the years, a part of him actually liked the fact that there was more of her to love.

Watching her breasts jiggle as she struggled to shove the hairpins in place reminded Mark that he was indeed a lucky man.

"What?" Sharla piped up.

"I'm just looking at you."

"Why?"

"Because you're beautiful."

She smacked her full lips. "Not beautiful enough for you to come home before midnight, though."

Why does she always have to ruin a good thing? Mark stuffed both hands into his pockets. As a matter of habit, he checked his phone's screen to see if there were any new texts or email messages.

Sharla rolled her eyes and carried on with the business of securing her hair. "That's what I thought."

He decided to backtrack. "Sorry I'm so late getting home."

"I'm not surprised," she quipped.

Mark leaned his weary body against the doorframe, trying to decide whether or not he had enough energy left to wiggle through his wife's brick-hard attitude and find out what was really bugging her tonight.

He gave himself the benefit of the doubt; maybe her problem had nothing to do with him. Anyone in her family could have put her in a bad mood. Amani might have said something crazy, something he'd been doing a lot more lately.

For the record, he'd give her a chance to vent. "What's really going on, babe?"

She shook her head. "If you don't know by now, I can't help you."

15

He racked the last bits of his brain. Nothing out of the ordinary. "I'm too tired for guessing games tonight."

"And I'm too tired to repeat myself."

She wrapped a black mesh thing-a-ma-jig around the base of her head. Somehow, it kept its place.

Mark figured there must have been some kind of Velcro strip holding it in place. Sharla was right up there with the best of them when it came to keeping herself up. As he understood it, this was something the women in her First Wives' Fellowship taught her she needed to do.

Mark remembered now. "The church?"

"Bingo. Mark, when are you going to start *delegating* more?"

"I do," he barely answered. "I delegate what I can. But some responsibilities at New Vision can't be pawned off on other people."

"How about the responsibility of being a husband to your wife and a father to your son here at eight hundred Evanshire Street?"

"What do you want me to do, Sharla? Ignore my calling?"

She pouted, "I know you have to do God's will. But I also know that I did not sign up to be a pastor's wife. I married a businessman, not a preacher."

With that, Mark dismissed himself and made his way back upstairs to the office. They'd had this conversation too many times in the past few months for him to count, and it never ended with compromise. Eventually Sharla would take a look around and see that she had it pretty good. Once she came back to herself, she'd offer to make him a red velvet cake—a most welcomed apology. He would have to wait out her current tidal wave of attitude issues.

16

In the meanwhile, all Mark could do was pray that the Lord would mature his wife in Christ to the point where she could appreciate what God was doing with New Vision. He'd keep praying for her until then, because it wouldn't be fair for him to have to choose between his God and his wife.

Mark set aside what had just happened with Sharla in order to finish reviewing his canned sermon. But the tension resurfaced as soon as he turned off the light in his office and headed back downstairs again.

Part of him hoped Sharla was sleep already. At least she wouldn't be awake to give him the cold shoulder. He always found it much easier to drift off with the comforting idea that Sharla didn't realize he was in bed than to think she was ignoring him.

Mark showered and climbed into their King-sized sleigh bed for what might as well be considered a nap. A captivating glow from the pool's lighting system streamed in through the window.

When he and Sharla spent their first night in the house, they had both been so spellbound by the blue radiance, they'd stayed up nearly half the night in the hot tub section drinking virgin strawberry daiquiris and enjoying sensual pleasures.

Memories of how much they used to enjoy spending time with one another kept Mark from sleep. *Really, how long has it been?*

He listened closely for Sharla's breathing pattern. Shallow and fast. She was still awake.

Slowly, he slipped his left hand across her waist. Rubbed his foot against her leg. Waited for some reciprocity.

Since she didn't show any sign of resistance, Mark nudged his chin against her neck. Kissed her ear the way he knew she liked it.

"Mark, if you want to make love, why don't you just say it?" Sharla blared.

"Because I'm trying to *show* it." He nibbled on her ear.

Sharla shot up straight in bed. "What I want you to *show* me is that you care about me and our son. You didn't even *ask* about the conference with Amani's counselor yesterday."

Finally, Mark had a clue about his wife's extended attitude. "Did you tell me about it?"

"Yes. I sent you a text, since I didn't see you Thursday *at all*."

Mark vaguely remembered seeing Sharla's text flash across his screen, but all it said was, "call me." He hadn't seen the message until after the YoungLife fundraiser at the community center. By then it was almost ten o'clock and he was on his way home. Sharla was sleep when he got back, so he guessed it must not have been important enough for her to wait up. Maybe she'd figured out whatever was on her mind earlier.

"Amani's grades are ridiculous. Four C's, a B, and only one A. And I had to sit there and let her tell me all this *without* you," she stabbed at him with words.

How the heck did we go from almost making love to discussing report cards? "I didn't even know, Sharla. I'm sorry. But can we talk about this *later*?"

"Like you're going to actually be awake and ready to talk when you finish doin' your business? Yeah, right." She gave a sarcastic laugh.

"How is it *my* business? This is *our* business," Mark corrected her.

"You can't just spend all day at the church, come home after midnight, spend another hour in your study, and then expect me to roll over and play lovey-dovey with you," she snarled, her delicate face marred with anger.

With his heart rate still slightly elevated, Mark tried again. "Look, I'll talk to 'Mani tomorrow. But right now, baby"—he ventured to kiss her shoulder again—"it's about me and you."

Sharla balled a handful of covers into her fist and yanked the mass over her head as she resumed her face-down, off-limits stance in bed.

It took every ounce of godliness in Mark to keep from entertaining the irony of refusing advances from a stranger only to come home and face rejection from his wife.

Chapter 3

Sharla was angry with herself for losing sleep again over Mark. She knew the routine, knew her husband's grueling schedule and his level of dedication to the church. For all intents and purposes, New Vision was Mark's mistress.

"Amani, take a bite of turkey bacon at least," she said to her son.

"Mom, I already told you. I'm not hungry." He frowned.

There it was again—that look of defiance on her son's face that sent something through Sharla every time she saw it. Made her count backwards from ten. "Get up off your behind and eat this doggone bacon right now," she ordered him.

Amani sighed heavily as he drug himself from his spot on the couch in front of the television to the kitchen bar. He shoved an entire piece of bacon into his mouth, chewed a few times, then swallowed it probably nearly whole. "Happy now?"

"You wait until I see your father."

"Good luck with that," Amani smirked.

Sharla flew to his side, pointed her finger in his face and threatened, "Forget your daddy, you gon' make me slap you."

With a blank stare, Amani asked, "You're going to slap me because I'm not hungry?"

"No, I'm gonna *slap* you for talkin' *smart*," she clarified.

"You want me to talk *stupid*?" he fired back.

Sharla shoved Amani's ear with her palm. He caught himself on one of the kitchen table chairs and slid into the seat laughing, "Man, Mom, that was amazingly hilarious."

"Have you lost your mind? Who do you think you're talking to?" She towered over him, breathing heavily. In an instant, Sharla had a vision: She was choking Amani with every ounce of strength in her arms. She could visualize him clawing at her hands, struggling to breathe while her French-tipped fingernails pressed deeper into his flesh.

The image was so vivid, so surreal that she had to take a step away from her son. *This child is literally making me crazy.*

Sharla shook her head, forcing herself back to reality.

Though Amani held onto his smile for its sarcastic effect, Sharla could tell her son was confused by her actions.

"Let's go."

She rinsed the breakfast dishes and quickly threw them in the dishwasher. She drove to Amani's school on autopilot and then went straight to the church.

"Hi Jonathan, I'm here to see Pastor. Is he in with anybody?" she panted from her rush into the building.

"No, he's alone."

"Thank God," Sharla sighed as she knocked on Mark's door while simultaneously opening it. She stormed into Mark's study and plopped herself down in the guest chair.

Mark closed the manila folder full of papers he'd obviously been studying. He tilted his forehead slightly and asked, "To what do I owe the pleasure of this visit?"

"I think I could have killed Amani today."

Mark's throaty laugh scraped up Sharla's right side and down her left. He rested his elbow on the desk, his chin in one hand. If she weren't so flustered, she might have appreciated her husband's buttery brown skin and perfectly straight, periodically whitened teeth.

"Sharla, he's a teenager."

"I know he's a teenager, Mark, but this is not about him. This is about *me*. I'm telling you that I nearly *lost* it today."

Again, the patronizing grin on her husband's face stood between them.

"Are you listening to me? Is *anybody in this family* listening to me?"

Once she raised her voice an octave, Mark seemed to be getting a clue. "Baby, I hear you. I'm just telling you that Amani is testing his independence, turning into a young man—"

"Well, he's a *young* man who won't make it to be an *old* man if he keeps this up. I don't understand what makes a teenage boy think he can talk to his Momma any kind of way—"

"Now, wait a minute. Being disrespectful is not part of the plan," Mark finally changed his tune.

"I'm glad you agree. You need to have a man-to-man with him, Mark. I'm serious. I sat there and actually thought through what it would feel like to choke our son."

By then, Mark had already flipped open his iPad case, entered the passcode, and swiped a few times. "I'm booked for the next couple of evenings. How about Thursday? Does 'Mani have track practice or an ROTC meeting?"

Sharla set both elbows on her knees and buried her face in her hands. "You're not listening to me. This is ridiculous. Saturday night you said you'd talk to him on Sunday."

"Yeah, but you know the elders' meeting went long after service. By the time I got home, 'Mani was already gone to...wherever you let him go most of the evening."

"What do you mean, wherever *I* let him go?" Sharla crossed her arms and leaned her body into one corner of the chair.

Mark shrugged. "If he's acting up, he has no business going anywhere. Like Saturday night. If his grades are as bad as you say they are, he shouldn't have been upstairs in the media room watching television. He needs consequences."

Never fails. "So this is my fault now, huh?"

Mark raised an eyebrow. "Stop putting words in my mouth."

Sharla slapped both hands on her thighs, a move she'd performed almost unconsciously since her high school cheerleading days. "I can see where this is going. I'm out."

She grabbed the handles of her Louis Vuitton bag and stood. In her most professional secretary's voice, she mocked, "Just, um, put your only child on your calendar whenever you get a chance, okay? In the meanwhile, I'll keep doing everything wrong, okay?"

Mark stepped around the desk, approaching her. "Sharla—"

Sharla held out both palms to stop him. "No, no. Don't get up, Pastor Carter. Sit back down and continue with whatever church or community business this is you've got going here, benefitting I don't know how many other little boys in Houston." She knew the act would soon be over because the tears were beating at the back of her eyes. "Carry on. Keep on servin' the Lawd, Pastor."

Mark followed Sharla all the way to the side exit asking her, calmly, to stop and come back to his office. But she wouldn't listen; couldn't listen without breaking down in front of him. She ignored his pleas, hopping into her car and driving away even as he stood at the door watching her leave.

The whole scene made her even angrier. He'd chase her only as far as he could go without walking outside of the church. He wouldn't leave his *true* home for her.

As she made a right onto the busy street, which was partially responsible for making their six-year-old church such a success, Sharla wondered if she was wrong for wanting her husband to put her and Amani before the church.

She'd been right by Mark's side when he founded New Vision in a vacated grocery story. No woman had been a happier helpmate than Sharla when this whole thing first started. She'd typed up church bulletins, helped clean up after services, called the visitors and personally invited them to return to New Vision.

Tears traveled down Sharla's cheeks as she made the short trip back home. When she thought of all the people who had given their lives to Christ at the church's altar, a sense of shame enveloped her. The church couldn't be a bad thing. *I'm being selfish.*

Maybe she was the bad one. After all, she'd just sat there and imagined strangling the life out of her own son. And then came another thought—one Sharla rarely entertained, but nonetheless one that surfaced whenever she second-guessed her parenting skills.

Maybe this is why God didn't bless me to give birth to a child.

Chapter 4

Rev. Jackson prompted, "Let the church say..."

"Aaaaaamen," the congregation answered, acknowledging the official benediction.

Mark wasn't too happy about the number of people who'd adjourned themselves early, walking out of the sanctuary during the final moments of service as the new members' names were announced. More and more, people seemed to be leaving when Mark walked away from the podium—especially the people in the balcony. They had their nerve, since they'd come late in the first place.

But he couldn't get too upset about their disrespectful behavior when his own son sat on the second row texting throughout most of the service. Amani knew better, and he should have been acting better after their talk the other night. Mark might need to add a little extra muscle to his next lecture. Though Amani was almost eye-to-eye, physically, Mark might have to resort to "laying hands" on Amani if he didn't respond to words.

"Pastor, you ready?" Jonathan asked, scooping up Mark's Bible and tablet from the stand next to the tallest chair in the pulpit.

"Yes. Let's go."

Swiftly, Jonathan led Mark around the east pathway and back into a smaller meeting room across from the church's small bookstore. This was where he met personally with the first-time visitors nearly every Sunday.

This "receiving room" as they called it, had been inexpensively yet classically decorated by Sharla, with a sparkling chandelier and beveled mirrors on one side that made the room appear twice its size. Silk flowers adorned each corner and the tables bearing fruit, and cookie trays sported festive tablecloths. Members of the hospitality committee served up the snacks with a double-dose of smiles, hoping to make a positive impression on the visitors.

Mark nodded at a few of the prospects from afar while Jonathan performed his weekly duty. "May I have your attention please?"

The room of roughly thirty adults and children quieted as the strangers found seats, holding food in one hand, plastic cups filled with punch in the other.

"The shepherd of this house, Pastor Mark Wayne Carter, III, would like to address you personally at this time."

Applause—first from the hospitality committee, then the visitors—followed suit. Mark raised his hand to stop them. Somehow he felt like he was supposed to stop them. "Thank you. Really, I should be applauding *you* for coming here today. It's always a blessing to see new faces at New Vision church."

Mark paused briefly as one face in particular caught his attention. It was *her*, wearing another tight shirt with her legs crossed and that same strip of skin on display. Truth be told, Mark really couldn't remember what she looked like from the neck up, but her body, the way she sat was unforgettable.

He forced his eyes to travel in another direction. "Here at New Vision, we have something for everyone. If you're into traditional ministries, we've got a choir, a lovely hospitality team." Mark extended an arm toward Miss April, the head of that ministry.

She gave a toothy smile and a humble bow, appearing almost giddy with the recognition.

Mark continued. "If you're the more contemporary type, we have ministries for artists, dancers, rappers; you name it we've got it. And if we *don't* have it, maybe you can start it. We believe God is calling everyone to service in these last days."

A soft "amen" trickled from the small crowd.

"So on behalf of my pastoral staff, my wife in her absence—she's serious about getting home and making sure that meat turns out just right, you know?"

The visitors laughed at his half-truth. Sharla was probably on her way home, but since she was in one of her moods, she certainly wasn't at home slaving over a stove in their kitchen. Mark hoped the Lord would charge that lie to his wife's account. If she'd been there, like a First Lady was supposed to be, he wouldn't have felt the need to make up stories about what might otherwise appear as his wife's lack of concern.

"And on behalf of the entire New Vision body, we welcome you with open arms and hope that you will be back again. I leave you in the hands of the membership team."

With that, Mark waved and left the room. Jonathan trailed slightly behind, but slipped ahead of Mark when he entered the pastor's suite so that he could unlock the door for them both.

"Pastor, the pastoral advisory meeting will convene in thirty minutes. Rev. Marshall has already printed the spreadsheets and placed them at your seat in the conference room."

"Great," Mark said.

"Can I get you anything? A bite to eat before we start?" Jonathan offered, following Mark into the inner office and laying the Pastor's belongings on his desk.

"Yeah. A two-piece from Popeye's. With fries and a Sprite, if you think you can make it back in time."

"I'm on it." Jonathan scurried out of the office.

That boy certainly was an eager beaver. For what, Mark wasn't quite sure. Maybe a shot at the podium? A chance to lead something? No matter, Jonathan would get nothing but high praise from Mark if he kept up this pace.

He was a good assistant. Not as good as Sharla had been, though. She used to ask him on Saturday nights what he wanted to eat Sunday, if he had a meeting planned. Then she'd pack the meal in his lunch bag. She used neat plastic containers and wrapped all necessary plastic ware in a napkin. She might throw in a piece of candy for dessert. Often, she would stick a little note inside: *I love you!* or *Got a surprise for you when you get home*. He'd almost gotten to the point where he looked forward to the notes more than the food.

Those were the good old days.

"Excuse me," a woman's voice called from the reception area.

"Yes?"

And there she was again, standing at his private doorway. Mark pieced it all together and realized that in his rush, Jonathan must have left the suite door unlocked.

Mark stood and walked toward her. He opened the door wider and ushered her right back toward the hallway where he knew a fair amount of after-church traffic would keep them both in plain sight.

Problem was, in his effort to keep this woman in front of him, he got a good look at her behind. Mark was just about ready to question the Lord as to why on earth He would give one woman *all that* to work with.

28

Granted, she wasn't the first beautiful woman to come on to him. But something about *this* woman, *this* time…Mark empathized with David, Solomon, Sampson and every other man of God in the Bible who had a weakness for women. He knew he didn't need to be within ten feet of her without a flock of witnesses.

He played with the change in his pockets. "How can I help you?"

She lowered her chin. "I was hoping we could meet alone."

"I thought you said you were already a member. Why were you in the visitors' receiving room?"

A grin slithered across her face. "I'm glad you noticed."

Mark wondered when the game had changed. When did women get so transparent about their intentions? Shouldn't she at least ask for him to touch and agree? Prayer for her chest area? Even if he were going to consider cheating on Sharla—which he was not—but if he *did*, he would cheat with somebody who had the decency to at least *act* decent.

"Sister, I don't know why you joined New Vision, *if* you joined New Vision, but this is a family church. I'm a family man, happily married to my wife of fifteen years, and—"

"Sixteen, Pastor," she cut him off. She waved the visitors' information brochure before his eyes. "You've been married *sixteen* years."

Mark coughed. *How could I have forgotten?* "Right. Anyway—"

"And your wife should have been here," she interrupted again.

"Don't tell me where my wife needs to be." Mark felt the heat rising in his face. "*You* need to be on the altar."

The woman dropped her face, laughing softly. She batted her eyelashes twice. "The truth hurts, but it *will* set you free, Pastor."

Mark fixed his lips for a rebuttal, but the woman turned and walked away, her hind quarters switching from side to side in perfect harmony with the stride of her long legs.

Mark tore his eyes away from the picture of temptation set before him and locked himself in his private sanctuary. He stepped to the side of his desk, swiveled the chair toward him and dropped to his knees in prayer.

"Lord, I need You. Your word says You always make a way out of temptation," he started. But he really wasn't tempted. Not *totally*. The problem was the situation more than anything. This woman's advances weighed heavily on top of Sharla's…fussing, resisting him in bed, nagging him about Amani, being off in her own world now that the church was up and running.

"God, I don't know what's going on, but You do. Show me. And help me. Amen."

Chapter 5

Rev. Jackson, who might have been a perfect mentor to Mark if he hadn't been so busy sneaking off to the boat to gamble on the first of every month, opened the meeting in prayer. Mark had done his best to surround himself with upstanding, older men of good character when he founded New Vision. Some of them had even come from Greater Fountain of Hope, where Mark had been spiritually fathered by that church's pastor, Dr. Kevin McMurray.

And yet, Mark had come to the realization that his pastoral staff, consisting of two older brethren and one younger, were still people. Each man had his struggles and problems. If not gambling, cursing. If not cursing, pride. Maybe a combination of all three, if the state lottery jackpot got to be over 50 million.

One good thing about his crew, though, was that they ran a tight ship with regard to church funds. Thanks to a sound system of checks and balances Mark set in place, New Vision had been nearly impeccable in handling its members' tithes and offerings. Though they weren't quite a megachurch, the membership was able to generously support four full-time (including Mark) and three part-time employees. These bi-monthly meetings were an integral part of sound fiscal management.

"Gentlemen, Jonathan has prepared the reports for our review," Mark said as he slid a packet to each man seated at the cherry wood table.

Despite the ornate appearance of the room, Sharla had once again, worked her decorating skills to create a professional, welcoming atmosphere without breaking the church budget.

Mark took his place at the head of the table. He gave his leaders a moment to digest the information contained on the spreadsheets, which included the departmental budget requests for the upcoming quarter, the average contribution of each adult member, and the demographic trends in new membership, as Mark had requested.

"Why does it cost three hundred dollars to host a free writing conference for approximately thirty-five people?" Rev. Kit, the youth minister, voiced an objection.

"Honorarium of fifty dollars to the speakers. Boxed lunch for each person," Jonathan read from the proposal as everyone flipped to the detailed proposal.

Mark opened his calculator app. "That's almost six dollars a box. What time is the workshop?"

"Ten 'til two-thirty."

"That's four and half hours of instruction, less thirty minutes for lunch. Ask them to schedule the workshop for 9 a.m. to 1 p.m. Serve continental breakfast, axe the lunch. That'll cut the cost to almost half. People eat lunch every day. They're coming to a writing workshop to get information, not food."

"Yes, sir." Jonathan made a note, as did everyone else.

They found a few more places to trim costs—printing in black ink instead of color for the men's breakfast programs, seeking a counter-offer from a contractor for striping the parking lot. Individually, these cuts wouldn't make much difference. But taken altogether, these were kinds of small adjustments that added up to tens of thousands of dollars annually.

"Mark, have you given any more thought to what we discussed about the television broadcast?" Rev. Jackson, the only one who addressed the pastor by his first name, asked.

Mark tried his best to mask his annoyance at this topic. Going on television would be a dream come true. Ministering to thousands or even millions of souls weekly had a nice ring to it. But he wasn't sure the church's budget could support a broadcast for as long as it might take to build up a substantial and steady flow from the TV offerings. "No, Rev. Jackson, I haven't. I don't think we're ready for it yet."

Not to mention the amount of time it would take to get into a studio and record the before-and-after sermon commentary. Mondays were booked with volunteer meetings, Tuesday mornings he met with the interfaith ministers' alliance to discuss issues they all wanted to address in the community. Tuesday evenings he tried to get his sermon together for Wednesday night service.

Thursdays and Fridays were busy on campus with paperwork, putting out administrative fires—not to mention funerals and wedding rehearsals. Nuptials on Saturdays, something with the youth every other weekend to keep those busy minds off the street.

His assistants, of course, helped—but everybody wanted *Pastor* there. And, quite frankly, Mark prided himself on being an in-touch shepherd. Even if Mark had *wanted* to do the broadcast now, God wasn't going to grant him more than twenty-four hours in a day.

"We could try a streaming broadcast. This younger generation is more likely to watch you on a tablet or a smartphone than a television station," Marshall suggested.

"This younger generation ain't come into no money yet," Rev. Kit shot down the compromise. "New Vision—and I mean *you*, Mark—needs to be on TV, that's all there is to it. Look at our numbers. Look at the demographics." He demonstrated an inch with his thumb and forefinger. "We're this close to becoming a megachurch. A broadcast could take us over the top."

"Or it could drag us under," Mark said.

"Since when have you ever backed down from a challenge? It's all on you," Rev. Kit instigated, bearing a smile that whispered: *I dare you.*

The competitive geyser began bubbling in Mark's stomach. By God's grace, he knew better than to let it control his mind.

Marshall jumped on board. "We could start small. Local. And as viewership increases, go national. Global. Members would come pouring in from everywhere. Not to mention the online offerings from people we'll never meet." His eyes nearly glassed over. "I say we go for it."

Mark surveyed the expressions staring back at him. He hoped that his leaders had New Vision's ministry at heart, but it was hard to know. Every man at the table knew that the higher the bottom line, the more left over for salaries. Plus ministry. But mostly salaries were at the forefront of their thoughts, Mark figured.

And they had a right to be concerned. Rev. Kit mentioned his finicky pension recently. Though Rev. Jackson was only part-time and wasn't supposed to earn more than $1200 a month because of his social security income, he wasn't at his max yet. Marshall and Jonathan, both having no seniority, were low on the pay scale, too, but could look forward to frequent raises as the church grew and their ranks rose with it. Eventually, each of them would be a chief with devoted followers under them.

"Let's take another look at the projections," Mark avoided a direct answer. "How long until we have two thousand regular members?"

Jonathan grabbed a pencil and sketched a line extending the graph he'd already formulated. "Nine months. Maybe a year."

"Okay," Mark shrugged. "Our growth has been slow and steady all this time. Why fix what ain't broken?"

"We could cut this lag time down to three months with a broadcast, I bet," Rev. Maxwell said, slapping one hand on the table.

"Slow your roll," Mark put an end to the momentum. "We don't make rash decisions. We never have."

"It's not rash, Pastor. We've had this talk. Everybody's in except you," Marshall let the cat out of the bag.

Mark leaned back in his chair and perched a finger over his lip. "Is that so?" One by one, their eyes averted Mark's, silently telling off on each another. "So *you all* have decided what direction New Vision needs to take."

Marshall backpedaled, "No, Pastor. We—"

"Look," Rev. Kit intervened, "I can only speak for myself. A few months ago, I got an offer from Fresh Start Community Church. I turned it down because I believe in New Vision. I believe this church is going somewhere. The people love you, Pastor."

"Aw, Kit, take your nose out the man's behind," Rev. Jackson groused. Then he pointed a finger and declared, "Mark, you'd be a fool not to take advantage of what God is doing here. Maybe it's so hard for you to see, considerin' as you don't *need* a pay raise like the rest of us."

And there it was for the third time in only a few months. Though Mark was the highest paid person on staff, he actually needed the church's money least. The residuals from his successful 15-year run in insurance sales before becoming a full-time pastor still had his family sitting quite nicely.

"Gentlemen, it's one thing to base a decision on dollars and cents when we're talking about printer ink. But this is different. We need to pray and seek God's counsel about exactly how He wants to grow this church," Mark preached.

Jonathan pushed his glasses up on his nose. He'd stopped taking notes and seemed more enthralled with Mark's message now than when he'd been standing at the podium only an hour before.

"God's been faithful to us for the past six years. I know He will continue leading us down the right road," Mark concluded.

Rev. Maxwell mumbled, "You can lead a horse to water, but you can't make him drink it."

Against his better judgment, Mark asked the reverend to explain himself.

"Don' you want it, Pastor?"

"Want what?"

"Think about it. T.D. Jakes, Creflo Dollar, Joel Osteen—those men are no better than you. They probably didn't even get as far as you have in six years. Why are you slowing down the progress of God's work in this church?"

Finally, Rev. Maxwell had asked a question that needed to be answered.

Problem was, Mark didn't have a good one that wouldn't come across as selfish or lazy. If he said, "I don't want to," the men would think he didn't care about their well-being. If he said, "I don't have time to," they'd help him open up a spreadsheet and analyze his time management.

He settled on a reply that they couldn't argue with—at least not for a while. "I hear your concerns. But I don't feel led to go down that road at this time."

Rev. Kit bristled. "Then what road *are* you taking to ensure the prosperity of this church *and* the people who've helped you build it?"

Mark was tempted to tell Kit to hit the road if he felt like he could do better at another church. Nobody was holding a gun to Kit's head, making him stay at New Vision.

And yet, the man had asked another fair question.

Suddenly, Mark realized the reason he didn't know the answer to where this church was going was because, in truth, he'd been so busy with ministry that he hadn't talked to the Head much lately.

Mark's only answer came as a request. "I need your prayers so I can hear from Him."

Chapter 6

The knot in the pit of her stomach twisted as she heard Mark's car docking in the garage. These meetings with the ministers and auxiliary boards and volunteers and whoever else needed her husband's ear were ridiculous. Sure, Sharla had her share of appointments with the ministers' wives and the Mother's Board, but they hadn't taken over her life. Somehow, women knew to back down when another woman said, "My child has a fever."

Maybe it was because of slavery or World War II that women had figured out how to step in for one another. No matter, Mark needed to get with the twenty-first century and learn how to leave things undone at church instead of at home.

She whispered to the Lord, "Please help me not to go off on my husband tonight." It was Sunday, after all.

Well, if she couldn't put on a happy face for Mark, she could at least put on one for Amani. At the sound of shoes on the kitchen tile, Sharla twisted her body toward the entry. "Hey."

"Hey," Mark barely responded.

She could tell the meeting had not been completely pleasant by the wrinkles in his forehead. Then Sharla felt the wrinkles on her own face. "Where's Amani?"

"I don't know," Mark scowled. "You tell me."

"I thought he was with you," she enunciated harshly.

Mark's mouth crimped in annoyance. "When was the last time 'Mani stayed with me after service for a meeting?"

Sharla jumped off the couch, yelling, "You're right. I should have known better than to think my husband might actually be with my son," as she stomped toward their bedroom.

She called Amani's cell and breathed a sigh of relief when he answered the phone. "Where are you?"

"I'm coming in the front door right now."

She ended the call and dashed back to the front door as Amani waltzed through with a McDonald's bag in one hand and a drink in the other.

"Where have you been?"

"I went to Derek and Desmond's after service," he chirped.

Sharla looked upside his head. "Did you not think to tell either me or your father where you were going?"

Mark joined her in the makeshift interrogation space in the main foyer. "Son, we didn't know where you were."

"I texted you and told you where I was going," Amani said to his father.

"First of all, you don't *tell* me where you're going. You *ask*," Mark took the wheel.

Sharla's breath steadied. She was glad to know that she and her husband were on the same page, for once.

"Second, after you *ask*, you don't follow through with your proposal until I actually *acknowledge* you and give you *permission* to proceed. You got that, Jack?" Mark threatened.

Sharla added her two cents, "And I've told you about hanging at the twins' house. I know they're your friends, but that little sister of theirs isn't so little anymore. I'm not comfortable with you being over there unless I know their parents are home."

Amani took the last, loud slurp of his drink. "Sorry about that, folks." He walked toward the kitchen as though all was well.

Mark stood frozen, his face twitching. He hissed at Sharla, "Is he serious?"

Sharla smacked her lips once and tipped her head toward the kitchen area. *"That's* what I've been trying to tell you." She couldn't have planned a better setup to let Mark witness first-hand how disrespectful their son had become in recent months.

She watched proudly as her husband dropped both his preacher hat and his father hat and slipped straight into you-don't-know-who-you-messin'-with mode. Some might have called it thug-mode or even street-mode, thanks to Mark's background. Whatever, Sharla didn't care. If it put the fear of God—or at least the fear of his parents—back into Amani, she would gladly be Mark's sidekick.

Together they approached their son, who was calmly chowing down on a burger at the table. Mark removed the burger and the fries from the table and handed them off to Sharla, who set them on the island. Mark grabbed one leg of Amani's chair and forced the boy to face the seat Mark took right next to him.

Though Amani was still trying to play it cool, Sharla could tell that the jerking motion had rattled her son.

"Dad, you know this is just like when Jesus got lost and his parents didn't know where he was for, like three days," Amani reasoned in his most intellectual tone, wearing a nervous grin.

"Be quiet," Mark ordered.

Amani gulped.

Sharla crossed her arms and stood behind her husband. She stood perfectly still, but inside she was dancing. She had to give credit where it was due; Mark looked darn good sitting there getting ready to go in on their son. This whole scene was straight sexy.

How long has it been?

Mark leaned forward and locked his eyes on Amani's. "I don't know what's gotten into you. I don't know why you've been talking back to your mom. And I don't know what's made you think you can talk to me like I'm one of your friends. But you betta get yourself together *real* quick and remember who you are and what kind of parents you're dealin' with 'cause if we have to have this discussion again, it won't be this nice and neat."

Sharla resisted the urge to add, "Yeah!" after every sentence.

Amani's gaze darted to his mother. She kept her poker face intact.

Amani dropped his head and grumbled, "Yes, sir."

"A little louder," Mark commanded.

"Yes, sir," Amani spoke clearly. "Can I leave now? I'm not hungry anymore."

Mark dismissed him with a nod.

In one motion, Amani scooted his chair back, tore away from the table and took off for the front door. "I'm gonna walk around the block, okay?"

"A quick walk," Mark permitted.

"What the heck is that supposed to mean?"

Amani slipped away.

"Mark, go get him," Sharla could barely murmur. Felt like her throat had cinched closed.

41

Mark laced his fingers and hung his hands between his knees. "No. Give him his space. He's got a lot going on inside. He's been telling us he wants to meet his birth family, Sharla. Looks like it's all coming to a head."

"Okay, we can put the whole birth family issue aside right now. You can't just leave him on the streets," she feared aloud.

"Yes, we can let him walk down the streets of the Honey Ridge subdivision alone, Sharla. Nothing's gonna happen to him. He needs some time to think. They warned us about this, remember, when we attended those adoption classes."

Yes, she remembered. Yet, she'd filed those cautionary speeches and case studies in the "It won't happen to me" category. Hadn't God punished her enough already by making it impossible for her to give birth?

"He needs counseling," Sharla snapped to a solution. "We *all* do."

"In the infamous words of Sweet Brown, Ain't nobody got time for that," Mark declined.

It was Sharla's turn to wonder if Mark was serious. She caught the hint of humor on his face as he stood. "You think this is funny?"

"Babe, I'm just trying to lighten the mood." He placed both hands on her shoulders and gently massaged the knots forming in her muscles.

As much as her body wanted to give in to Mark's comfort, she couldn't shake the idea of her son walking around aimlessly, even if it was only four in the afternoon. What if the cops stopped him? What if a delusional neighbor thought Amani was trying to break in somebody's house, like Trayvon Martin?

She grabbed her purse and keys. "You coming with me?"

"No. I already told you he needs to blow off steam. He's probably going to walk to the park and pick up the next basketball game. He'll be back."

"Whatever. He's hurting and he needs someone. Since we obviously can't depend on you, I'll have to do it myself."

Chapter 7

His first real opportunity to seclude himself and get in God's face didn't come until Wednesday. For one thing, his attitude was bad until Tuesday night, when Sharla finally gave in to his sexual advances, probably out of a purely primal urge. Mark had gotten so desperate he simply took it however she would give it, but quickies weren't his preference.

Sex was definitely on the list of things Mark wanted to put on the prayer list in this quiet hour. Along with Amani. And New Vision. And Sharla, period. Not to mention his message for Wednesday night service, which was only hours away.

Mark had made it a point to dress down that day. Denim, a Dallas Cowboys T-shirt and a Kangol 507 cap. He unlocked the suite, secured the door behind him, then entered the sanctum of his office.

Jonathan had taken the initiative to meet with a bereaved family on Mark's behalf as they made preparations to funeralize their loved one Friday. Not meeting with the member's family might lead to a nasty letter via email, but Mark couldn't run on "E" anymore. If he didn't get some time alone with the Lord, he wouldn't be any good to anybody, least of all the people who leaned on him in troubled times.

He'd planned to have words at the funeral, though, to make up for it.

Therein laid the first issue Mark wanted to bring before God—being there for all these people. Sixteen hundred adults and their families was a lot of people to shepherd, not counting the sporadic members. What would happen when they had 2,000? 4,000? 6,000? What if they grew faster than he could manage?

Mark kicked his feet up on the couch in classic psychiatrist's-chair position. He selected the "Worship" playlist on his phone and listened as Bishop Paul Morton, Smokie Norful, and Crystal Aikin filled the atmosphere with praise. The melodies seemed to push the sense of worry right out of the room as Mark meditated on the words of each song.

Next, he lowered his knees onto the floor and assumed a prayer posture before the Lord. After thanking God for Jesus and salvation, Mark's concerns rattled across his lips as though they'd been bottled up, waiting to expel themselves from his mouth. "God, I don't know what to do. The ministers want to move forward, but I don't think this is what You want. Sharla's acting like...well, you know. Amani's going through his teenage adopted child phase; I guess that's what they call it."

Following a good thirty minutes of talking to God as though one might talk to his best friend, Mark sat up on the brown, suede couch and took out a notepad and his Bible, waiting anxiously to receive guidance about his concerns. He also opened the Bible search app on his iPad to search for scriptures that might shed light on the things he'd mentioned.

Sitting with the Father in this special time reminded Mark of why he'd become a pastor in the first place. He loved God. Loved His Word and wanted to share the good news of Christ with people. And on that note, the divine lesson began.

Mark grabbed his tablet and scrolled back through the messages he'd preached over the last month. Though some had indeed been downloaded from the internet, he had to admit that even the sermons he'd managed to scrape up on his own were void of the essential Element of the gospel: Christ.

He'd preached on success, self-esteem, overcoming your haters, letting go of the past, and a number of other subjects people could have just as easily heard at a business seminar. But as he read Romans 10:17, he recognized a gap. He read the verse aloud again from the NIV. "Consequently, faith comes from hearing the message, and the message is heard through the word of Christ."

Where was Christ at New Vision—other than tacked on at the end of every sermon with the invitation, the call for new members, and the benediction?

"Forgive me, Lord," Mark uttered to the Master. Without a doubt, he knew what He'd preach that night, Sunday, and for however long the Lord wanted him to stay on Christ, he would.

Mark waited for another prompting from the Spirit about the other matters bothering him that morning. He prayed again. He worshipped again. He put his nose to the carpet and begged for guidance, but just as quickly as the Father had started class, He'd concluded it.

These were the kinds of lessons Mark disliked, the ones where God showed him one faith-required, blind step at a time what to do.

Mark sat back up in his chair. "God, why? Why won't you just tell me what I need to know? Isn't that what You said in Jeremiah thirty-three and three?"

In frustration, Mark turned to the verse. He would put God in remembrance of His word and, hopefully, force His hand to give an answer quickly. "Says right here, 'Call to me and I will answer you and tell you great and unsearchable things you do not know.'"

No sooner than he'd read the NIV, he got the urge to tap the verse into the tablet's Bible app and read it in the New King James version. The word "tell" was translated "show."

This complicated things, of course. A search of the original Hebrew said "shew" which had several meanings, one of which was "make known".

Mark didn't like the sound of "make known". He didn't want one of those long, drawn-out life lessons that could only be understood retrospectively. He didn't want a trial-filled testimony. All he wanted was some simple answers. Was that too much to ask? Step one, step two, step three, and BAM! It was done in Jesus's name.

All this "shewin'" was for the birds.

And yet Mark knew there was no other way. No other *perfect* way. It would either be God's will or Mark's made-up, bootleg plan which would fail miserably and lead him right back to God's will. He could do this the hard way or the easy way.

"I surrender, Lord."

Though Mark hadn't gotten exactly what he'd wanted from God, there was no mistaking the joy that had flooded his heart after submitting to whatever it was God had in mind. This joy, which the Word had promised to believers through Christ, was the subject of his message Wednesday night.

Typically the mid-week crowd was an older, more studious group. They came with Bibles in hand after long, hard days at work to press in for a refill through the praise team and to hear a message from Mark that would give them another boost for the last half of the week. Yet they sat there and stared back at him the way he might expect from the second service Sunday crowd.

It was no secret that at almost every church with more than one service on Sundays, the early crowd is the serious crowd. They're older, traditional, they're established so they have more money.

The second crowd came in still smelling like the clubs. If they hadn't been out all night dancing, then they'd been up all night with small children. This was a younger group with less to put in the collection plate, but they were much more forgiving toward program diversions and much freer with their praise.

Mark sometimes altered his sermons for this youthful crowd the way a good teacher differentiates her lessons to meet her students' learning styles. He couldn't go too deep too quickly with second service or he'd lose most of them.

But the Wednesday night group was a faithful mixture of people who presumably cracked open their Bibles more than once a week. Mark wasn't used to the blank stares facing him now. *Why would joy in Christ be such a hard concept for this bunch to grasp?*

Mark racked his brain for another verse to make the message come alive. "Let's turn to Romans chapter fifteen. Here Paul speaks of the joy that even the Gentiles have in Christ. This joy is not necessarily the kind of joy that makes you smile because you and I well know that a smile can be a cover-up."

He scanned the audience, finally landing on the small, practiced smile laced with impatience set on Sharla's face. Mark believed that God Himself had planned for him to speak those exact words as his eyes met Sharla's, because he

48

suddenly felt the depth of his wife's suffering deep within his own heart. Though he couldn't put his finger on the source of her pain, he felt it the same way Jesus must have felt when Mary wept at his feet because her beloved brother, Lazarus had died.

Something in his beloved Sharla had died, too. *How could I have been so blind?*

Disturbed by the revelation, Mark struggled to resume his train of thought. "Where were we?"

"Romans fifteen," they mumbled.

"Y'all give the Lord a hand praise," he stalled as the church responded obediently. He quickly scanned the chapter again, trying to find his place. *God, help me.*

"Amen, let's read verse thirteen," he decided. "'Now the God of hope fill you with all joy and peace in believing, that ye may abound in hope, through the power of the Holy Ghost.'"

They mumbled in agreement, as though these words alone weren't enough to rejoice about. The very idea of God filling His people with hope and joy and peace was completely amazing to Mark once he really started thinking about it. "Did you hear what I said, church?"

A few, "Amens," squeaked through the silence as roughly four hundred people sat waiting for him to say something extremely interesting.

He tried again. "Don't you see? Christ has given us *His* joy for our pain, *His* joy for our sufferings, *His* joy for our lives. He gave us all of Himself on the cross. So you see, we're not waiting for a blessing. Jesus *is* the greatest blessing we could ever receive."

"Make it plain," from a man to his left.

49

"Bring it home, Pastor," from a familiar voice behind him, Reverend Jackson.

Make it plain? Bring it home? The comments, which were probably meant to encourage him, actually ticked Mark off. If they didn't want to hear about Jesus, what *did* they want to hear?

Mark decided he'd conduct a little private experiment. He grabbed the microphone from its stand, which was Robert's cue to start backing him up on the organ. "You see, church, Jesus died on the cross to set us free."

"Mmmm hmmm," they agreed.

"Free from sin and shame," he continued.

"Yes."

"And now that we're free..."

Robert hit the keys once.

"We can be all that he called us to be."

A few people in the audience stood to their feet. "Preach, Pastor."

"I don't know what kind of problems you had. I don't know what your Daddy told you, what your Auntie prophesied over you, what kind of notes your teachers wrote in your little manila folder, but I'm here to tell you—you *are* somebody!"

Several of the deacons got up, crossing their arms and shaking their sanctified heads.

"I don't care if you rode the long bus or the short bus...if you had to walk to school with holes in your shoes 'cause there was no bus...it does not matter where you come from, what matters is where you're going!"

They were with him now! Clapping, standing, waving their hands and cheering him on.

"All you got to do is believe," Mark roared.

50

"Yes!"

"Believe!" he roared again.

They echoed, "Believe!"

"Believe that you can be anything you want to be! You can have anything you want to have! Nothing is too good for you!"

"Yes!"

"And what do we as saints of the Most High believe in?" Mark thrust the bulb of his microphone toward the crowd and then read as many lips as possible. Of the six or so he was able to see, none of them mouthed the same thing.

"I say what do we believe in?" He repeated the question and tried again to get a handle on their responses. This time, the word 'yourself' could be clearly heard.

Though Mark couldn't possibly have read everyone's lips or heard everyone's response, he was one hundred percent certain that none in the sampling of responses he *had* heard came near God or Christ.

"Sit down," Mark said, fanning a hand for them to take their seats.

Robert mistook this as a signal to rile them up on the organ again. He took off with a fast beat and led the church on a three-minute praise party. Out of respect for the fact that God is indeed worthy, Mark didn't stop them.

He stood there and watched as God supernaturally lifted the veil from the faces of some of the most dedicated members of New Vision. They jumped, they hollered, they yelled out—but for many, it wasn't praise. It was pain.

My God.

He'd seen that same scene play out hundreds, maybe thousands of times, but *that* time, Mark's eyes and ears perceived the massive uproar differently. The people were desperately waiting for a blessing, eagerly waiting to receive the carrot-on-a-stick breakthrough that would bring them the joy and peace he had just tried to convince them they already had in Christ. If only they believed.

In those moments, Mark realized that in obedience to preaching the gospel, God had *shewn* him New Vision in a new light. The question at that point was what God wanted Mark to do about it.

Chapter 8

Sharla used to enjoy the monthly First Ladies' Fellowship founded by Lady Candace Gibson of The Way Church. Candace freely welcomed every woman whose husband was in ministry— whether he was actually a pastor or not. When Mark had opened New Vision six years earlier, that group of women had been Sharla's life preserver.

Though Sharla was used to helping her husband with his insurance business, taking on the title of First Lady had been a hundred times more daunting, partly because Sharla didn't appreciate being thrown into a role she wouldn't have wished on her worst enemy. She had watched her own grandparents struggle with their church—taking in strays off the streets, living in the back of the sanctuary at times, pawning the church's drum set to pay bills, basically bending over backwards for the sake of the church and its ungrateful members.

Granted, Mark was no Grandpa Smiley. Grandpa was a musician-turned-minister who'd never really had a decent "gig" before becoming a pastor. In fact, he'd spent most of his 20s and 30s playing in juke joints and chasing after other women before the Lord changed him.

Mark was the polar opposite. He'd gone straight into multi-level marketing after finishing high school. Alongside successful mentors, he'd learned the art of networking and perfected his charismatic pitches, mastering techniques better than his peers who were sitting in university classrooms. He was a brilliant speaker, an even better salesman. He ran a tight ship and made good decisions based on the bottom line.

That was why, initially, Sharla put her own niggling

objections aside and wholeheartedly stood beside Mark with New Vision. She didn't believe he would turn out to be like her grandfather, selling his wife and his family short to tell people about Jesus. No, Sharla thought Mark would have better sense than to go "all in" with church. He should have been able to run the church like he ran his insurance franchise—keep a level head about things.

Sharla, at one point, had been glad to be a part of the First Ladies' Fellowship. The other pastors' wives in the group had walked Sharla through the unspoken, unwritten, often unrealistic expectations she would encounter in her role. Though they didn't agree on how a First Lady should dress or whether it was okay for a First Lady to read erotica, they always gave her food for thought and a safe place to air her feelings.

"So why am I dreading this meeting?" Sharla wondered aloud. She sandwiched her Benz between Jasmine Pritchett's Beamer and Candace's Lexus.

After growing up in poverty, Sharla knew she should be thankful that Mark's hard work had paid off. By the time Amani reached kindergarten age, her husband was making enough so that Sharla could quit her job as an office manager to homeschool their son. Even at that point, Mark's residuals combined with his pastor's salary had brought them to the point where they were pre-approved to finance her dream home. She had an appointment with the homebuilder coming up in just a few days.

Mark was a wonderful provider who also loved God. Most black woman—shoot, most women, *period*—would be shouting in her shoes. But for as good as her husband was, there was one thing he wasn't: home. Especially not since the church took off.

Sharla lifted the silver sandal straps in place over her Achilles heel and stepped out of the car. She repositioned her Ray Ban shades to serve as a headband, then pulled a swath of virgin Brazilian hair under the shades to produce a messy bang. She performed the classic lower-blouse-smoothing technique with a flattened hand almost unconsciously as she walked toward the door marked with the number twelve.

She wondered if, one day, New Vision would have twelve entrances. *God, I hope not.* All those entrances could just as easily serve as her exits, especially the way she felt that day. If the Lord had any kind of mercy on her, he'd leave New Vision where it was and send all those new people looking for a church home to other churches.

Upon entering the building, Sharla slapped her smile into place and made the first left into their meeting room.

"Hey, Sharla!" Candace welcomed her with open arms. As the woman of the house, Candace had said more than once that she made it her duty to stand at the door and greet every attendee of the First Ladies' Fellowship.

The two hugged quickly. Sharla then made herself a plate of fruit with yogurt dip and grabbed a bottled water. Before sitting she made her obligatory rounds, briefly embracing all ten of the women seated at five tables arranged in U-formation.

Sharla could remember how she'd once adored this space with its scraped walls, wood trim, and custom lighting. Even if the gold tablecloths and centerpieces hadn't been exquisite, the walls and stained concrete floors themselves could have been in a magazine.

Candace had been kind enough to "school" Sharla on how to make New Vision look like royalty, too, though

Sharla didn't have the same budget.

"You gotta start somewhere," Candace had told her as they scoured the outlets for church decor. "Don't despise the little things. God will honor your faithfulness."

After taking a chair next to Beverly Knight, who was the third wife of the pastor at the arguably stale Fresh Life Outreach, Sharla decided to get over herself long enough to enjoy fellowship with these women. Candace was a friend, and Beverly definitely needed a friend under her circumstances. The third wife of any man was going to need some serious help.

Prayer opened their official time together, followed by the reading of the agenda, which was always fairly loose. They discussed the upcoming Juneteenth celebration, for which Janice distributed flyers so that the women could take them back to their respective churches.

"The libraries are really hoping to see a greater turnout this year," Janice added. "They say that since President Obama took office, interest in events that celebrate African American culture has declined."

"Mmm," the room mumbled.

"I guess some folk think we done made it to the Promised Land," Beverly mocked. That comment, of course, led to a sidetrack conversation about the pros and cons of Obamacare.

Sharla wasn't one to debate politics, but she listened attentively and patiently as her peers aired their true feelings in a forum where what they said wouldn't be misconstrued, quoted out of context in a post on somebody's Facebook page, and eventually come back to reflect poorly on their husbands or their church. Here, it was understood that whatever they shared with each other was off-the-record.

Candace managed to get everyone back on the agenda by reminding them all that if they really wanted to have a say-so in politics, they needed to vote in every election. "And we should all remind our congregants the same. Can I get a witness?"

They all agreed with, "Amen".

Sharla sat in unusual silence as the meeting proceeded with a recap of the plans for a first annual combined Samaritan's Purse effort for Christmas.

"I hope you ladies are holding on to your shoeboxes," Candace cooed. "And by looking at all these fresh-off-the-runway sandals you ladies are wearing today, I know we will have plenty."

Novelette Hampton remarked, "The way I hear it, everybody who's not at Joel Osteen's church is here at The Way, so I know your congregation will have plenty to donate."

Candace pointed a perfectly manicured index finger at Novelette. "God is good."

"All the time," Novelette finished the phrase with a raised eyebrow.

Though the women might have been open and honest with each other, Sharla knew full well there was some...well, not exactly jealousy, but a sense of competitiveness that reared from time to time. This shoebox drive was going to bring out the former pageant contestant in Candace. Judging by the amount of effort she obviously put into The Way and the professed success of her personal training business, Candace liked to win. All the time.

Sharla's self-esteem demon crept up, causing her to wonder if maybe there was something wrong within. She should care about New Vision the way Candace cared about

Bishop Gipson and The Way after more than twenty years of service to their congregation. *Maybe I just need to get a life.* She had actually toyed with the idea of starting an event planning company or writing a book.

But how could she commit herself to something else when, basically, she was a single parent to Amani? She and Mark had taken the initiative to adopt him, to rescue him from the foster care system and a life of only God-knows-what with his birth parents. He didn't deserve to be abandoned again during the most crucial years of a young man's life.

Sharla's older sisters had both become pregnant during the hours of three and six p.m., the time between school's dismissal and parents returning home from work. Sharla wasn't about to leave her teenage son home alone to experiment with girls, drugs, and whatever else his hands could find to do. The world was too crazy. Sharla wasn't about to let herself be the mother of a child who was building bombs in his bedroom unbeknownst to his parents. She didn't "straighten up" his room regularly for nothing.

If only Mark could remove his super-hero cape long enough to drop down to the people who needed him most.

Now that the official agenda had concluded, the ladies were free to chat and catch up with one another.

"Oooh wee, Prophetess Alex Murphy just finished a revival at our church. I'm telling you, it was on fire," Beverly gushed.

"Where's she from?" Jasmine asked.

"I believe New Orleans," Beverly said.

"Nuh uh," from the youngest attendee, Ria De'Garmo. "I don't mess with people from New Orleans. They all got screws loose, if you ask me."

"Who dat talkin' 'bout N'awlins?" Candace, a native New Orleanean contested in her native dialect.

Ria's face fell. "You're from New Orleans, Candace?"

"Born and raised."

"Oop, let me shut up then."

"But my family is crazy," Candace confessed.

"Whose isn't?" Novelette agreed as she turned toward Beverly again. "So, did Miss Murphy prophesy or prophe-lie?"

Beverly nodded, "She brought the word the first night. But after she preached the second night, she walked through the aisles and called out a lot of stuff. She told our choir director he needed to go ahead and marry the woman he was already living with. Told one of the deacons to quit playing scratch-offs. After that, a lot of people didn't come back."

The nonchalant manner in which Beverly ended the narrative sent a ripple of laughter through the room.

"You are too funny," Jasmine wailed.

"What? I'm just telling you all the truth," Beverly shrugged.

The ladies continued to share church news – vacation Bible school plans, upcoming conferences and the like. Once the banter died down, Candace asked for prayer requests so they could close in conversation with God.

Jasmine asked for continued prayer for her mother, who had been diagnosed with pancreatic cancer. Beverly's brother, a diabetic, had suffered a foot injury and doctors said he would probably lose his foot if it didn't heal soon. Ria wanted them to bring one of her high school classmates before the Lord as she recovered from the aftermath of a serious car accident.

Novelette, who seemed to always make it her business to

get on the prayer list some kind of way, piped up, "My daughter. She's got an ear infection that won't go away. She's miserable and so is everyone else. I *had* to come here today or I would have run out the back door screaming."

Sharla smiled, remembering the days when Amani was a baby. With his chubby brown cheeks, that cute button nose, and those long eyelashes, she'd made sure he only wore blue so people wouldn't mistake him for a baby girl. Despite the small port wine stain under his left eye, Amani had been absolutely adorable. But Sharla was thankful that with time Amani's skin darkened, masking the birthmark almost completely.

"Hey!" Candace nearly yelled, causing Sharla to blink rapidly as she returned to the present. "Did you hear me?"

"I'm sorry. No. What did you say?" Sharla asked.

Candace laid her pen on the table. "What's going on with you, girl?"

"You've been too quiet today," Jasmine probed. "What gives?"

Sharla wondered if she wanted to take up the group's time with this old-news conversation. *No one wants to hear me whine.* Everybody in there had signed up to marry an ambitious man and should have known that his aspirations would equate to many-a-lonely night. Lonely days, too, if he was actually good at what he did. It came with the territory. *I need to put on my big girl panties and get over it.*

She should be thankful. There were more serious prayer requests on the table. Sharla gave a fake yawn which, thankfully, morphed into a real yawn half-way through. "I'm just tired, that's all." She was tired, alright. She hadn't told a complete lie, at least not in her head.

She might have escaped the other women's trouble-radar, but the look on Candace's face told Sharla she hadn't fooled the hostess.

"You know, we're all here for each other," Lady Gipson scratched the surface of Sharla's heart.

Instantly, tears threatened to ruin Sharla's façade. Those women cared about her and her husband's ministry. She had no reason to be ashamed—by that point, they'd all seen each other with mascara running down their faces.

Yet, something in her didn't *want* the women to help her. She wanted to savor her bad attitude, savor every drop like a blue coconut sno cone. Besides, they'd just pray and ask God to change things. From where Sharla stood, God was part of the problem. He probably wanted her to be humble, submissive, stop being selfish, put all her feelings aside and suck it up for the sake of the church.

"Yes, I'm okay. Thanks for asking."

Candace carried on with the prayer requests, though Sharla felt as though the older woman was keeping an eye on her.

She can keep one eye on me all she wants. Maybe Candace was part of the problem, too. People like her were the reason so many pastors' wives were held to such a ridiculous standard. *Always gotta look nice, come alongside your husband, be his helpmate.* All this straight 1960s mumbo jumbo and it was all because men were too sorry to figure out how to multi-task like women do every minute of the day.

Besides, who was going to help Sharla while she helped Mark? Did God think women didn't need help? Pulleaze! *No wonder we have so much heart disease.*

Sharla barely caught the "amen" at the end of the prayer.

She grabbed her purse and headed for the door, offering yet another lie about needing to get to an appointment.

She even pretended not to see Candace through the rearview mirror trying to flag Sharla down as she peeled out of the parking lot.

Right or wrong, Sharla was no longer content to play the "good wife" role when Mark obviously didn't care about *his* role at home.

Chapter 9

For the next few weeks, Mark focused on one thing at church—Jesus—and one thing at home: making Sharla happy by making more time for Amani.

The church had seen an increase in the number of people giving their lives to Christ at the end of each service, which gave Mark a renewed sense of commitment to New Vision.

On the home front, he and Amani texted each other more often than usual. They also spent a couple of hours playing video games together one of those Saturdays. Mark tried to get Amani to open up and talk a bit, but Amani seemed reticent, responding to every question with one-word answers. Mark decided to lay off. His son would open up if and when he felt like it. "I just want you to know that I'm here for you if you need me," Mark had assured Amani.

"Cool."

Mark had gone out of his way to make sure Sharla knew of his efforts with their son. He'd made a few comments about the video games, mentioned the few minor details Amani leaked through texts, and even printed the latest progress report from the school's parent online portal.

"Looks like he's doing better, Baby," Mark remarked casually on their way to visit Sharla's grandmother in the nursing home. Even their trip to visit Grandma Smiley, which he was only able to make because of a rained-out picnic, should have earned him brownie points.

"Mmmm," she barely acknowledged.

Mark exhaled loudly.

She looked up from her tablet and asked, "What are you breathing all hard for?"

"You wanted me to connect with him, right?"

"Yeah."

He spelled it out for her, "So the least you could do is say something good about it."

Her face soured. "What? You want a *cookie* for doing what you're *supposed* to do?"

Okay, that's it. He'd had enough of Sharla's *fonk* attitude to last him a lifetime. Every ounce of "Pastor" Carter slid out of Mark as he aired the thoughts he'd been holding back in hopes of avoiding a massive blow-up with his wife. But it was clear there was no way around it. No way to make her happy, no way to please her, period.

Mark made a quick swerve to the right and abruptly parked the car in the back corner of a grocery store. It was as good a place as any to have a come-to-Jesus meeting.

"Why are you stopping here?" Sharla demanded an answer as she slapped her tablet closed.

"What's wrong with you?" he asked. The words came out with less force than he'd imagined they would, definitely due to the fact that God had given him insight into his wife's pain.

"Nothing," she replied softly.

"Stop lying to me. You've been treating me like a dog for the past few months, trying to act like I'm not doing my job in our marriage, making me feel bad about my role as a father. You come to church with a bad attitude; you put on a fake smile while I'm preaching. I know something's wrong, but I can't help you fix it unless you tell me what it is."

He waited. The swish of the windshield wipers punched through the silence intermittently.

"You can't fix me, Mark," she finally snapped, pounding her thighs with her fists. "I'm a human being. I have emotions and feelings and needs. I'm not some kind of corporate branding experiment."

Bewildered, Mark sat with his mouth open. "What are you talking about?"

"This!" she threw her hands in the air. "We're so far apart, you have no earthly idea what I'm going through."

"No. I don't," he admitted. "You *said* you wanted me to spend more time with 'Mani, so I did."

"It's not just Amani," she revealed.

"What do you expect me to do? Read your mind?" Mark gasped in exasperation.

"Read my *heart*," she demanded.

"That's impossible," he stated.

"It didn't used to be. When we were dating, and before the church, you used to know when something was bothering me. You'd stop to see what it was. We'd take a weekend off, go somewhere and reconnect, make a plan to overcome. And I felt safe. But now..." her voice cracked with emotion.

A flood of anxiety rushed through Mark's veins as he realized his wife was about to start crying. Her lips quivered, her eyes watered, and her button nose flushed red. He'd been expecting a barrage of smart comments from his wife, but not *that*. Not *crying*.

"Baby," he tried to sooth her with words as well as a hug across the console.

"No." She gave him the hand.

"Sharla, honey, I'm only trying to help."

"Don't touch me right now," she wiped her nose, her dainty fingers shaking.

Mark sat in amazement, watching his wife try to compose herself while her body betrayed her attempts. The tears kept flowing, her hands kept trembling.

Suddenly, his mind flashed back to his Aunt Jackie, his mother's youngest sister. Aunt Jackie had been perfectly fine until Mark's cousin, Kendrick, drowned in the lake. Mark was too young to know what a "nervous breakdown" was, but he remembered the day before the mysterious occasion. Aunt Jackie had been sitting in their living room crying uncontrollably. Rocking herself back and forth. And he distinctly remembered her fingers shaking the way Sharla's shook now.

This is not the time for Sharla to be having a nervous breakdown, Mark thought, *not with the church on the verge of a huge paradigm shift, not when I've finally gotten back into the groove of hearing from God and walking in His direct guidance.*

Sharla's condition had to be the work of the enemy, Mark surmised. "Baby, let's pray."

"No! I don't want to pray!" she practically screamed. "I'm tired of you and all this pastor stuff. I want my husband—Mark Wayne Carter, III—back!"

Now he *knew* she had flown the coop. But Sharla's tears kept Mark from flying off with her. "Okay. We can go to counseling like you wanted."

She sniffed. Gave her eyes a sloppy wipe. "Thank you. I already have an appointment set for Amani Tuesday evening."

No! Not Tuesday night! Mark was scheduled for a live guest appearance with Joey Z, the metroplex's gospel radio station's praise-and-pray DJ. Rev. Marshall had schmoozed for months to get Mark on that show. The hope was that

Mark would become a regular commentator and bring in new members.

"What time did you set the appointment for?"

His voice must have hinted at his conflict.

"Why?" Sharla baited him.

"What time?" Mark repeated.

"Six-thirty."

The interview was from 5:30 – 6:30. "I'll do my best to make it."

"So…you might be there, you might not."

"Isn't it Amani's counseling session?"

"Yes, but it would be nice if we could both go to show support," she explained.

Mark didn't quite understand how sitting on a couch while someone was in another room being questioned was actually a show of support. "I'll be late," he said, "but I'll be there by the time he comes out of the room."

Sharla rolled her eyes. "Let's just get to the nursing home, please."

Chapter 10

A quick glance across the sanctuary gave Mark cause for question. There were definitely fewer people in attendance that week. Mentally, he ran through a list of possibilities, including the previous night's musical, where he had taken the liberty of sharing the good news about Christ and extending the invitation to meet Him, although he wasn't on program to do so. Mark was well aware that some people "counted" any event where a preacher spoke as their weekly visit with God. Once they met the quota, that was it—especially with this second service.

After the announcements scrolled across giant screens, the praise dancers rendered a routine that totally rubbed Mark the wrong way. The chorus of the music, "God, please don't turn away from me," was impossible. God had already promised in His word that He would never leave or forsake His people.

Several people in the audience stood, raising their hands toward heaven as they mimicked the dancers' begging gestures. *Have these people not been listening to a word I've preached for the past two Sundays?*

Maybe Sharla was right. Perhaps he should cut back on his efforts at the church. If they weren't going to listen to him, what was the point?

Or maybe he was expecting too much too soon. The fact was, he could only point the finger at himself for their misunderstanding. What was two weeks' worth of truth supposed to accomplish after years of politically correct social teaching on his watch, not to mention the preachers they might have had before him? No matter, he tapped a memo to himself to develop a sermon on entering God's rest through Christ, Hebrews chapter 4.

The choir's last song didn't help. Though it was a classic, Mark cringed at the first line.

"The race is not given to the swift nor to the strong," Valeria Newsome sang her heart out, "but to the one that endureth until the end."

Mark could remember when he used to quote those words, but last year he'd stopped when he found out the saying wasn't actually a scripture in the Bible. And he'd told the church about it, too, but obviously they'd decided it didn't matter. It sounded good, so they sang it anyway.

There again, Mark made a note, this one to be discussed with the elders: No more unbiblical songs.

But was he being too harsh? Legalistic? Was it the end of the world if the choir's songs and praise dancers' music was a little…off? Even more, how was he going to micromanage every single move the worship ministry made?

Not possible.

Finally, the song ended with yet another partial-verse-scramble and Mark took the pulpit. His message that day was almost the same as last Sunday's: Free from sin.

"If you have your Bibles with you, go ahead and turn to first John, chapter three."

While he knew that some congregants were busy swiping virtual pages, the familiar melody of thin pages flipping, flipping, flipping sent a pleasant ripple through Mark's soul. Breaking the bread of God's word with people filled him more than a six-course meal.

"I have to forewarn you," he started, "some of you may not like this sermon. It's what I like to call a mirror sermon."

"Ah hah," from Mother Herndon, sitting on the second pew. "Preach it anyway."

Her words made Mark laugh inside. He had been encouraged when Mother Herndon joined New Vision. She'd been a long-time Mother at Dr. McMurray's church but, according to her, the Lord wanted her to follow him and Sharla as they started their own ministry.

"You need the old and the young alike at every church," Mother Herndon had wisely stated.

He had no doubt that she prayed for him and his family on a regular basis. He hoped the Spirit would lead her to add a little extra for Amani and Sharla.

Mark spotted Amani in the crowd. Arms folded, eyes looking as though he might fall asleep at any moment. But at least he wasn't texting anymore during service.

Sharla sat on the front row to his right, where she always sat. Same fake grin. Different hairstyle.

After focusing himself with the thought that at least his family was physically present in the house of God, Mark trained his eyes on the Word again, reading verses one through nine. "May the Lord add a blessing to the hearers and doers of His word."

"Amen," the congregation agreed.

"My brothers and sisters, I want to talk to you today about the fact that you don't have to live in sin. You don't have to live in obedience to your flesh. Because Christ died and rose again, those of us who believe on Him have died with Him, according to Colossians three and three. And we find here in First John the product of a life lived in Christ—freedom from the rule and reign of sin, even as we go about our lives in this mortal body."

The audience resembled deer in the headlights.

70

"You see, before Christ, you and I didn't have a choice. We had to obey our flesh because it was our master. But once we believe and receive Christ, we exchange our lives for His."

A few amens.

"Now, Paul did say in Romans that there is a war going on inside of us—the flesh still wants what it wants."

"You right about that!" from someone.

"You still have cravings and desires and suggestions that rise out of your body," Mark continued.

He got a whole chorus of amens on that one. But his heart sank as he realized his congregation could relate more to their human shortcomings than to the victory already secured in Christ.

He had failed the people miserably, and he'd have to answer to God for it. *What do you want me to do?*

Mark yanked the microphone from its holder and stepped down from the pulpit. Jonathan quickly followed behind him, wearing a confused look on his face. Mark pointed for Jonathan to sit down next to Sharla.

"Saints of God, members of New Vision, I have a confession to make."

An audible rattling swept through the building. People straightened up in their seats. The balcony seemed to lean in closer. He could see Jonathan shaking his head and mouthing the words 'I don't know' to the fellow ministers.

Mark knew that he was making everyone uncomfortable, perhaps most of all his wife. To calm Sharla, he flashed a quick smile in her direction.

"The Lord has been dealing with me about something," Mark continued. "For the past six years, I've been preaching to you about many, many things."

71

"Mmmm hmmm," they prodded.

"Many things that are beneficial."

"Mmmm hmmm."

"I've taught you how to pray more effectively, how to get out of debt, how to get healed, how to get whatever you want from God."

"That's right," they played along.

"I've given you plenty of how-to's, but not the *who*."

"That's right," Mother Herndon bellowed. "Help him, Jesus!"

"I stand up here week after week telling you all stuff that I thought you all needed to hear when, really, all you need is in Jesus—the very last part of what gets mentioned every week. But you can't know peace, you can't know love or joy or prosperity without Jesus Christ.

"When you think about the one person you love more than anything, even when they do wrong, you don't want them punished to the fullest extent possible. We got people in this church who have given all kinds of collateral—houses, cars, savings accounts, taken second and third jobs—to get a good attorney to argue the case for a child they *know* did wrong. But even though they know that boy did wrong, they still want mercy.

"That's exactly what Christ did for us. He sacrificed Himself so you and I could have mercy. Hebrews seven and twenty-five says He ever lives to intercede for us. And then he turned around and gave His life for us and *to* us so we wouldn't ever have to submit to sin again. Even when we get off track, the sacrifice He made for us is still in effect. It is finished.

"The only requirement is to believe. If you've been listening to sin, if you've been trying to argue your own case

72

before God, trying to do everything right so God will forgive you—you can stop. He already has. Fall in love with Him the way He's already in love with you.

Mark felt the leading to give the invitation a different way. "Every head bowed, every eye closed. Right where you are. You don't have to stand or walk down the aisle. You don't have to give us your name or your number or your address. You don't even have to raise your hand. Right where you are, if you feel Christ knocking at the door of your heart, just open it. If you've already accepted Christ but you've been wrestling with sin, just surrender to Christ. Believe on what He has done and give it all to Him. Sin is broken. The same rest you will have in heaven can start *now* because He's the same God there as He is here. Right there, where you're sitting, open your mouth and let Him know that you receive Him."

The revelation flowing from Mark's mouth stunned him. He hadn't planned it, had never even considered the idea that believers didn't have to wait until eternity to experience an inexplicable rest in Christ today.

The words were not his own, and he could not have been more humbled by the fact that God had used his lips to speak them.

Soft music began playing as Mark held the microphone to his chest, rocking from side to side in the manifest presence of God. He could hear people whispering soft prayers. Someone in the balcony began sobbing from the pit of her soul.

Mother Herndon started singing, "Oh, it is Jesus." Robert picked her up on the organ as her sweet voice caroled, "For I have touched the hem of his garment..."

A wave of worship flowed through the congregation as they all joined in the simple, powerful tune. Valeria took the microphone again in the choir stand and sang the verse. "I tried all that I could..."

Without prompting, people began to come forward and gather at the altar. Shoulders heaving as they cried, hands lifted in total surrender.

"Prayer team, we need you," Mark beckoned the warriors to pray with those who were following an unction to meet Christ at the foot of the pulpit. Within minutes, the altar area was filled with people praying for one another.

"Right where you are," Mark moved with the Spirit, "if you need to pray with somebody, just ask your neighbor. Ask them to pray with you, ask them if you can pray for them. Saints of God, let's edify one another in Him right now."

He lost track of time in the Spirit and thoroughly enjoyed every second—or minute?—of it. However long it was, it hadn't been long enough before Rev. Kit took the podium and brought the impromptu worship service to a close. "Amen, amen. You all can go back to your seats now in Jesus' name. Amen, amen. Let's continue on with the message. Amen, and amen."

Jonathan appeared at Mark's side, holding out his arm, directing Mark back to the pulpit. The sudden, unwelcomed jolt back to the program left Mark feeling confused. Actually, drunk was probably a better word. He wondered why on earth Rev. Kit had quenched the move of God in the building.

Lord, show me what to say next.

And, almost audibly, he heard the reply in his Spirit: Nothing.

Mark whispered to Jonathan, "I'm finished preaching." He turned toward the side exit doors.

Jonathan rushed to his side so that their conversation couldn't be heard by the congregation, which was settling back into their seats. "But, sir, there's twenty minutes left in the service."

A righteous anger rose up in Mark. "Tell Kit he can take it from here."

Chapter 11

Mark gave a short reply to the texts from Marshall and Kit requesting a meeting Sunday evening. In all caps, he typed: BUSY WITH FAMILY. Mark refused to answer a call from Rev. Jackson, who never texted. Jackson would probably leave a long, drawn out message so lengthy the system would cut it off before he was finished.

But, really, Mark didn't care. They all needed to feel what it was like to get cut off—like they'd done the Holy Spirit in service.

Who's the pastor, anyway?

But before getting carried away with the whole situation, he thanked God for showing Himself strong in church that morning. There would probably be no official count of how many people gave their lives to Christ, but he knew there were many more converts than on an average Sunday. And wasn't that what mattered most?

He propped his bare feet up on the ottoman and made another note on his iPad: record the number of people who come to Christ, not just the number of people who join the church.

Somewhere in these past two weeks, God had begun girding Mark up for something. More members? A television show? A new building? A book deal? Whatever it was, Mark knew it was big. He wanted to be ready for it.

He slipped into His study for another moment alone with God before Sharla and Amani came home from church. Half an hour later, he heard the garage door lifting. Amani bounded up the staircase, breezing past Mark's office without a word.

"Hey," Mark stopped him.

Amani froze, then turned to face his father.

"Did you enjoy yourself at church today?"

"It was weird," Amani remarked, but nodded, "in a good way. Your sermon was nice and short. I liked that part. But then Rev. Kit talked for a long time afterward. Where'd you go?"

"Here."

"You came *home*?" Amani seemed surprised.

"Yes. Is that so hard to believe?"

Amani bunched his lips to the side as though it took every ounce of home-training in him to refrain from saying something smart.

Mark rescued him. "I know it doesn't seem like it sometimes, but I *do* live here."

Amani put a hand on his father's shoulder. "They say admitting it is the first step, Dad."

That boy still managed to sneak one in. Mark could only laugh at his son's snide comment. "Yeah, yeah. Did you and your momma get something to eat?"

"Yeah. Barbeque from Pappas. She got you a plate."

Mark made a bee-line to the kitchen. He opened the refrigerator and beheld the sack bearing the restaurant's emblem.

He felt a sharp poke in his side. "You're welcome," Sharla purred.

Thank You God, she's coming back to normal. "Ouch," he played along.

"You deserve more than that," she flirted.

"For what?"

"Why'd you sit up there and make Rev. Kit look like a fool in front of everybody?"

Mark ran a finger across his sauce-soaked chicken. "Baby, that man brought it on himself."

"Well, it wasn't pretty," she said. "He brought the whole service down."

"Not my fault." Mark placed the container in the microwave and set the timer for forty-five seconds.

She leaned against the counter and crossed her arms. "I suppose you have a meeting with the advisory board tonight."

"Nope."

"No?"

Mark repeated, "Nope."

"What *are* you doing tonight?"

The timer went off. "First thing I'm gonna do is eat this here food you got me. I sure do 'preciate it, Mamasita." He grabbed a spoon from the drawer and sank himself into the couch with the food on his lap.

Sharla followed him to the living room. "So what was today all about? Another power struggle between you and Kit? Or Jackson?"

He rarely talked church business with Sharla anymore because, quite frankly, she didn't seem to care much about New Vision. She only seemed to get angrier when he told her about forthcoming initiatives.

Now Mark jumped at the chance to reason with her and invite her to pray with him on this matter. "It wasn't a power struggle between me and them. It was between Kit and God, I'm guessing. Of course, Kit lost."

"Okay, you have to admit, though—you went old school today," Sharla pointed out.

"Honey, Kit's older than *me*. He knows what happens when the Holy Spirit takes over. You go with Him."

"But Mark, if you plan on someday doing all the stuff you said they used to nag you about—going on television and all—you can't just change the order of the program and do what you want to do."

She remembered. "It's not what *I* want to do, it's what *God* wants to do," he corrected her. "Who am I to tell God what He can and cannot do in His own house?"

"But God is not the father of chaos," she quoted scripture.

Mark missed those kinds of conversations with his wife. He took a bite of meat. "I know. I wouldn't exactly call what happened chaos, though. Did you get a sense that things were...chaotic?"

"No."

"What *did* you feel?"

"I don't know. I just praised God."

"Exactly," he agreed. "Nothing wrong with that. People always come to church to *get*. How about *giving* sometimes?"

Sharla slapped her hands on her thighs. "I'll leave all this up to you and your people." She took off toward their bedroom.

"Wait. Can you bring me a glass of lemonade?" he asked.

She doubled back to the kitchen. "Now, you knew you were going to need something to drink before you sat down, Mister."

She was right. But he liked it better when she got the drink for him. "Thank you, Ma'am."

"Mmm hmm."

She set the drink on the end table closest to him, buffering with a coaster. "Please don't fall asleep with this television on." Snoozing in front of live screens was one of Sharla's pet peeves.

"I can't promise you anything."

"Mmm hmm," she said, rolling her eyes.

"Babe. For real, though," he said, seizing her arm gently. "I need you. I need your opinion about things at New Vision."

Her lips puckered. "You don't want to know what I think."

"I wouldn't have asked if I didn't."

"I think you ought to slow this whole thing down," she reiterated for the umpteenth time.

"We wouldn't be able to move into the dream house," he stated.

"Yes we could. I could get a job as soon as Amani graduates."

"Four years from now?"

"Just keep everything at the status quo until you are able to better balance your church life and your home life. How hard is that?" she contended, her chin jutting forward.

Times like these, Mark was completely baffled. Sharla claimed she wanted a husband who gave the minimum at work but got the maximum benefit from work, so she could move into a mini-mansion. She also wanted a husband who was a great father, who attended to her needs all at the same time—*if* he was interpreting her correctly.

He snapped the top half of his carryout container on top of the bottom, sat up straight and patted the seat next to him. Now that she seemed rational, he could have a long-overdue conversation with her.

Sharla followed his directive, sitting with one leg crossed over the other.

Mark faced her head-on. "Sharla, I've got two questions for you. I'm not obligating myself to do what you say, but I want to know the truth. Got me?"

She nodded.

"Number one, do you still support me and the ministry of New Vision?"

Her top leg bounced nervously as she sighed heavily. "Mark, I support *you*. But I don't like what the church has done to our family."

"That's fair," he gave her. "Number two, how, exactly, do you feel I'm lacking as a husband to you and a father to Amani?"

Again, she hesitated before answering. "I'll be the first to admit that I am a high-maintenance person. You know my family background is crazy. And you know when we went through that marriage class that my love language is affection and spending time together. Those things can't be done without physically being with me."

He remembered those classes. In fact, he recalled the sense of dread that overcame him when he realized that he and Sharla were nowhere near each other when it came to what they desired from a mate. He wanted domestic support—cooking and cleaning—and sex. She wanted smooching and a whole bunch of talking. How they'd managed to get married in the first place had to be the work of the Lord Himself.

"As for Amani," she answered the second part of his question, "I don't know exactly what a man's supposed to do with his son, but whatever it is, I can't do it."

Really, Mark didn't know what "it" was, either. His own father had provided—albeit intermittently and illegally—for their family, which led Carter II to count jail as his second address. But other than a few lectures on how to avoid the cops and cheat con artists at their own game, Mark's father hadn't done much by way of training him to be a man.

Mark knew full well that if it hadn't been for the Lord keeping him, he would have continued in the tradition of the two Mark Wayne Carters before him, living a life of perpetual hustling and womanizing.

Mark watched his wife's backside twitch off to their bedroom, again thankful that she was in the final phase of her mood swing. If he played his cards right, he'd have a certain meeting of his own with her later that night.

Chapter 12

Rev. Marshall's text was more of an FYI than a request to meet at six Monday evening. Mark knew that he couldn't put it off forever, so he agreed.

After a full day of prayer, Bible study, reviewing the church's numbers, responding to email messages, and giving the main address at the Brothers-for-Books inaugural gathering at a local bookstore, Mark barely had enough time to prepare his mind for the meeting with his advisors.

On his drive back to the church, he decided it was probably just as well that he hadn't prepared himself. He wanted to be fresh, hear them out without having already practiced his rebuttals. After all, Mark *was* the founding pastor of New Vision. He was, ultimately, accountable to God for what happened there.

No one was late for that meeting. In fact, they were all in place ten minutes ahead of time, so Mark convened with prayer accordingly. He'd barely uttered the "Amen" when Rev. Jackson took the floor.

"I think I speak for all of us when I say you'd be a fool to pull that crap you pulled Sunday ever again," he spat out the words as though he'd been chewing the nasty bits all day. "We're all trying to build an empire here, a legacy. Stick with the program."

"I second his thoughts," Kit added.

Mark could almost see steam forming on Kit's glasses. The fact that he was still angry even after a 24-hour cooling off period was even more proof that he'd messed up royally after Mark left the church.

"Pastor-I-I…" Jonathan stumbled through, "I guess we're all wondering why you left."

"I ain't wonderin'," Marshall piped up, "he left because he didn't want us telling him what to do." He laid his eyes on Mark. "If that's how you feel about the advisors' board, then all you gotta do is say the word. We'll be out of your way and you can run this church your doggone self."

"Gentlemen. Brothers," Mark slipped into charismatic mode, "there's no need for us to argue—"

"Cut it, Carter," Kit jumped in again. "If you want to run some kind of new age spiritual mumbo jumbo church or even an old holiness fallin'-out-on-the-floor church, that's fine. Just let us know so we can make a move."

Mark had had enough of Kit making tacit reference to the offer he'd supposedly received from Fresh Start. And the fact that Kit had just called him 'Carter' instead of Pastor didn't escape notice. "If you need to bounce, bounce. Don't let me stop you from doing whatever it is you think you gotta do."

Kit took a deep breath, obviously holding back words that weren't appropriate for the house of God.

Mark held his breath, too, hoping Kit wouldn't walk out. He had been with Mark from day one of New Vision. Mark couldn't imagine continuing without Kit's help. But by the same token, Mark's gut instincts wouldn't dare let Kit have the upper hand.

Rev. Jackson laced his fingers together, held them behind his head, and leaned back in his chair. He stared at Mark. "What's really going on with you, brother-in-Christ to brother-in-Christ?"

Mark decided to do the best he could to explain what was happening inside his heart. These men deserved to know. "God's changing me. And I think he's changing the vision for New Vision."

84

"Changing it to what?" Marshall demanded.

"Changing it from a focus on programs, this so-called empire and even me—back to Jesus."

"You don't think Jesus is a part of what we already do?" Rev. Jackson quizzed.

Mark laughed slightly. "That's the problem. He's a *part* of what we do, but He's not the *center*. He's like…a sidebar. A footnote."

Kit reached into his back pocket and threw a small scrap of paper to the center of the conference table. "Read this."

Mark reached his hand forward. Rev. Marshall helped by passing the paper the last few feet. He read the note aloud, "We didn't come here to get beat down about sin. Keep that in mind."

Slightly confused, Mark asked, "What's this?"

"A note that was paper-clipped to a hundred dollar bill in the offering plate."

"*And?*" Mark said.

"*And* if what you're preaching is scattering the sheep rather than reeling them in, you have to ask yourself if you're being a good shepherd," Kit filled in the blanks.

"Kit, I'm giving everything I have to this church. I'm ten seconds from losing my *family* behind this church. Don't *tell* me I'm not a good shepherd," Mark defended himself.

"You're missing the point," Rev. Marshall voiced calmly.

Taken together with Rev. Jackson's demeanor, Mark shelved the near-personal beef with Kit long enough to hear the other two out.

Marshall continued, "Maybe you need to focus on what the research tells us about church growth, solid programs that have been proven to work in today's busy, ever-changing world. People need stability. Inspiration. They need to be able to relate to what you're preaching and apply it in a practical way. That's how we got to where we are now."

Mark listened.

"That's all we're trying to say," Rev. Jackson reasoned. "We've come this far by doing what works. Plus, it's not just about you, Mark. It's about the souls at stake."

The thought of people of New Vision dying and going to hell on his watch scared Mark. Was he preaching over the heads of most of the people in the congregation? Did he make them feel alienated? Was he trying to feed the congregation meat when they were only capable of digesting milk?

Rev. Jackson and Rev. Marshall had made their points well. "Jonathan, do you have anything to add?"

Noticeably caught off guard, Jonathan straightened up his glasses and coughed a few times. "Um…yes, I've done a lot of reading on church growth in the new millennium. The group of…um…twenty and thirty-year-olds today are called screenagers. They…I guess *we*…grew up in front of screens, sir. We have low attention spans and we need a lot of interaction in order to stay focused."

Mark and the older gentlemen exchanged puzzled glances.

Jonathan pressed forward "In fact, I was thinking maybe we should put your main points up on the screen in a PowerPoint presentation. It might help people follow along better."

Kit pointed at Jonathan. "That's the kind of stuff I'm talking about. Relate to the people. Meet them where they are. Otherwise, all this talk about sin and death and hell and...whatever else turns people off is going to turn them away. That's the *last* thing churches need to do."

"What about Jesus?" Mark asked.

"Nobody's saying leave Jesus out," a much calmer Kit explained. "We're saying *find a better way* to bring Him in."

As eloquent as Kit's words sounded to the ear, they repelled Mark immediately. He shook his head. "You know, three weeks ago, I might have agreed with you, Kit. But not today. I have to do what God is calling me to do. Maybe we need to do something else. How about if I preach first and third Sundays, and somebody else preaches whatever else you all feel led to preach on second and fourth?"

Jonathan sharply turned his head. "Sir, that would be...difficult. From a financial perspective."

Rev. Jackson nodded. "He's right. The offering is sometimes down by a third when you don't preach."

"Maybe we could put a stop to letting anyone know who's preaching," Marshall recommended. "At least first service wouldn't know ahead of time."

Mark raised his hands in the air. "Are you listening to this? People shouldn't be coming to New Vision to hear *me*. They should be coming to hear from God, no matter whose mouth He uses."

"I know that and you know that, but obviously they don't. It is what it is," Rev. Jackson put an end to Mark's argument. "The best thing is for you to keep doing what you've been doing. Stick with the plan. Everybody at this table wants to see New Vision rise to a higher level. Once we have our thousands and thousands of ducks in a row, perhaps we can ease the people into appreciating different preachers' styles. Starting with the Wednesday night crowd."

Mark noted the simultaneous nods at the table signaled agreement with Jackson's suggestion. It did sound reasonable.

"We have to stick together if we ever want to be recognized with the Potter's Houses and Lakewoods," Marshall fired them up.

Mark had to admit, the term "mega-church" did have a nice ring to it. Still, his chest thumped with unease. "I have to be true to what God is calling me to do," he pressed.

Jackson leaned forward now. "Do you honestly believe God would lead you to take off—"he swished one hand across the other, "in a direction that leaves a sizeable portion of your congregation behind to be devoured by the enemy?"

Of all the things said in the meeting that night, these would be the words that chased Mark and held him down until he conceded that, maybe…just maybe he had misunderstood what God wanted him to do.

Chapter 13

Thursday morning nearly did Mark in. He sat for hours with the Humbert family, whose son was nearing the end of a nineteen-year battle with cerebral palsy. As friends and fellow church members filed in and out of the room, Mark listened to their awkward, bitter-sweet attempts to comfort the family.

Mrs. Joyce Hubert, understandably, was taking it hardest. She'd given up her life when her son was born with special needs. Now, her own mother was trying to prepare her for the boy's imminent death.

"Baby, he's tired," the wise grandmother whispered into Joyce's ear. "Let him go on."

Mark felt drained of all spiritual juice whatsoever. How on earth could he expect to get alone with God and get direction to finish preparing for Sunday? Let alone do a run-through. He wondered how hundreds of thousands of men of the cloth before him had managed to make it all look so easy. How did they lead congregations, take care of their families, and keep their sanity? No wonder neither Jesus nor Apostle Paul recommended marriage for everyone.

Still, Mark believed he needed to be grateful and not get caught up in grumbling and complaining. After watching the young Hubert boy hooked up to all those machines, Mark remembered how blessed he was to have a son who had always been able to breathe, sit up, talk and walk in his own power. *Thank You, Lord.*

Mark swung by the high school and sat in the stands for half an hour watching Amani's track practice. He'd been there ten minutes before Amani even saw him, and that was only because someone else pointed him out to Amani. Mark waved a big country wave. Amani barely moved his hand in response, but the joy painted all over his face gave Mark a rush that propelled him through the rest of the day's tedious obligations.

The impromptu trip to the track put Mark off schedule by about an hour, which meant he wouldn't quite get an opportunity to round out the notes for Sunday's sermon that night. He hoped he wouldn't have to supplement again with Sermondepot.com.

Then again, what did it matter? The people didn't want to hear about Jesus. They didn't want to hear what God had told him to say, obviously. They wanted to hear about practical things—things they could check off a checklist so God would, in turn, do His part because they had been faithful. A nice, neat system.

Only problem was, sitting there with the Humberts was a testament to the fact that life doesn't go by a formula. People needed to hear the truth, and the truth was Jesus. But if people didn't want to hear about Christ just yet, what was he supposed to do—*make* them want to? *Force* the meat down their throats? That didn't make sense, especially when Jesus Himself doesn't force His way into people's lives.

Nothing made sense, especially not after the meeting Monday. Mark had prayed about this to God, but He seemed to be in talk-to-the-Hand mode.

He had even tried to talk to Sharla, but she gave the same pat answers she always gave when it came to the church, "Do what you think is right." Though she was no longer in her funky mood, she still had no interest in seriously discussing New Vision.

She did, however, have an interest in discussing her job hunt. She was shooting for something that paid in the high 50s or low 60s so they could live comfortably in the dream house while Amani was in college. "We're going to need lots of furniture, you know?" she chirped.

The thought of Sharla going back to work wasn't quite happiness for Mark. If she got into some high-powered position, he'd surely be relegated to even more fast food and even less sex. He remembered what it was like before Amani came along, how they had both been dedicated high-achievers at work. Neither of them knew how to do anything half-way.

The last thing Mark needed at this point in his life was to feel like a single man. Alas, Sharla was her own woman. Expressing his dissention would only lead to days, if not weeks of the silent treatment. Way too much drama. It was easier to keep his mind off of home and stay focused on work.

Praying with citizens of Oak Manor Nursing Home was one of Mark's more pleasurable obligations. Once a month, Mark made his rounds at the center along with New Vision's outreach team. Greeting people who hadn't had visitors in weeks always made his chest stick out like a mini-hero while somehow humbling him at the same time.

"Oh, bless you, young man," the elderly women would say, planting kisses on his cheek. The men always had war stories to share, most of them exaggerated with pride, faulty memories, or both.

Sitting in their circle by their large-screen television, Mark reveled in the sense of being in an assembly with elders. Sometimes, they grilled him on his savings and retirement plan. "You got enough money saved up so you won't have to spend your last days in a dump because of Medicare?"

"Yes sir," Mark could answer truthfully.

Other times they got into heated debates about the government. There was usually a little cursing and a crude joke or two, but they respected him enough to say "excuse my French" and "you might want to cover your ears, preacher" before they gave their worst lines.

Tonight was no different. Thankfully, there was no news of anyone passing. And when it was all said and done, Mark prayed for his quasi circle of elders one by one.

At a quarter past seven, he left the nursing home, still trying to decide if he wanted to go back to the church and pick up his parallel Bible or go home and do the research via the digital versions.

There was something about the paper version—actually touching and writing in the physical books—that drew Mark back to the church to get the book. He made a promise to himself that he would get in there and out of there, be back in time to surprise Sharla with a pre-midnight arrival.

He decided to send her a text: *On way home. What you got for me?*

No matter how she replied, Mark knew she'd have to be happy. He hoped Amani had mentioned the show of support at track practice. Coupled with the fact that he'd shown up to the counseling session—late, but still—he should be well into the positive on brownie points. Anything to let Sharla know that he was at least trying to be the man, the father she wanted him to be.

Quickly now, Mark got in and out of his office. He was actually proud that he hadn't let himself get distracted by the million and one things still in his never-shrinking "To do" pile.

He approached his SUV from the driver's side, opened the door, shut it as he buckled in. He laid the coveted book on the floorboard of the passenger's side and, suddenly, the passenger's door swung open.

"What the—"

"I'm sorry. I need to talk to you."

It was *her* again. The curvaceous woman who had tricked her way into his office weeks ago and later, tried to make plans with him after visitors' meet-and-greet. Though she wasn't dressed in tight, provocative clothes, he somehow managed to recognize her face. Even if he hadn't, he certainly would have remembered her perfume.

"Lady, are you crazy? Get out of my car!"

"Just give me a minute," she pleaded. "I'm not trying to do anything crazy, okay? And I'm sorry I tried to hit on you before. That was wrong. I just didn't know any other way to get to you."

Mark opened his car door, stepped out. "So are you going to get out *now* or when the police get here?"

She was still sitting there in the seat from where he'd only seen one woman's face staring back at him—Sharla's. The audacity of this woman to hop in his car! She must have been following him.

Mark took a quick look around and noticed that the nearest car was at least fifteen spaces away. This crazy lady must have been hiding on the other side of his car. His father would not have been proud that he'd let this woman catch him slipping.

"Don't call the police. I need to talk to you," she begged desperately.

Mark was amazed at her acting skills, but they wouldn't be working today. "I told you to make an appointment with my secretary. He can get you in touch with the counseling team."

"I don't need to talk to the counseling team. You have what I need."

"What *I* have belongs to my wife," he clarified.

"Not exactly," she argued.

"Yes, it does." Mark stopped himself. *Why am I arguing with this lady?* He extracted his cell phone from his pocket and began to dial 9-1-1.

"Fine!" She screamed, finally opening the passenger's door. She looked at him from a standing position outside of his car, talking over the two front seats. "You have something that belongs to me."

Mark stopped shy of pressing the send button. With some distance between him and the woman, he felt like he might be able to work this out without sending her to jail tonight. "Look, you obviously need help. I don't have anything that's yours, lady."

"My name is Bria, and you *do* have something that belongs to me. Will you listen to me? Please? For a minute?"

Maybe if he listened, he might get this woman out of his hair once and for all. So long as they were separated by two humongous car seats and a console, he could tolerate her for sixty seconds. "Go."

She took a deep breath, as though she'd just finished running a sprint. "Okay. First of all, I am a member here. I joined for the wrong reasons, but anyway, I'm glad I did. I met"—she choked—"I met Jesus this past Sunday. Thank you for introducing us."

Mark froze. How long had it been since someone actually spoke such words to him? Months? More than a year? "You're welcome. My pleasure."

"Secondly, you do have something that, well, *used* to belong to me." She flicked her long hair back. "And it was wrongfully taken away."

"What?"

"Amani."

"Amani?" Mark had just begun to connect the dots when the unmistakable whiz of a bullet arrested his attention.

In an instant, Bria looked behind herself, then flew back into Mark's car.

A set of headlights sped toward them in the parking lot.

"Get in! He's coming!"

Mark jumped back in, too, cranked up the ignition. Threw the car in reverse. Forward.

Bria shrieked in terror, "Go!"

Chapter 14

Sharla could have kicked herself. She should have known better than to get all excited about Mark coming home early. Though Mark normally kept his word, there had been a few times when something unexpected came up and he'd been detoured.

The fact that he'd sent a text saying he was on his way home only made matters worse. He would have been better off saying nothing than to take forever to make the ten-minute drive.

Sharla hid the red velvet cake on the side of the refrigerator. Mark would still see it, but not immediately. The last thing she wanted him to do was walk his late behind into the kitchen and see that cake waiting for him like "Hi! We're glad to have you *any*time you come home!"

She threw on her most despicable house robe and her favorite house shoes—the ones with the bunnies missing their eyes—and snuggled up in the bed watching a recorded episode of *Bridezilla*. She felt like a *Wife*zilla right now, but that was only because Mark made her go there sometimes.

Overhead, she heard Amani and his friend Jadan yell regarding whatever video game they must have been playing.

Mark wouldn't have been too excited to know Amani was playing video games with friends so late on a school night. But if Mark wanted to run things his way, he needed to be there.

How's that?

By the time Jadan's mom blew her horn to pick up her child, Sharla's anger had been punctured by worry. She tried to remember the names of their sick church members listed

96

in the bulletin. Had one of them taken a turn for the worse? Had someone approached him with an urgent need the moment after she got the text from him?

An hour later, Sharla gave up trying to call Mark and started calling her husband's comrades. "Hi, Reverend Jackson, this is Sharla Carter. How are you?"

"Lady Carter, so good to talk to you."

"Same here," she lied. "Listen, Mark said he was on his way home a while ago. Do you know if he got sidetracked with some kind of emergency business?"

"No, not that I know of. I think they went to the nursing home tonight, but visiting hours are over at seven, if I'm not mistaken."

"I see," Sharla mumbled as she tried to think of a likely scenario that would make the short trip home from the nursing home morph into an expanded wilderness experience. "Did he have to stop anywhere else afterward?"

"You might better call his new assistant, Jonathan. He keeps Pastor's calendar. Let me give you his number."

"I tried him already. But I'll call him again. Thank you."

"Sure thing. Tell him to call me when you find him."

"Yes, Rev. Jackson. I will."

Instead of calling Jonathan, Sharla got dressed and hopped into her car. Her stomach twisted in knots. Now, she felt like she could almost kick Mark for being so inconsiderate.

"There better be some kind of problem, buddy," she said under her breath.

As she neared the main intersection by the church, traffic slowed to a crawl. "Man," Sharla fussed impatiently. She struck the steering wheel twice with her palm. There was nothing she hated more than sitting in traffic; it always felt like moments of her life were slipping away into nothingness.

She wondered what kind of construction, malfunctioning light or other ungodly foolishness must be happening up ahead. Though the street was a busy one, the speed limit was only 45 MPH. Even if there was an accident, Sharla presumed it couldn't have been serious enough to tie up traffic like this.

In the next five minutes, she moved roughly ten feet. If Mark was on the other side of this mess coming home from Oak Manor, this would certainly play a huge part in his explanation of what had taken him so long. Didn't explain why he wasn't answering his phone, but she knew from her days working at a telecommunications company that anything could happen with technology.

Sharla tipped her right blinker into action. Forget this. She was going back home. At this rate, Mark might actually beat her back to the house, if he'd found an alternate route already.

After a few honks and a maneuver to forcefully secure a lane change, Sharla bluffed her way into the right lane and into a shopping center's parking lot, hoping to find a back alley shortcut to a parallel street. If nothing else, she could visit the shoe stores until the congestion cleared because no one in the vicinity was going anywhere soon.

She took a quick glance down the road. Squinting, she barely recognized the mass of metal being hauled onto a tow truck as a car. It looked more like one of those transformer characters, half-car, half-robot.

A shiver ran through her as she realized the accident had been a bad one indeed. Someone must have been going way over 45 to do that much damage to the passenger's side. "Bless whoever was in that car, Lord," she prayed.

The final few feet of the car were raised high enough for her to make out the back end of an SUV. White. No fancy rims.

"Oh my—" she gasped as the vehicle's familiarity hit her. This was a Cadillac. An old Cadillac.

Sharla crept through the lot so she could get a better look. "God! No!" She banked a hard left and parked. She grabbed her purse and keys, running much faster than traffic would have allowed her to travel. With each hurried step, the vision of Mark's Escalade grew clearer and clearer. The peculiar tint, the Ichthys symbol on the back window.

Her only comfort was the fact that Mark wouldn't have been sitting on the passenger's side.

Sharla ran faster now, her heart's pace racing as she squeezed between cars that were stuck on a feeder street. She heard her linen pants rip on someone's license plate, but she was immune to the damage to her clothes and her knee.

With eyes set on the mangled mass of metal only, she stumbled as she stepped down from the curb into the street. Two other damaged cars littered the street, but neither looked as bad as Mark's.

"Ma'am, I need you to step back." An officer blocked the view of her husband's car.

"That's my husband. I mean, that's his car." She pointed over the officer's shoulder.

For all intents and purposes, the man was invisible to Sharla. She couldn't take her gaze off Mark's SUV. As the tow truck drove away, she could see that the windshield had been nearly destroyed.

"Where's my husband?"

"Ma'am, they took 'em to the hospital."

Sharla managed to focus herself. "Which hospital?"

"Well, the man they took to Southwest Memorial Hermann, I believe. The woman was care-flighted."

"Woman?"

"Yes. Female passenger."

Mark must have been transporting people from the outreach ministry. "W…was there anyone else in the car?"

"No. Just those two. Ma'am, we're trying to clear the premises now, I'm going to have to ask you to step back on the curb. I'm about to move this cone so we can open up this lane."

Sharla fumbled through her purse and found her phone while speed-walking back to her car. She scrolled through the call log. "Rev. Jackson, Mark's been in a car accident."

"Where is he? Is he okay?" Rev. Jackson fired.

"He's at Memorial Hermann Southwest, I think."

"I'm on my way."

Sharla pressed the red "END" button. Calling Rev. Jackson was as good as sending out an Amber alert. Every leader at the church would know in a matter of minutes.

Sharla amazed herself with her calmness. Somehow, hearing that someone other than Mark had been taken away by helicopter gave her a sliver of comfort.

However, the consolation was short-lived. She reached her car and jumped inside, her hands shaking with a heart-wrenching thought: Maybe they hadn't put Mark on a care flight because he was too far gone. Was someone pronouncing her husband dead at that very moment?

Horrifying scenarios raced through her mind. Sharla struggled to gather her thoughts and steady her voice long enough to call her son. Hopefully, she could get to him before social media did. "Amani?"

"Yes."

"Honey, your dad's been in a car accident. I'm headed to the hospital now."

"Wait! Come get me!" he croaked.

"I can't. There's too much traffic." Even with one opened lane, Sharla was still crawling through the aftermath. In retrospect, she thought she should have asked the officer for an escort. "Call Reverend Jackson and ask him if you can ride with him to the hospital. The number is on the refrigerator."

"Mom, is he going to be okay?" Amani asked, concern lacing his words.

Sharla's voice wavered. "I wish I could answer you, but I don't know. I *promise*, I'll call you as soon as I know something. Bye."

She dismissed Amani before she could throw him into even more turmoil.

Already, she had omitted the slight detail about the female passenger when talking to Rev. Jackson and Amani. There had to be a reasonable explanation.

Even if there wasn't…well, Sharla would have to get to the bottom of that later.

Chapter 15

The throbbing in his head wasn't overwhelming, but the pain in his right arm had to come from the devil himself chewing into Mark's nerves. He wanted to yell, but the holler came out more like a moan.

"Baby?"

He recognized Sharla's voice. Moaned again, nearly gagging at the nasty fire within his mouth and throat. Now he understood how the rich man must have felt when he requested a measly drop of water from Lazarus's fingertip.

"Dad?"

Amani? Mark wondered who else was there, wherever they were. He wanted to open his eyes, but the simple task would take far too much energy and incoming light might make his head pound even more.

His lips burned, too. He faintly rolled them inward and rubbed his tongue across them. The cracked, dry veil of dead skin registered in his brain as a bad sign.

He heard shoes shuffle toward him on a tile floor. They stopped. Then, the bed jarred slightly, sending a tidal wave of pain through his right arm. Agony propelled the word, "Stop," from his mouth.

"I'm sorry, honey."

"Bless God!"

"Amen! He's talking again!"

Rev. Jackson? Rev. Kit?

Why were these men in their bedroom with his wife and son?

"Amani, go get a doctor. Tell 'em your Daddy is awake again."

A doctor?

102

Unfamiliar women's voices mixed in with his wife's. They were telling Sharla that they had her back, they were praying for her. Something about the First Ladies.

A flood of church members who came to visit. They were too loud. Even with lowered tones, the slightest emphasis on a word reverberated in his head.

Perhaps because they thought he couldn't hear, there were soft questions about a woman. An accident. A gunshot. None of it made sense to him behind the thick curtain of blackness in his head.

The haze of anesthesia wore off, almost making Mark wish he could be put back under again. His entire body ached as though he'd climbed a ten-story building and jumped off. Twice.

Not to mention the hunger pangs writhing through his stomach. He opened his eyes and beheld the white ceiling tiles. They moved about two feet to the left, then back to the right. Mark shut his eyes tight.

"You up?"

He tilted his head toward Sharla's voice. He hoped that this time when his lids parted, the room—including his wife—would be stationary. Slowly, he let the light in again.

"Thank God," Sharla inhaled, cupping her mouth with both hands.

"Yes," Mark croaked. "Water."

Sharla rushed to the sink. Mark was too exhausted to follow her with his head. He waited, his neck fixed in same position. Now, in lieu of Sharla's face, he saw the opposite wing of the hospital. Rows and rows of windows, behind which must have been dozens of sick people.

And then it occurred to Mark that *he* must be sick, too, because he was laid up in bed looking out of one of these sick-people windows. "Sharla," he mustered a whisper.

She rushed back to his side with the small cup of water in hand. Seeing her standing there, Mark realized that he couldn't possibly sip from the cup lying flat on his back.

As though she'd read his mind, Sharla asked, "You want me to raise the top of the bed up a few inches?"

The proposal didn't sound like a good idea to Mark. "Get a straw."

Sharla laughed. "The doctors were afraid you might have sustained permanent brain damage. I'll be happy to tell them you're just as sharp as ever."

Sharla returned with the straw and cup. She bent down and stuck the straw through the bed railings.

Mark took small sips. The cool trickle soothed his throat tremendously. "Thank you."

She withdrew the straw. "Are you in any pain?"

"My arm."

"Okay. I'll get the nurse in for meds." She reached down, producing a white box. Mark watched as she pressed a button, then spoke to a woman through the mechanism, requesting pain relief.

"I'll be there in a second," blared through the speaker.

A second seemed like far too long to wait for relief. Perhaps if he knew the reason for his suffering, it might be easier to bear. "What happened to me?"

Sharla stared down at him. "You were in a car accident."

Mark squinted, trying to rack his brain for a memory. "When?"

"Three days ago," Sharla said.

"What's today?"

"Sunday."

"Who's preaching?" he wanted to know.

She rolled her neck to one side. "Mark, that's the last thing you need to be worried about. You could have lost your life," she informed him in lecture-mode. "And you *almost* lost your entire right arm."

He almost wished he didn't have the limb at that moment. He could feel every pump of blood pulsing through the arm's veins. There should be some kind of special pill for this degree of pain. Surely, modern medicine could find a way to give him some ease. If not, he might have to resort to his father's methods: 100 proof whiskey.

A nurse, dressed in Mickey Mouse scrubs, entered the room. "Hello there, Mr. Carter," she said cheerfully. "It's nice to see you alert."

"Mmmm," he moaned in the most upbeat manner possible.

She injected a solution into the IV line. "This'll take effect shortly. It'll probably make you drowsy at the same time, though. Can't have it both ways."

"Thank you," Sharla said on behalf of her husband. She stood over Mark again, breathing deeply.

Mark could tell there was something else on his wife's mind. Was he dying? Were both of his legs actually there or was the feeling only a phantom? To assure himself that he had use of his arms, Mark attempted to raise his left hand to Sharla's cheek. Thankfully, his body obeyed.

"What's the matter, Mamasita?"

She shook her head. "We can talk about it later. I don't want to waste the time we have before you drift off again. I love you, Mark. I thank God for sparing your life."

He traced her chin with his forefinger. "What are you not telling me?"

Sharla shifted her weight to one side. Her eyebrows drew close together.

"Go ahead," he encouraged her gently.

"There were other…people…involved in the accident."

"What? How many people?"

"Two other cars, but they weren't too bad."

Mark sighed, "Bless God."

Anxiety seeped through Sharla's glare. "And there was a woman. In your car."

"*What* woman?"

"I don't know exactly who she is…to you. They took her to a different hospital."

"Is she okay?"

"I'm not sure. Her injuries were a lot worse than yours since it was her side that got rammed into the concrete median."

Median! Mark remembered careening out of control. And then, somehow, a large, flaming cat entered the picture. "A lion."

Sharla gave him duck-lips. "What?"

His wife's image grew fuzzy. "I saw a lion on a bookstand."

"It's okay, Mark. The drugs are kicking in. Go on and get your rest before half of New Vision comes in to visit after first service, and the other half after second."

He couldn't have kept his eyes open if he'd wanted to.

"Faster!" she yelled. She twisted her body in the passenger's seat, looking back at the driver in hot pursuit. "Oh my God! He's crazy!"

Mark made a left out of the lot onto a sleepy street, then another left leading to the intersection. Somehow, he imagined that they'd be safer on a busy street; the chaser wouldn't endanger dozens of lives, would he?

The SUV's back windshield shattered as another bullet zipped between him and the woman, and lodged in the dashboard.

On second thought, the person in that vehicle was a lunatic. A four-way light wouldn't save them. Mark ignored his own stop sign, barely missing a convertible as he fishtailed onto the main street. If he could get a good thirty yards ahead on a long stretch, the Caddy would do the rest of the work.

"He shot me!" the woman screamed.

Quickly, Mark glanced over at his passenger. Blood seeped through her white shirt at the shoulder, momentarily arresting his attention from the road.

A moment too long.

When Mark looked up, there was a truck coming straight-on. He couldn't fathom how he'd gotten into that position, but the only way out was to swerve into the median and hope for the best.

In that instant, he felt a Presence pressing against him, bracing him for the impact.

"Aaaaah!" Mark shouted.

"Baby!" Sharla was suddenly at his side along with a host of other church members towering over him.

"You alright, Pastor?" and "It's gon' be okay," came from the small crowd.

Mark could hardly get air with all these people in his space. "Sit me up."

Sharla took hold of the white box again. The incline came quickly, sending sharp jabs throughout his body. Mark grimaced, holding his breath while his bones and muscles fought against the movement. "That's enough," he exhaled.

Amani pushed through the visitors and took first place at his father's side. "Dad, you were having another nightmare."

Peering up at Amani loosed another flashback. The woman, whose name he now believed started with a B had said that Amani belonged to her. Now, comparing Amani to the last face Mark saw before the accident. Same doe eyes, thick eyelashes, chiseled cheekbones.

For Amani's sake, Mark had to know. He blurted out, "What happened to the woman who was in the car with me?"

The crowd around his bed thinned quickly, giving one another awkward glances. Only Amani and Sharla were left to answer the question.

"Honey, we don't know who she was, so we really can't get any information about her." Sharla tried to keep a calm demeanor, but embarrassment etched itself into the lines around her mouth.

"Do you know who she is?" Amani asked innocently.

"I'm not sure."

"Amani, go sit with everyone else for a moment," Sharla ordered their son in a hushed tone.

He obeyed reluctantly.

Sharla inched in closer to Mark. With her back to the visitors, she whispered between clinched teeth, "Who is she?"

"She said we'd wrongfully taken Amani from her."

Sharla clutched her shirt. A touch of anxiety stained her voice. "What? Who...who was she? His aunt? His...mother?"

Mark couldn't be sure of the details. "I don't know, but he does look like her. Her named starts with a B...Brittney, Brenna...Do we know somebody with that name?"

"No," she replied quickly. Tears welled in Sharla's eyes and, immediately, Mark regretted spilling the beans. His wife had always been insecure in her role as Amani's adoptive mother, a fact that had loomed in their family since their first rounds of counseling when Amani became officially theirs. "Honey, it's okay."

"It's *not* okay. Wh-what were you doing with her?" She stuttered.

"She got in my car and—"

"How did she *get in* your car?"

Sharla's high pitch pierced Mark's skull. "Can you keep it down, please?"

"No. You had no business riding *anywhere* with another woman," Sharla spoke louder.

Rev. Jackson entered Mark's line of vision. "Pastor, I think we're all going to head on out now. You get some rest."

Mark recognized the Reverend's effort to do damage control. "Thank you, Jackson."

"And don't worry about anything at the church. We got it covered. Let's have a word of prayer."

The visitors gathered around Mark's bed, joined hands, and bowed their heads for prayer. Rev. Jackson added a generic strand for the "others" who had been involved in the accident.

They all followed the prayer in unison, "Amen," and scattered out with half-hearted promises to return soon.

Chapter 16

"Church members are rallying around their pastor after he was involved in a serious, *suspicious* car accident," the ten o'clock news anchor blared.

Mark winced but sat up in bed and focused on the television, wondering who on earth had suffered the same terrible coincidence as he.

"Members of New Vision Community Church"—*Wait! That's my church!*—"are speaking out against reports that their pastor was fleeing from a known gang leader, which led to this accident at the seven hundred block of Denbow Street."

The footage of Mark's garbled Cadillac nearly made him vomit. He couldn't believe he'd been in that vehicle. "My God," he murmured to himself.

Rev. Marshall's wife, Esther, appeared on screen. From the background, he could tell she was on the church's front lawn. "Our pastor is *not* a criminal. He does *not* run with shady types, and we do *not* appreciate the media painting him in a bad light. He's an upstanding man of God, and we're all behind him."

Applause erupted as the camera panned out to reveal at least thirty people standing behind Esther.

A lump rose in Mark's throat.

Just then, Sharla entered the room with a bag from Panera Bread. He could have sworn she was ten pounds lighter.

She took one look at Mark, then looked at the television screen. "Honey, you don't need to be watching the news. Let me turn—"

"No." Mark wrapped his hand around the white control box.

A grainy picture of Mark appeared on the screen. "Officers continue to investigate the accident. The pastor, seen here on the church's website, is thirty-eight year old Mark Carter III." The anchor's face returned. "A female passenger in the pastor's vehicle, who we understand was *not* his wife, was also injured in the accident. That woman remains in critical condition. We'll keep you updated as we know more."

"What the heck?" Mark bristled. That "investigative report" was ridiculous! They might as well have said he was dealing drugs and sleeping around on his wife.

Sharla yanked the remote from Mark and switched off the TV. "I can't stand the media. They've been at the house all day trying to get a story out of me. Been trying to get in here, too. We've had to just about shut your room off to visitors."

"Let 'em in. I need to defend myself," Mark said. "I didn't do anything wrong."

"No. I've already talked to Danny Hernandez. The best thing for you to do is keep quiet," she said.

"You talked to our lawyer?"

"I've talked to plenty of lawyers this week," she informed him.

"About what?"

She motioned toward the blank screen. "You just saw it for yourself, Mark. You were in a high-speed chase, running from a criminal. Your car had bullet holes in it. You weren't wearing your seatbelt, which is against the law. It's a miracle you didn't fly out the window.

"Anyway, neither the car insurance nor the health insurance companies will agree to do anything until you're cleared after the investigation." Sharla put a hand on her forehead. "I don't know what we're going to do. The investigation could take weeks."

Mark felt as though Sharla had dumped the weight of the world on his lap. He couldn't imagine what it must have been like for his wife to carry the burden alone, even if only for a few days. "Baby, I'm sorry. I didn't mean for any of this to happen. I'll make some phone calls. I still have contacts with StateWay."

"I want to know why there was a woman in your car," Sharla changed courses, her hand flying to her hip.

"I told you, she jumped in."

"A total stranger jumped into your car," she added incorrect words to his.

"No. I've seen her before. She's been at the church," he stumbled through.

"So, you've talked to her?"

"A couple of times."

Sharla smacked her lips. "When and where?"

Mark knew he'd better address his wife's real concern before she extracted any more dubious details out of him. "Sharla, I have never cheated on you. This woman was not a mistress, she was not an old friend, a new friend, she was not even an acquaintance. She *did* try to come on to me, but I shut her down—just like I've shut down every other women who has tried to take your place since the day I said 'I do.' Please don't turn this into something that it's not."

Sharla sighed. "Well, the media sure has."

"Don't let them get into your head. Baby, come here." Mark reached for her with his left hand. Slowly, Sharla

113

responded. Once she was within a few feet, he pulled her even closer and wrapped his arm around her waist. She dropped her bags and leaned over him, embracing his head.

Her hair swept against his face as warm tears dribbled onto his neck. "We could have lost you," she cried. "I was so scared."

He rubbed her back. "But I'm still here." He kissed her cheek gently. "I'm still here, Mamasita. Let's pray." He led his wife in a prayer of thanksgiving, a request for strength and peace, and a petition for the passenger woman's recovery.

Now that he was aware of all the drama his wife had been dealing with while he was laid up in the hospital, Mark was past ready to make a move. "When am I getting out of here?"

"A few more days," Sharla said as she resumed her composure. "Your right arm was…almost ripped off just below your elbow. You've got more surgeries ahead of you. Physical therapy."

"Yeah, but we don't have to do all that *today*. Let's get a doctor in here so we can get the ball rolling. And whatchu got in that bag? It smells a whole lot better than whatever that was they brought me for lunch. Ulk!"

With that, Mark made up his mind that he would do whatever it took to get out of that hospital, take over the things Sharla had been handling, and clear his name, which would mean getting in touch with the woman who'd jumped in his car—if that possibility existed.

He split a sandwich and soup with Sharla. She looked so much thinner; he almost felt bad taking food from her. "Baby, you need to get yourself another batch of this tomorrow."

"No. I haven't been too hungry lately."

"I see."

"Been too worried about you. Your Momma called to check on you. She wants to know if she should go ahead and get a plane ticket to come see you."

"You told her 'no', right?" Mark wanted to know.

"I wasn't sure for a while there," Sharla said. "Until they finished all the x-rays and tests, we didn't know how seriously you were injured. I did call her later and told her you were much better."

"Thank you," Mark sighed. "I don't need her coming down here with my sister and all their superstitious cures. I'm glad she called, though."

"What'd you expect? She is your mother," Sharla reminded him. "Amani's been worried about you, too. He's dealing with it his own way, I guess. Staying in his room, keeping to himself."

"Hmmm. I'll get Rev. Jackson to spend some time with him," Mark said.

"That might be good. He thinks of him as a grandfather."

Rev. Jackson was about the only grandfather-ish person in Amani's life. Sharla's father passed away when she was a teenager, and Mark's father wouldn't have been a good influence. Suddenly, Mark wondered if Amani had any older male relatives who could have just as easily stepped in from time to time to give his son guidance. Maybe including them in his life, as Amani wanted, wouldn't be the worst thing to happen.

But rather than run his thoughts by Sharla, Mark kept them to himself. She'd been through enough.

Chapter 17

Sharla had nearly passed out when Mark hinted at the woman's name. Sharla knew exactly who Bria Logan was. She was the woman who had given birth to Amani. The woman who needed to let the past stay in the past and stop trying to ruin the life Sharla had so carefully tried to secure. Even if it wasn't her first choice—which would have been to give birth to her own child—Sharla had done a good job of making sure plan B ran smoothly. How dare Bria Logan try to come and mess with the Carter family.

Sharla wasn't having it. Not now, not in a million years. Amani had expressed a desire to see his "birth" family since the age of eight, but Sharla figured what the boy didn't know couldn't hurt him. Truth was, the Logans were an ungodly, sheisty bunch with a history of alcoholism, repeated incarcerations, abuse, poverty, and teenage pregnancies.

Sharla knew all too well what it was like to grow up under those circumstances. She was thankful that God had pulled her out of the vicious cycle. Even more grateful to pull someone else out of it, particularly an African-American boy. Maybe Sharla hadn't done everything right when it came to adopting Amani, but like the saying goes: You can't unscramble eggs.

Sharla stood in her bathroom mirror checking out her appearance. Rather, someone else's appearance. The short curly wig, ruby red lipstick and Bamboo earrings were definitely not her style. And the dumpy denim button-down shirt with those cotton pants that shouldn't ever be worn in public, denied all sense of class. She would fit right in with the type of around-the-way girls she imagined Bria hung with.

She grabbed her broadest, darkest pair of shades from the collection atop her dresser and headed to the garage, then on to Ben Taub Hospital. After a bit of online research, Sharla guessed Bria had been transported there because they are a Level 1 Trauma care hospital. She couldn't get any information by phone about Bria's condition other than the ambiguous one-word medical term: critical.

Critical didn't tell Sharla what she needed to know. Would Bria live or die? If she lived, would she retain her mental capacities? Most importantly, would she be coherent enough to continue with her effort to butt back into Amani's life?

There really was no plan for this visit. Sharla wasn't even sure what she would do once she got there, but she needed to see Bria's condition for herself. Beyond that, she wondered if Bria looked like Amani. How *much* did she look like Amani? Did her other children look like Amani, too?

The curiosity was eating Sharla alive. In previous years, she'd been almost obsessed with Bria Logan, searching for her back in the MySpace days, looking for her Facebook profile, Googling her name and image, all to no avail. Who was this woman who had given birth to the son Sharla loved?

Sharla stopped at the information desk and got the room number. Bria was still in ICU.

"Thank you," Sharla said, thanking God that hospitals were nothing like airports, making sure everyone had official business before allowing them beyond the perimeter.

However, when she reached the proper floor, she learned that she'd have to wait until three o'clock to visit, nearly twenty minutes, because the nurses were changing

117

shifts. This unwelcomed news made Sharla uneasy. *What am I doing here?*

Nonetheless, she'd come this far. She had to see it through. She joined about fifteen people in the ICU waiting room. Some looked as though they'd been camped out there most of the day, with blankets and empty McDonald's sacks scattered around their campgrounds.

These people were the *real* visitors. They had loved ones who were hanging in life's balance and, presumably, were gathered out of genuine concern. The wall-mounted television blared an old *I Love Lucy* episode that always made Sharla smile. But she knew these people in the waiting room probably couldn't have smiled if they wanted to.

Sharla could almost feel the guilt pressing down on her trunk, causing her to sink into one of the room's cushioned seats. She grabbed a magazine to take her mind off the situation, but there was no mistaking the idea that she should leave.

"You get in touch with Bria's job?" a lady in a purple maxi dress asked the elderly man sitting next to her.

Sharla nearly jumped at the mention of the name. She buried her face between an ad for perfume on the left and one for lipstick on the right, her ears at full attention.

He answered, "Yeah, I told them. Didn't you see the flowers the company sent her up on the counter by the light switch?"

"Ooh, that was nice. She works with some really good people," a grandmotherly figure commented.

Flowers? The fact that Bria had a job was a shock to Sharla—let alone a job that actually sent flowers to its sick employees. The last time Sharla peeked into Bria's life, the girl had been failing drug tests; she couldn't have gotten a decent job to save her life.

The grandmother sat on a different sofa, which led Sharla to wonder just how much space Bria's relatives had taken up in the room. For all she knew, she could be sitting next to Bria's best friend.

Sharla stole a glance at the woman who'd started the conversation. She was slender, with a killer white Michael Kors bag and a natural nail manicure. Buffed. Not quite the triple-acrylic, rhinestone-bearing claw nails Sharla had expected to see on members of Bria's entourage.

"I just hope we get to the bottom of this and the pastor does right by her," maxi-dress girl added.

"Yeah, me, too," from Grandma. "Wonder why he didn't swerve to hit *his* side of the car instead of Bria's. A man of God ought to sacrifice himself before innocent people."

Innocent? According to Mark, Bria had taken it upon herself to hop her happy behind in Mark's vehicle. These people had it all wrong!

Maxi-dress woman wagged her finger. "All I know is, when Bria wakes up again, I'm going to tell her to leave Boomie the heck alone forever. He is crazy. I hope they get him, shootin' all in people's cars like a maniac."

The news of Bria having been conscious and possibly able to comprehend, stirred Sharla in a way she hadn't anticipated. For Amani's sake, Sharla hoped she would live. But for her own sake, Sharla wanted Bria to…well…not *die*, but not pose a threat to her own stable life with Mark and Amani.

As far as the courts were concerned, Bria had no right to have any part in Amani's life. After months in Sharla and

119

Mark's home as a foster child, they had fallen in love with the baby and asked about adopting him even though the social worker, Demetria, had told them from the beginning that Amani would probably be returned to his mother. The father was unknown to everyone, including Bria. She claimed to have narrowed the possibilities down to three men, but there was no test conducted.

Bria had been taking parenting classes and learning to be a good mother, supposedly. But after the social worker discovered that she'd given the six month old a heavy dose of cold medicine to keep him knocked out while Bria went clubbing during one of Amani's weekend visits, the case changed dramatically. Bria was charged with child endangerment and suddenly, the door to claim Amani as her own forever cracked opened for Sharla.

Amani celebrated his first birthday with the Carters. By that time, there was no way on earth Sharla could give him back. She'd fallen hopelessly in love with the baby, and it was obvious Amani had bonded with his new parents. She couldn't imagine that a court would jeopardize the good life she and Mark could provide.

The only One who seemed to be oblivious was God. Sharla and Mark were also busy trying to make a brother or sister for Amani, but Sharla's body wasn't cooperating.

When it was clear that Bria was in no position to get Amani back, some of her family members tried to step forward and claim the baby. It was clear to Sharla, by way of Demetria, who was more than sympathetic to Sharla by that point, that the only reason they wanted to adopt Amani was because they would receive some financial support from the state for having adopted him out of the foster care system.

Both Sharla and Mark had talked about how stupid it was to consider removing Amani from their stable home to place him with the very people who'd raised Bria to be an unfit mother.

With Demetria's help and a little work from a private detective, Sharla had put a stop to all those endeavors. By that point, Amani was almost two. Bria had cleaned up her act, or so she claimed, and wanted Amani back.

Sharla wasn't giving him up, and she blamed the court system for dragging the whole adoption thing out so long. Ridiculous government bureaucracy. Sharla would move to Mexico before giving up the only child she would ever have.

Right or wrong, Sharla had done everything within her power to make sure Amani didn't return to his birth mother…by any means necessary.

After reviewing the big picture as it pertained to Bria and Amani, Sharla didn't feel so guilty anymore. If anybody was wrong, it was Bria for having put them all in that situation. At least that's what Sharla had to keep telling herself in order to hold her place in the waiting room.

"Has anyone from her church been by here to check on her?" a teenager half-way engrossed in her cell phone asked. Sharla noticed the exceptional quality of the girl's weave. Definitely not cheap. "She's been going there for, like, three weeks now, and she had even asked me to go so I could be part of this new family she said she had in Christ."

"Please," from Maxi-dress woman, "the church is what got her in this predicament to begin with. The last thing she needs is somebody from her church coming by here. I hope she sues that no-good pastor."

No-good pastor? Sharla could call Mark all kinds of ugly names in her head, but no one else had the right to do so—

121

especially not out loud! She tried to think of a way to butt into their conversation, but nothing appropriate came to mind.

Unsure of what or when to speak, Sharla kept her mouth shut. It was bad enough she was snooping, worse to try to pick Bria's family for information.

Speaking of such, Sharla tapped the name "Boomie" in her phone's notes. The police seemed to be unsure of who had been chasing Mark and Bria, but obviously her family knew. Maybe they were adhering to the unspoken no-snitch rules of the hood in keeping this clue from the police, but Sharla didn't have to play by those rules anymore. She was going straight to Detective Rozanno with the suspect's name.

The grandmother checked her watch. "We should be able to go back in to see Bria now."

Simultaneously, six people, including those Sharla already knew were there for Bria, began shuffling. They slid shoes back onto their feet, folded up the blankets, and stuffed reading material back into backpacks.

Sharla hadn't expected to see so many people there in support of Bria, the baby-abandoner, baby-drugger. They knew her as someone else. Bria the friend, the sister, the granddaughter, the loved one.

Come to think of it, Bria probably had more family support than Sharla would have had if she'd been in ICU for several days. Besides Mark and Amani, the only others she could count on to at least act like they cared would have been the members of the church.

"Oh, excuse me," the young man said as he stepped over Bria's dangling foot.

"No, you're fine." She glanced up at his face and caught a vision of what Amani would surely look like in another ten years.

He paused. "Don't I know you from somewhere?"

Sharla's heart pounded. She lowered her face, burying it in the magazine again. "No. I don't think so."

"Mmm. I'd *like* to know you."

Thank God, he was only flirting. "I'm married," she muttered.

"Happily?"

"Yes, thank you."

"Francis, leave her alone! Married women are off limits," maxi-dress-woman said, slapping him on the arm.

"I'm just asking," he joked with the woman as though Sharla were suddenly invisible.

Francis...Francis...Francis! He was one of the money-hungry uncles who'd tried to get custody of Amani when he found out there was a small paycheck to be had by adopting him.

The grandmother rested her hand on Sharla's knee as she passed by. "You'll have to excuse my grandson. He thinks he's Casanova."

With her head down, Sharla obliged, "Yes, ma'am."

"We ain't seen you here the past days. Who you here for?"

Out of respect, Sharla answered the nosy woman. "Oh...umm...a...co-worker."

"My goodness. What happened to her?"

"She had...a...stroke."

"Yeah, that'll do it every time. She lucky to be alive, my mother passed after her stroke. You reckon your co-worker gon' pull through?"

123

"I hope so," Sharla said with uncertainty.

"I'll be praying for you." She tapped Sharla's leg twice more and then tagged along with the rest of Bria's family.

Francis had almost done Sharla in with that near-miss. Plus, now that she'd lied to the grandmother, there was no way Sharla could get in that room without a million questions from Bria's family.

What am I doing here anyway? Sharla slapped the magazine closed, grabbed her bag and left the waiting room. *I don't need to be here wearing this silly disguise. What if Mark found out? What if the church found out? The media? What would I say?*

This whole thing is stupid. Amani was hers, Mark would heal, and her life would be fine in about six months, hopefully. She had no business at the hospital pulling this soap opera-ish stunt. *I am a grown woman with better things to do with my time.*

Sharla sped to the elevators and pressed the down button repeatedly, despite the fact that the light indicating her request had been processed was already lit. She couldn't get out of there fast enough.

Ding! Finally, the elevator arrived. When the doors parted, Sharla found herself face-to-face with someone whose image sent ice up her spine. *Lisa Logan.* Bria's mother. Dressed in a too-tight jumpsuit and six-inch platforms. She looked more like she was going to the club than to visit her sick daughter. *Some things don't change.*

Sharla looked past Lisa, waited for the woman to exit the elevator, then quickly traded places. She took a breath, thankful to have escaped notice, and pressed the button that would take her back to her car, back to a life of sanity.

But just as the doors were closing, she heard, "Sharla."

Out of sheer habit, Sharla lifted her head, locking eyes with Lisa.

Sharla cringed inside as she realized she'd just given herself away.

Chapter 18

Though the fate of his right arm was still undetermined by doctors, Mark had made up in his mind to believe God for full restoration. In the meanwhile, he was more determined than ever to live his life the way God wanted him to. If that meant a megachurch, great. If not, whatever. Through the dreams, visions, and hit-or-miss memories Mark had experienced while partially sedated, one thing stood clear to him: God had delayed Mark's transfer to heaven for a reason. People like Bria needed to hear the life-changing, eternity-sealing gospel of Christ, and Mark would preach it, megachurch or not.

As far as Mark was concerned, the fact that his medical insurance was in question actually worked in his favor. The hospital was eager to release him as soon as he could take a meal without gagging. A social worker had come to talk with him about following up with local clinics and charities. He'd listened patiently to the woman, who exuded a sense of compassion for the misfortunate.

"God bless you, ma'am, but I won't be needing the free services. My insurance will pay once I'm cleared through the investigation," he said as soon as he found a break in her speech.

"Well, just in case they don't," she said by way of a warning, "here's my card."

Mark took the card from the middle-age woman, thinking that she would be an asset to New Vision if he ever got the opportunity to hire more staff. He read her name. *Hope Green.* "Miss Green, if you died today, would you go to heaven or hell?"

She sucked in her breath, leaned back in her chair as though he'd just taken a swing at her. Her eyes widened behind her bifocals. "Heaven, I hope."

"Do you *know*?"

"I guess," she faltered. "I've lived a good life, followed the golden rule. I go to church sometimes."

Mark smiled gently at her. "But have you met *Jesus*?"

Her thick, pink lips poked out. "Yeah. I pray to God."

Surprised that she was still with him at that point in the conversation, Mark wasted no time. "The only way to God is through Jesus. We've all sinned, but Christ came to forgive us for being…human. No matter what we do, it's not good enough. But Christ is good enough for you and me. He wants to come into your life and be your salvation, Miss Green. Will you let Him in?"

She smiled, her eyes brimming. "No one's ever explained it to me like that before."

"I've never had the courage to share Him like this, either, close up and personal," Mark admitted. "But He *is* good."

Miss Green blinked rapidly, steering herself out of the trance. "I will definitely keep this in mind, Mr. Carter. Thank you."

He'd settle for a watered seed. God would be responsible for the growth. "I'll be praying for you. Thanks for sharing the resources."

He was surprised to see that Amani had come with Sharla to take him home from the hospital. It was one of the last days of school. Amani didn't need to miss any last-minute reviews before the final exams.

"He begged me. He wanted to help make sure you got home comfortably," Sharla intervened when Mark accosted Amani about his absence.

Mark wished she'd let the boy speak for himself, but now wasn't the time to argue. "Just don't let this be the reason you get a bad grade on a test."

"I'm cool, dad. You know I always pull through when it counts."

Mark had to give it to his wife; she'd done an excellent job of making sure Amani mastered the basics when he was homeschooled. With a firm foundation in reading, writing, and math, the only real challenges Amani faced in high school were due to lack of organization and perseverance—never his academic ability to complete the work.

Sharla and Amani had just finished gathering up all the flowers and cards when Rev. Jackson arrived to help as well.

"Pastor, you ready to blow this joint?"

"Most definitely. I'm ready to get back into the swing of things. I'm already thinking about Wednesday night's sermon."

Jackson sucked in air through his teeth. "You might want to slow down there a bit, Pastor. Take it easy."

Sharla took care of all the final paperwork, then they were off to the front entrance with a nurse pushing Mark's wheelchair all the way. He'd grown increasingly uncomfortable with people waiting on him.

When Sharla drove up the circle in her Benz and opened the passenger's door for him, it struck Mark that he couldn't have driven home if he wanted to. He had no significant use of his right arm. He might have to master the art of steering with his left hand. Wait a minute—he didn't even have a *car*. Was he still an insured driver?

"Watch your head," the nurse guided him into the car.

He wanted to tell her he was temporarily handicapped, not a doofus. But then he lost his balance and ended up bopping his noggin on the window frame despite her warning.

"Mr. Carter, you're going to have to take it slow," she reprimanded him.

He grunted an "okay."

At home, Rev. Jackson and Amani helped Sharla bring in his things while Mark took a rest on the couch. Just walking from the car into the house had taken the wind out of him. Why was he so tired? How could his legs be so weak when it only seemed like he'd been in the hospital a couple of days?

Mark reminded himself that it had been more than a couple days. It had been six days, actually, according to the calendar back in the hospital room.

Rev. Jackson brought in the last of the balloons and set them on the kitchen table. "That's it."

"Thanks, Rev.," Mark said.

"No problem."

Rev. Jackson sat alarmingly close to Mark on the couch. Any movement near the arm posed the threat of pain. Mark stabilized himself, putting a pillow beneath his arm.

"How you feelin'?"

"Fair."

Mark watched as Rev. Jackson spied on the action in the kitchen. Sharla and Amani transferred items to the bedroom, beyond the Reverend's view. When they were out of hearing distance, too, he leaned in and said to Mark, "Pastor, take all the time you need to recover."

"Oh, no." Mark shook his head. "I'm chomping at the bit to get back in the saddle. The sooner I get busy doing what

God told me to do, I believe the sooner He will get to working on this arm. If I have to set up a webcam and preach by satellite, I'm ready."

Rev. Jackson clasped his hands and looked away for a second. "Well…no…you don't need to go through all that trouble. The church ain't goin' nowhere."

"But just last week, you all told me that I couldn't stop preaching. I mean, I know I've had a car accident, but look at what God has done. He spared my life. He gave me another chance to do what He told me to do before I backed away from it. No offense, Rev., but I realize now that I shouldn't have listened to you. I have to preach Christ as the main course because He *is*. If that means people walk out of New Vision, so be it. They can roll out and take their itching ears with them."

"Hold on there, Mark. You got to take into consideration…the circumstances."

"What circumstances?"

Mark searched Rev. Jackson's face for clues. There, in the slight tremble of his lips, lied the hint that a waterfall of bad news was just on the other side. "Give it to me straight, Rev."

"I wasn't going to mention this tonight, but since you brought up preaching again, I guess I have no choice. This whole incident's got the church in a bind. We need to protect our image. The advisory board feels that right now, it would be best if you stepped down for a while."

"Step *down*?"

He nodded. "Yes. Until this all passes. We believe it will. Soon as something else bad happens, the media will focus its attention elsewhere, you know how they are."

Mark made the mistake of shrugging "Ow! Doggit!"

130

"Watch out there now," Rev. Jackson gave a sincere caution.

After recomposing himself, Mark tried to make sense of Rev. Jackson's words. "What do you mean—'this whole incident'? It was a car accident."

"A car accident with you and another woman," Jackson added.

"Another woman who hopped into my car without invitation. I didn't do anything wrong." Mark wondered why he needed to defend himself with Jackson. If *that* man held something against him, Mark didn't have a chance against the world.

"I believe you, Pastor. I really do. But you know the Bible tells us to avoid the appearance of evil," he referenced. "This whole thing looks bad."

"Is the media coverage really that serious? I only saw one report when I was at the hospital."

Rev. Jackson ran a hand along his neck. "If it were only the few reports on TV, that wouldn't be so bad. But it's more than that—it's...what do you call it? Blogs, stuff on Facebook. They say you got some tweetin' stuff. You got your own pound sign."

"Hashtag?"

"Yeah, that's it. Hashtag."

Mark turned his head toward the staircase. "Amani! Bring me my iPad!"

The boy's steps came too quickly to have looked through the office, retrieved the tablet, then come downstairs.

He entered the living room empty-handed. "Where is it?"

"Uh, yeah, Dad...about that iPad. I'm pretty sure it was in the car when you had the accident, so...um...no luck with that."

Sometimes, Amani picked the most inopportune times to try his hand at sarcasm. "Well, bring me your laptop."

Horror gripped his face. "For real? Mine?"

"Yes, yours. And you'd better not have anything crazy on it."

"Is this constitutionally *legal*?" Amani asked.

Rev. Jackson chuckled.

Mark gave his son a look that said he'd better bring that laptop down before he found himself without access to any computerized device for a long time.

Amani turned to go back upstairs.

"Now, before you go on the internet lookin' at all the foolishness people been writin', you need to know what we're doing to counteract it while you're...away. We got a crisis plan. Kind of like that show, Scandal."

"You watch Scandal, Rev?" Mark teased.

He denied unconvincingly, "No, not me. The Misses."

Amani returned with the laptop. Mark clicked on the icon that would take him to the worldwide web. With only one hand, it took him longer to conduct a search of his name, but in only a fraction of a second, he got over forty thousand results. The headlines were wretched. "Another Pastor Bites the Dust", "A Call for Change in the Church", "Pastor Mark E. Carter—the Apple Doesn't Fall Far From the Tree," "Pastor Has Accident in Car with Baby Momma".

Slowly, he raised his eyes to meet Rev. Jackson's, who could do nothing more than apologize. "I hate things have come to this. But I think you see now why we have to take precautions to save the church."

"Do people believe this crap?" Mark asked, though he already knew the answer. People who aren't full of the love of Christ love strife and salacious news; and that wasn't just his opinion. He already knew the Bible said so in Proverbs 17:19, a fact he'd tried unsuccessfully to preach to Sharla so she'd stop watching all those strife-filled reality television shows. Somehow, she didn't get that feeding herself, that drama was a problem.

"Unfortunately, they do. Some of the members have already let us know that they're leaving, and we got a lot of people who opted out of the newsletter."

"That's all it takes, huh? One car accident. One circumstantial lie from the enemy." Mark chewed his bottom lip.

Jackson cleared his throat. "Look here, Kit...*we* think if you maybe make an apology, take off a month or two, things will work out fine."

A spasm of irritation jerked Mark's body. "Make an apology for what?"

"For...this fiasco? The appearance of evil? Whatever you want to say so the people know you're sorry the church is going through this."

"Rev., we're believers. We have an enemy in the land. We shouldn't have to apologize to one another for being attacked—we all go through it."

"This is what the advisory board *recommends*," Rev. Jackson rephrased his words. "Besides, you need time off to rehabilitate. Recuperate."

Rev. Jackson gave a fake sigh. "Of course, with attendance going down...in your absence and all...and with everybody stepping up to fill your role...it only makes sense the salaries should be more...spread out...at least for the next few months, you see."

"Yeah, I see," Mark echoed with a trace of sarcasm. The money thing wasn't a surprise. Maybe they'd all been waiting for him to split their beloved pie more equitably all along, for all Mark knew.

Both men sat in silence as Mark rolled the "recommendation" around in his head. If he did what they asked him to do, including the apology, he'd be admitting guilt at some level. If he didn't follow their suggestion, he'd put himself in an awkward position—up preaching to people who hadn't had the time to digest what had happened. It was bad enough trying to reach them when he wasn't under a cloud of suspicion. Getting in front of them now might do more harm than good.

Mark wasn't sure. He couldn't make such an important decision without praying first.

"So," Rev. Jackson pressed, "what do you say? Agree with the recommendation?"

"I'll let you know."

"When?"

Mark didn't appreciate being strong-armed, even though he knew it was Rev. Jackson's style. "I'll let you know as soon as I know."

Chapter 19

The only thing worse than being pressured to step down was the fact that he'd been *told* to step down previously, but hadn't obeyed. All that time, Mark had been thinking God was preparing him for some wonderful promotion. *Some promotion this is, he thought.*

Should he go to New Vision on Sunday? He'd already skipped out on Wednesday, partly because his arm was bothering him. What about advisory meetings—could he still attend? How often should he get in touch with Jonathan?

Mark also wondered if it would be appropriate to contact the family of "B," the woman who'd been riding with him. He'd been in a life-or-death situation with this woman. He'd seen her bleeding, possibly breathing her last conscious breaths, sitting less than two feet away from him. No one in their right mind could move on from a situation like that without looking back, checking on the other person—especially knowing this person was most likely a blood relative to his son.

Cutting the French toast with his left hand was awkward and tiresome, but he wouldn't let Sharla or Amani help. The sooner he mastered doing things with his weaker arm, the sooner he'd be able to get back to himself while the Lord continued the long-term process of healing the right.

"These are good," he complimented Sharla.

"Thank you."

Amani hadn't thanked his mother with words. The way he inhaled the breakfast showed his appreciation. "I'm ready."

"Okay." Sharla stood and took Amani's plate to the sink while he went back to the living room to grab his backpack.

Mark wished Sharla wouldn't baby him so much. He could put his own plate in the sink—wash it, too, though Mark had never actually seen Amani so much as lift a finger to clean up anything around the house. The boy needed some chores, but Sharla had that territory all sewed up. From the housekeeper to the gardener to the pool serviceperson, all domestic duties were outsourced.

"Baby, I might stop at the post office after I drop Amani off at school, but I won't be long," Sharla said.

"Wait up." Mark had had enough of wrestling with his food. "I'll ride with you."

Both Sharla and Amani looked at Mark like he was crazy. "You want to ride with me?"

"Yeah. What's wrong with that?" Mark laughed.

"You've never ridden with me to take Amani to school."

"I've never been home with a messed up arm, either, have I?"

Amani gave a smug nod. "This is true, Mother. This is true."

She glanced at her son, then back at her husband. "If you say so."

Mark didn't take for granted the fresh spring air whipping across his face. The sunshine, the sound of birds calling for mates. All of this could have been taken away in an instant. As they sat at the stop light waiting to leave their subdivision, Mark declared, "This is beautiful."

"What?" Sharla asked.

"Everything God made is beautiful."

"Except snot and farts," Amani blurted out.

Mark couldn't help but laugh at his son's ill-placed humor. He'd certainly learned how to enjoy getting on his mother's nerves. There's just something about being able to irritate a woman ever-so-slightly...lets a man know he's still got his place in her heart.

Sharla scolded, "That's gross, Amani."

Mark took up for the boy. "It's a man thing. You wouldn't understand."

"I don't *want* to understand," she bit into both of them, rolling her eyes.

They dropped Amani off at school. Sharla actually made three more stops before returning home: the post office, as she'd already mentioned, as well as the cleaners and the office supply store so she could purchase toner for Amani's printer. Mark waited in the car while she handled her pressing tasks. All of this kept them out for an extra hour.

"Mamasita, is this what you do all day? Rippin' and runnin', as my grandmother would say?"

"This is just the beginning," she informed him.

"What else you got to do this week?"

"Turn in books at the library, buy toiletries, go grocery shopping, couponing, go to the farmer's market to pick out the best fruits and vegetables. Then there's me. Gotta keep myself up by going to the gym, getting my nails done, getting my hair done."

Mark couldn't object to Sharla doing things that kept herself appealing.

"I *do* take care of things at home as well. I have special projects I do once every few weeks—might be painting the baseboards, defrosting the freezer, or taking down all the blinds so I can hose them off and let them dry in the sun.

137

And on top of all that, I have to straighten up between housekeeping."

Mark squinted. "Straighten up between housekeeping? That makes no sense. What's the point in having a housekeeper if you still have to straighten up?"

She laughed. "Because things still get *messed up* in between visits. How do you think our bed gets made every day? You think we got little fairies that go around picking up socks and shoes that *some people* leave all over the house? And for your information, the housekeeper does not clean up your office. I do that myself."

He gave an exaggerated frown, impressed. "Really?"

"Yes. What do you think I do all day—sit on my behind?"

"I plead the fifth."

Her mouth dropped. "I cannot believe you."

"Hey, I didn't know."

"Obviously not. I think the bigger question is what do *you* do all day?" Sharla retorted playfully. "You only preach on Sundays and Wednesdays. What else do you do, Pastor Carter?"

This, of course, led to a never-to-be-settled bet about whose life was more challenging: a pastor's or a mother's. Mark had to acknowledge that Sharla presented a pretty good case. He'd never given much thought to the fact that there was always soap in the dispensers and a new toothbrush magically appeared in his holder every three months.

Though he hadn't done much more than wait in the car and deny Sharla's claims, Mark needed a nap by the time they got home. "Baby, there must be something in the

138

medication the doctor prescribed because I get tired real quick."

"Yeah," she agreed, "the label says it might make you drowsy."

He yawned. "They ain't *never* lied."

She parked in the driveway without raising the garage door. "Let me get you settled in. I've got some more things on my to-do list." She hopped out of the car and came around to his side to open the door for him.

"What time are you coming back?" he wanted to know.

"I don't know."

He hoisted himself out of the car. "Why don't you know?"

She led the way inside the house. "Look, I don't clock in and out when I run errands, okay? I do what I have to do and juggle it with playing taxi to Amani. I don't need you messing up my groove here, okay?"

Sharla fluffed up Mark's pillows and made sure he was comfortable on the couch. She gave him his morning dose of medication, then kissed him on the forehead. "Call me if you need me."

"Um..." Mark stalled. "What am I supposed to eat for lunch? Will you be back by then?"

Sharla put a hand on one hip, obviously holding back a smile. "Maybe. If not, you do still have one good arm. All you have to do is press a few buttons on the microwave."

"I'm calling the people on you," Mark joked.

"What people?"

"The treating sick people *mean* people."

"For your information," she sashayed back to him, "I'm actually helping you today while I'm out. I did a little...let's just say I really, really think it was Bria's boyfriend who was

139

chasing and shooting at your car. I'm going to the station to share my suspicion with Detective Rozanno."

Mark stared into his wife's face. "*Bria*."

Sharla hung her neck forward. "Yeah?"

"Bria—you said her name was *Bria*. You're right."

Sharla squeaked, "*You* said her name was Bria."

"No," he disagreed, "I didn't remember her name until just now, when *you* said it."

"Oh." Sharla jiggled her keys. "Whatever. All I know is her boyfriend's nickname is Boomie. I hope they already have him on file for something. I'll let you know what they say. Bye."

She rushed out the door as though suddenly panicked.

Mark's gut quivered with the realization that his wife was hiding something.

Chapter 20

Sharla collected her wits in the car. *How stupid was that?* She'd said Bria's name aloud before Mark did. Shouldn't have surprised her, though, for as much as she'd been *thinking* Bria's name.

She could only hope that Mark's drugs would fog his memory or recreate her faux pas in a way that left him second-guessing what had just transpired.

She lowered her visor and flipped up the mirror. Makeup still flawless, not a hair out of place. "Come on, girlie. Get yourself together." The pep talk did little to calm her nerves, but it did strengthen her resolve. She needed to take action. The hospital financial counselor had said that there was no way to stop or delay the bills or collection actions from coming before the police investigation was complete.

Even though Sharla felt strongly that the insurance would kick in sooner or later, she didn't even want to *see* a six-figure "amount owed" with their names next to it unless it was for the dream house.

For whatever reason, Detective Rozanno and his alleged team seemed to be dragging their feet on her husband's case. Every time she called, all the detective could say was, "We're asking questions and following up on leads."

Well, she certainly planned to give them a lead that would bring this whole thing to a close soon and clear Mark of any wrongdoing.

She waited on a bench outside the secured doors for Rozanno. He'd have to escort her behind the fortress. Sharla couldn't help the jitters crawling around in her belly. The last thing she needed was to be talking to anyone in law enforcement about Bria Logan.

That chapter of her life was supposed to be over. She couldn't afford to open it back up now. Maybe after Amani was an adult, but not while there was still the possibility that someone might probe into things too deeply.

She heard a buzz, then Detective Rozanno stepped into the waiting area while keeping the door ajar. "Mrs. Clark, come on in."

"Carter," she corrected him.

"Right, Carter. Sorry about that."

He was a short, dumpy man with pronounced male pattern baldness who had probably once been a young, energetic officer. Sharla imagined that maybe he'd taken a bullet to the leg, which caused him to be unfit for the streets. He'd been assigned to a desk job and started eating too many jelly donuts. All downhill from there.

She'd surmised all of this not only from his appearance, but from the way he slumped down the hallway toward his office, where he asked her to sit. "How are ya?" He said it like a disgruntled cafeteria lady might ask, "What'll you have?"

"I'm fine, thank you," she answered.

His office boasted several plaques and certificates acknowledging dedication and selfless service. As Sharla suspected, none of the awards had recent dates.

"I've got some information you might find helpful in your investigation."

He raised an eyebrow. "You doin' my job for me?"

"No," Sharla denied, "I just thought I'd help."

"We don't need your help," he very nearly lectured her. "We'll catch the bad guys."

The first time she'd met the detective, he seemed nonchalant. Today, however, he was just being downright

142

rude. "Detective, I'm not trying to overstep my boundaries, but I *do* have a vested interest in resolving this case quickly. Are you going to take what I give you or not?"

He gave her a condescending scowl, grabbed a pen, and prepped to write in the margin of his desk calendar alongside several other hastily scribbled, nearly illegible notes.

"Don't you have some kind of *file* for my husband's case where you need to record this lead?" Sharla insisted.

"I got this. What's the information?"

"The man who was shooting at my husband's car was Bria's boyfriend, I think. His name is Boomie, or at least that's what they call him."

He wrote the name on the pad. "Anything else?"

"Well, aren't you going to find out if he's in the system? Run an alias check?"

"Lady, you've been watching too many crime TV shows."

Dumbfounded, Sharla's jaw fell open. "Are you kidding me right now? I'm giving you a lead on my husband's case. It may not mean anything to you, but we're trying to save his reputation and keep from going bankrupt."

"Ma'am, your husband's lucky to be alive. Be grateful. And for your information, I've already been in touch with the other victim's family. The moment she wakes up, if she confirms this Boomie character, we'll have reason to move forward. But like you said, you've got a vested interest in clearing your husband. I don't. I only want to get to the truth. I want to know who was shooting at his car and why, and if he was involved in any criminal activity that led up to the crime."

"Alrighty, then." Sharla bit her tongue. "How long do you think this will take?"

143

"I don't know. We're understaffed, underpaid, all that. But…" he swiveled in his chair and focused his attention on his computer screen. He clicked a few buttons. "Wait a minute. Your husband is the pastor, right?"

"Yes."

He clicked a few more times. "Looks like you've saved me a trip." He pressed a red button on his phone, then dialed four numbers.

"Yes, Detective?" a raspy female voice came through.

"Do we have an interrogation room open?"

"Number six," she replied.

"Thanks."

Interrogation?

"Mrs. Carter, I need you to come with me."

"For what?"

"Got a few questions for you." He snapped the pen and placed it in his shirt pocket. And *now* he wants to get up and pull a file from a cabinet, Sharla snarled to herself.

Sharla stayed glued to her chair. "Why do you want to question me?"

"To clear you as a suspect…if I can."

"I don't think so," Sharla barked back.

Rozanno raised his sagging belt back to its long route around his stomach. "Ms. Carter, Bria's family has advised us that you were at the hospital staked out in the waiting room, which raises a flag."

Sharla couldn't believe her ears. What did her being at the hospital have to do with the investigation? "So, what if I was there?"

"What reason would you have to be there?"

She countered, "Why does it matter?"

"*Someone* was shooting at the car…" he alluded.

"Uh, everybody knows it was some criminal guy. They even said so on the news. Plus, Bria's family said it was a man named Boomie."

He crossed his thick arms. "Those reporters don't know what they're talking about. They get all their news from bystanders tryin' to get on the news and say something outrageous so they can become the next YouTube star."

Detective Rozanno might have been right about the spectators' motives, but if Bria's family concurred with the news report, why would the police divert to a wild goose chase—especially one where *she* was the goose? "This is ridiculous. I'm not speaking to you without a lawyer present."

His lips dripped with contempt, making Sharla wonder if it might be better to cooperate rather than wait for her attorney. Maybe if she answered his questions now, he'd show mercy. She had an air-tight alibi for her whereabouts that evening. There was no way they could prove she was anywhere else but home the night of the accident.

"Fine. Let's get this over with."

As she shadowed the officer down to what was presumably room six, Sharla mentally replayed as many episodes of the crime show, *48 Hours,* as possible. Detective Rozanno was treating her like a person of interest, which was right up there next to suspect. The suspects always broke down when the interviewers suggested that they might spend the rest of their lives behind bars. Even the toughest, hardest criminals changed their tunes when prison hung in the loom.

But I'm not guilty of shooting into my husband's car, Sharla reminded herself. She had nothing to hide. If the detective started to sound like he was trying to trip her up,

145

she'd end the interview and call her lawyer without another word crossing her lips.

To Sharla's surprise, a dark-haired, frail-looking woman was waiting for them in the interrogation room. The lady didn't speak. She didn't even offer a hint of a smile. She just sat there in a chair on the far side of the table. Rozanno joined her while Sharla sat alone on her side.

"Who is this?" Sharla felt she had a right to know.

"Monica," Rozanno barely replied.

"What's she doing here?"

"Observing. Training."

Sharla didn't like the idea of being somebody's case study, but there was something about having a woman's presence in the room that offered some sense of female camaraderie, taking the scary edge off the cameras and sound equipment conspicuously placed throughout the room.

Monica set up her notepad with its little keyboard and began typing something or another.

Rozanno jumped right in. "State your full name."

"Sharla Denise Everson-Carter."

She answered a few more run-of-the-mill staple questions before he got to the pertinent ones. "Where were you on the night of your husband's accident?"

"I was at home watching television while my son, Amani, was upstairs playing video games with his friend, Jadan," she answered with a slight upward tilt of the chin. Once she'd given him an account of herself, that should have been the end of the interview, as far as Sharla was concerned.

But the detective pushed on, "What time did Jadan arrive at your house?"

She guesstimated, "Six, six-thirty."

146

"And what time did he leave?"

"Around eight-thirty. His mom came and got him."

He poked out his lips. "Were you there when his mom arrived?"

"Yes, I was."

"Did you see her?"

"Yes…I mean, no, I didn't *see* her see her. She blew her horn. Jadan came downstairs. He left."

"So, you were downstairs while they were upstairs."

"Yes."

"Did you *see* Jadan when he left?"

"No, but I heard him come downstairs." Sharla grew impatient. "You can verify all this with Jadan and my son, you know?"

"No, I can't," he said with a faint smirk on his mouth, "because if you didn't *see* them, then they obviously didn't *see* you for those two hours."

"I'm not an irresponsible parent. I wouldn't leave two teenage boys in my home alone for two hours," she smacked.

Rozanno started with the second round, "Mrs. Carter, where do you park your car?"

The momentary flicker of Monica's eyes set off warning bells in Sharla. "No more questions without my attorney. This interview is over."

Chapter 21

Wherever Sharla went, she sure is taking a long time to come home. If she doesn't come through that door in a heap of sweat from working out and with a couple of bags of something-or-another as evidence of shopping, I will have to check with the IRS to make sure she doesn't have a job I don't know about.

He hoped no one from the media had stopped her. Mark had gone so far as to turn off all ringers on the house phones. The reporters and ambulance-chasers somehow actually thought he would give them an inside scoop for a story or a scenario that might lead to a wacked-out lawyer representing him. No matter how many times he told them that there was nothing to report, they kept calling. "What's your relationship with Bria Logan?" "Is Bria Logan your child's mother?" "Pastor Carter, why would anyone want to kill you?"

He could end the phone calls with the simple flip of a switch. But the blogs were merciless. There was no way to stop people from slandering him in cyberspace. People were comparing him to fallen '80s televangelist, Jim Baker, calling him a "pulpit pimp" and saying he had to be a con artist because he'd also been an insurance salesman. Someone, perhaps one with sense, had linked an aerial photo of his house, saying that obviously the Carters weren't "rich". To which, there were several replies from other people that pastors often have more than one house.

People posted that they knew for a fact he drove an Escalade, but there was no mention that the car was going on ten years old or that he'd bought it before he was ever a pastor. Comments ranged from "leave God's people alone"

148

to "I wouldn't be surprised if he was gay or one of those black-power reverse racism preachers." Of course, several women posted that if Mark was gay, they wanted the opportunity to "turn him back straight." To which one man wrote, "Please don't. He's hot! LOL!"

They laughed, they joked, and applauded the accident as though it were punishment from God. They made nasty comments about Sharla's curvy thighs and even made fun of Amani, saying he looked like an alien. *An alien?*

He'd read a lot of stupid stuff online, but that one took the cake. Who did these people think they were to read an article full of speculation and then comment so negatively? What gave them the right to judge him and his family from clear across the country? And these weren't all the watch-dog types, either. When he followed their profiles back to their Facebook pages, most of them claimed to be Christian. They had families of their own. Children Amani's age. Why were they—his brothers and sisters in Christ— slandering him instead of praying for him? Really, even if he were guilty, prayer would still be in order.

Even if they weren't Christians, whatever happened to innocent until proven guilty? The American way?

Out of curiosity on one semi-intelligent blog post about the Pastor Carter incident, Mark left an anonymous comment stating that people should not hold pastors to a higher standard. He added, "God will, of course, but the most important thing for a Christian to do is to grow in the knowledge of God through Christ."

In just a few moments, the replies started pouring in: "Pastors are shepherds", "Pastors keep the flock in order", "Pastors have to be held to a higher standard, or else they'll lead the people the wrong way."

149

He politely thanked them for sharing their thoughts, then exited off the web. Mark promised himself for the fifth time since Rev. Jackson left the other day that he wouldn't go back on the internet and research himself. But with his best arm still healing and no way to get out of the house, he didn't really know what else to do with all his free time. Even ESPN had gotten boring to him—a sure sign that he was going down.

Examining the books on Sharla's bookshelf, he hoped to find one that might pique his interest. Nothing. He'd read all the magazines twice. He even got the urge to make dinner, but gave it up when he couldn't open a jar of mayonnaise for the sandwiches. He'd have to ask Sharla or Amani to put mayonnaise in an easy-to-open plastic container.

The list of things he needed her for was growing every day. Earlier, he'd done his very best to shave with his left hand. He stopped halfway through the massacre, so frustrated that a few choice words slipped out. He needed an electric shaver. It wouldn't cut as close, but it would have to do.

Of course being right-handed, Mark had known that it would be hard to cope without his dominant side. But he had underestimated how difficult it would be to make concessions with his left. He looked forward to rehab so that he could get his life back.

Mark carefully positioned himself in the corner of the couch so he'd stay upright. He turned off the television and sat in silence for a moment before it occurred to him that he was actually home alone with no Sharla, no Amani, no distractions from church, nothing pertinent on the to-do list. He'd already done the micro-exercises the physical therapist printed off and recommended he do on his own, since it was clear he wouldn't have insurance to pay for services any time soon.

Now what was he supposed to do with himself?

And where on earth was Sharla?

Mark got a text from Jonathan: Get well soon!

He decided to return with a phone call because, God knows, he desperately needed to interact with a human being. "Hey, Jonathan, how is everything?"

"Great, Pastor, just great."

"Uh huh." Mark wondered how could that be, especially since the founding pastor was officially on reduced-pay, in light of a bogus scandal. "Jonathan, could you email me the week's numbers?"

"Oh," his voice dropped, "Pastor Carter, I really don't think you want to see those."

"Yes. I do. That's why I asked."

Jonathan sighed. "Yes, sir."

"When's the next advisory meeting?"

"Tomorrow. Ten a.m."

"Why are we meeting on a Friday?"

"Sir, I can't answer that question."

"Listen," Mark said, "I'm going to check with my wife's schedule to see if she can bring me. If she can't, you come get me."

"Awesome. But sir, your arm. Should you be out?"

"Thanks for your concern, Jonathan, but it's an *arm*, not a brain. Anyway, First Lady keeps me in tight bandages and a sling. I couldn't move it if I wanted to."

Jonathan managed an uneasy laugh. "Yes. I understand. I'll wait to hear from you about whether or not your wife is bringing you."

151

It sounded like a good plan until later when he told Sharla about it. "Absolutely not."

"What?"

"No way are we going to risk infection. Honey, you have metal screws in your arm, you've got a section that's still an open wound. The less you get out in public and risk infection, the better."

"But baby, I'm getting cabin fever here," he came close to whimpering.

"No. I'm not taking you, and you can tell Jonathan to save his gas money. I'm not going to have you going to the meeting, then your arm starts hurting and you have to take a pill, then you need to hurry up and get back home because you're getting sleepy and you need to lie down. Absolutely not."

She swished on back to their bedroom. Mark noticed her empty hands and perfect hair. Again, he wondered where she'd been—especially since she'd returned with such a nasty attitude.

"I won't hold it against you if my arm falls off!" he yelled to her.

"No!" she hollered back.

Who does she think she is? But despite his outward dissent, Mark knew he was blessed to have a wife who made such a fuss over him.

He saved face with Jonathan by saying that something else had come up. It wasn't actually a lie. Something *had* come up—his wife's veto.

"Pastor, maybe you could join us virtually," Jonathan suggested. "You could use the FaceTime app on your iPad and I'll connect using mine."

"Oh. So, like a videoconference?"

"Exactly."

"That'll work. Email me the agenda and the numbers. I'll figure out how to use the app thing on my wife's tablet by tomorrow."

Mark fiddled with the app for a while and decided that his office was the best place to set up shop for the meeting. Then he opened the agenda Jonathan had sent him. Immediately, he realized why Jonathan had been so persistent about Mark's attendance.

Chapter 22

Jonathan's image was the first to appear onscreen. "Can you hear me?"

"Yes," Mark replied. "Can you see and hear me, too?"

"Loud and clear," Jonathan confirmed. "I'm going to set the camera up at the table where you'd normally sit. How's that?"

"Excellent."

The streaming video bounced around before settling in a spot that gave Mark a clear view of the men surrounding the table. "Where's Kit?"

Rev. Jackson answered, "He couldn't make it tonight."

"You didn't answer my question."

Marshall obviously wasn't used to videoconferencing. He gave Jackson a silly smile that he probably wouldn't have if the pastor was physically present in the room.

Mark put him on the spot. "Marshall, where's Kit?"

"Uh...he's..." Marshall's eyes darted to the other men for help. When they offered none, he came clean, "He took off today."

"I see." Exactly what Mark thought.

"Let's pray." Jackson took over, opening their meeting with a request for guidance and understanding. "First thing is to look at last week's numbers."

Mark switched his attention to Amani's computer. Jonathan reviewed the data, pointing out the most significant stats. "Attendance was down by approximately thirty percent, offering by forty-five."

"How many came to Christ?" Mark asked.

"One in each service, sir," Jonathan said.

There must have been something about viewing the men from a different perspective that gave Mark even more insight, because that camera told it all. "Why isn't this information in the report, like we discussed?"

"I was…later advised not to," Jonathan reported.

"Advised by whom?"

Rev. Jackson intervened, "We've decided that information can't actually be determined. Some people accept Christ while sitting in their seats, without ever coming to the front altar."

Jackson had a point, but Mark needed to make his. "If I *ask* for a report, I expect to have it."

"Duly noted," Marshall spurted with a mocking expression that was amplified by the underside of his chin, which Mark happened to be able to see well.

Mark wondered how being gone for a little over a week could usher in such disrespect. One man talking crazy, another man didn't even show up for work.

Rev. Jackson charged ahead with the agenda. "Understandably, the numbers aren't good. But we've had setbacks before. We'll bounce back. Amen?"

"Amen" from all.

They reviewed the bids for choir robe cleaning and decided on a new company that was trying to gain traction in the community. The process for the children's baptism program had been revised so that the children didn't have to attend four classes before professing Christ publicly.

Rev. Jackson read the next item on the agenda. "Partnership with local chapter of fraternity, Theta Phi Mu, to host an event at New Vision."

"That's a no," Mark quickly stated.

"Well, I think we ought to table it for now since Kit isn't here. This was his idea," Rev. Marshall said.

"It's a no today, and it's gonna be a no tomorrow, next week, next month, period," Mark made himself perfectly clear.

"Pastor, I don't think you understand. We're in a *crisis*," Marshall stressed. "New Vision is being dragged through the mud. We *need* to partner with a well-known, well-respected organization to let the community know that we're still the place to be despite the smaller numbers and all the...you know...the scandal you've put us in."

It's a good thing the meeting was taking place on a couple of tablets instead of in person. Mark wanted to yell in Marshall's face so hard, spit flew out, "You know me! You know I haven't done anything wrong!"

But thanks to God's infinite wisdom, the setting had been altered.

"Rev. Marshall, even though this is a scandal, the best thing we can do is assure the congregation that nothing scandal*ous* has actually taken place. Furthermore, even if I had done something scandalous—which I have not, for the record—but if I *had*, that wouldn't necessarily be a reason for members to leave their God-appointed posts in the church."

"Yeah, yeah, I get all that," Marshall jived. "What I don't get is why you have a problem with Theta Phi Mu. What—you wanted to pledge when you were in college and they wouldn't accept you?"

Mark wasn't sure if Rev. Marshall really thought that was funny or if he was insulting Mark double-time by pretending to forget the fact that his pastor hadn't gone to college. Again, the cyber-space between them had served its function well.

"It's got nothing to do with this particular fraternity or any Greek letter organization, for that matter. Maybe *Jonathan* doesn't know, but *you* and especially *Kit* know where I stand about keeping the exalting of Greek letters and the exalting of Christ separate. We don't mix the two at New Vision."

"Like I said, that's Kit's thing," Rev. Marshall bowed out of the battle. He must have known there was no way he could win that one.

Rev. Jackson resumed the lead, covering the next month's budget requests. Then Marshall discussed the temporary redistribution of salaries. Mark listened quietly, waiting for the bottom line. "Pastor, since we're all going to be taking up the slack while you're…out indefinitely…we propose to reallocate thirty percent of your salary."

He and Sharla could survive off of thirty percent less from the church. It wouldn't be pretty, but they could swing things until he was released to resume normal duties. Though he really didn't like the thought of fulfilling what he believed to be Kit's agenda—which was to get as close to "rich" as possible through ministry—he had to admit that the proposal was reasonable. The advisory board had always done its best to be fair, if nothing else. "What's the schedule?"

"Schedule?" Marshall repeated.

"Yeah. Who's preaching when? I'd love to come and be fed, myself."

Marshall shuffled through a few papers. "I'll do this coming week's sermons—Sunday and Wednesday, since it's the first week. Kit'll take second, Jackson third. We're still thinking through the fourth."

"I'll do it!" Jonathan piped up.

Rev. Jackson and Rev. Marshall looked at Jonathan like he was crazy. Actually, they looked at him more like he was trying to steal money from their pockets, which would be in order if he actually stepped into the rotation.

Jonathan took advantage of their silence. "I've been to seminary, I've studied under some of the best preachers, had my sermons critiqued. And isn't fourth Sunday youth Sunday? It would make sense for me to preach then."

The thought of Jonathan preaching in the near future was definitely not on Mark's radar. Sure, Jonathan had studied and was an excellent resource when it came to researching the context of scriptures. More than once, Mark had been able to add insight to his sermons based on information that Jonathan produced—that is, when Mark wasn't downloading them from SermonDepot.com.

But could they trust the flock to a kid?

Mark leaned toward his iPad, which only captured Jonathan's profile. "I have to say, this is a surprise."

Rev. Marshall laughed, "Most definitely. Jonathan, you've only been here…what? Six months?"

Jonathan pushed his glasses up higher on his nose. "Yes, I understand. But this wouldn't be my *first* first sermon. I preached at my cousin's funeral. I-I spoke at my niece's kindergarten graduation."

Rev. Jackson and Marshall busted out laughing. Mark had to cover his mouth.

"Whoo!" Marshall slapped Jonathan on the back. "Aw, man, you got me!"

"Did anybody get saved?" Rev. Jackson joshed.

Thankfully, Mark could see that Jonathan himself recognized the humor in his statement.

"Okay, okay. That wasn't the best example," he admitted, "but I came to this church not just because I needed a job. I needed a place where I could grow, where I could learn to run a church. And I know that preaching is part of what makes a church run well. I gotta get my start sooner or later. Everybody does, right?"

Jackson and Marshall calmed down long enough to acknowledge Jonathan's addendum. That's when Mark, for the first time, recognized that if Jonathan had the ability to win over two men who stood to lose money because of him, he might have a future in sharing the gospel on a large platform.

"So, Jonathan, do you mind if I ask you something?" Mark probed. "It's a question I ask every potential minister at New Vision. One I've never written down, one that I ask you not to share with anyone else who might be interviewing with me for such a position in the future."

"Shoot," Jonathan consented confidently.

Marshall tilted far back in his seat. Jackson folded his hands on the table.

"If you died, were suddenly standing at heaven's gate, knocking, and God asked you why He should let you into His kingdom, how would you answer?"

Jonathan looked at his two comrades quizzically. They stared back. Stoic. For some reason, Mark felt his chest tightening.

Jonathan laughed nervously. "I mean, that's…like…a trick question. God would never ask me that."

"Explain yourself." Mark prompted.

The camera shifted. Jonathan talked to Mark face-on. "Because that would be like me going to my best friend's house, knocking on the door and him asking me why he should let me in. That wouldn't happen because we would have talked earlier that day, we might have talked while I was on the way over—when I got there, he wouldn't do anything else but open the door wide and welcome me in. That's how it'll be with me and God because of Christ. He'll welcome me like a friend because that's what we've been all along the way."

In all his years of asking men and women that same question, Mark had never heard or seen a more sincere, passionate answer. And with His unmistakable power.

Jonathan turned the camera back toward its previous arrangement, capturing the astonished expressions of his elders, who sat speechless.

Mark spoke for them all. "You're in the rotation, Jonathan."

Chapter 23

If he didn't get out of the house soon, Mark was going to pull his eyelashes out one by one. The marvel of watching Sharla run the household had worn off. And now that Amani was out of school for the summer, Mark found it hard to watch how his wife and son interacted. She fussed at him perpetually, and he bit back with comments that bordered between hilarious and disrespectful.

Then Mark had to jump in on his wife's side, but a part of him wished Sharla would just be quiet and stop pestering the boy about every little thing. "Amani, you didn't make your bed right," "Amani, sit a little further back from the television," "Amani, those shoes don't match your outfit."

Really, it was enough to make a grown man wild, let alone a teenager trying to express himself. Mark wondered when Sharla had gone from simply being a detail-oriented person to being a control-freak. He appreciated all the hard work she obviously put into managing their household, but was it really *that* serious?

He couldn't take much more of it. The visitors from the church had stopped coming by except for Rev. Jackson, who always joked around with Amani every time he dropped by. Though Mark and Jackson might disagree about a lot of things with regard to New Vision, they were friends and brothers in Christ nonetheless. They had both mastered the art of weaving in and out of their roles with ease.

He whispered to Jackson, "My wife's driving me crazy. I gotta get back to the office. Can I borrow your old pickup truck?"

"Now, Pastor, I would let you, but you know that truck is a stick. You'd need both arms to drive it."

161

"Aw, dang." Mark chewed another nail and tapped his foot.

"Where you wanna go? I'll be glad to take you somewhere."

"Anywhere, I don't care."

"Let's roll."

Mark seized the opportunity. He sprang from the couch. "Sharla, I'm leaving with Rev. Jackson. We'll be back later."

She was in the living room before they could make a move. "Where are y'all going?"

"Riding around," Mark said.

Sharla spoke to Rev. Jackson, "Mark's on medication, you know? He can't go long without it or those nerves might start to acting up. And he can't have a lot of jarring action."

"Sister, I'll be extra careful with him." Rev. Jackson put an arm around Mark's shoulder and escorted him to his own front door.

"Rev., are you sure?"

"Yes indeed. Talk to you later."

"Bye, baby." Mark quickly walked toward his friend's car and hopped in before Sharla could come up with another reason why he shouldn't go.

Jackson started the car. The rumble of the engine swept through Mark's body. "Freedom!" he yelled.

"Aw now, Mark, don't get so upset with her. You know that's how women are. They ain't happy if they ain't got nobody to worry after."

"This is exhausting," Mark confided. "It's like she's always trying to make sure everything is perfect, and I don't know why."

"Some people just like that." Jackson backed out of the driveway and headed onto a main street. "Where to?"

"I don't know. You hungry?"

"Not really," Jackson said.

"Me, either." Sharla made sure he ate so his body would have the energy and nutrients to heal itself.

Jackson turned up his Neal Roberson CD. The old-school gospel rhythms, the guitars, the tambourine, and the blues-like composition seemed a perfect soundtrack for the moment. Mark rocked to the song, *My Mind is Gone*. The heavy beat thumped deep down inside him.

They rode, listening to music for about fifteen minutes. Mark thanked God for Jackson. Sharla couldn't have ever just ridden in a car without an agenda, without talking—unless she was purposely giving him the silent treatment which, actually, was louder than words.

The highway wasn't as crowded as he thought it would be. They cruised another five minutes before nearing the exit to the hospital where Mark had been a patient the week before. He was glad to be looking at the rows of windows from far away.

Suddenly, the question plagued him: Was Bria still in the hospital? "Rev., you heard anything else about the lady who was in the wreck with me?"

"No, sir, I haven't."

"You think we ought to find out?"

"I reckon it couldn't hurt. Maybe your *lawyer* can find out for you," he obviously tried to nip Mark's wild idea in the bud.

The attempt didn't work. "I was thinking...maybe we should go by there. Check on her."

"Now Mark, I can't sign up for no kind of foolishness. We already got the reporters coming to church and picking the members for dirt. Last thing we need is you pokin' around the hospital bed of the woman they think you seein' on the side."

"But I've got you with me. We're going on behalf of New Vision. If the paparazzi are anywhere near, they'll get their Sunday evening feel-good story—Injured Pastor Visits Fellow Accident Victim," Mark drew a rosy picture.

"Or Suspect Visits Victim on Death Bed to Finish What He Started," Rev. Jackson dumped a bucket of black paint on Mark's scene.

"Look, this isn't about just me. It's about 'Mani." Mark knew he'd struck a chord. Rev. Jackson had a soft spot in his heart for Amani. "I think Bria is some kin to him."

"Bria?"

"Yes. That's her name."

"Sounds like one of them young names," Jackson estimated. "She his cousin or something?"

"I'm not sure. I need to find out. I think Sharla already knows, but she's keeping her lips sealed," he confided.

"Did you ask her what she knows about Bria?"

"No. 'Mani's been dropping hints lately that he wants to get more information about his birth family, but every time he does, Sharla gets touchy. I think she feels like he's trying to fill her spot in his life with someone else," he explained. "I've tried to tell her that no matter what, she'll always be the one who heard his first words, saw him take the first steps. It's weird, Rev. She'd never help me check on Bria."

"So I gotta ask," the elder probed, "if you know what can of beans you might open if you go see this Bria woman, why do you *really* want to go see her the first minute you get out of the house without your wife?" He gave a sideways glance.

Mark couldn't believe his ears. "Rev., are you kidding me?"

"I'm just askin' for the record."

"You of all people should know me better than that. I'm not a cheater."

"Don't get all bent out of shape," Jackson griped. "You was a man before you was ever a minister. We all got temptations. I needed to hear it straight from the horse's mouth, that's all."

A hundred darts pierced Mark's heart. If Rev. Jackson thought his pastor capable and possibly guilty of sneaking around with Bria, it was no wonder the rest of the world assumed the worst.

The rest of the trip to Ben Taub was unmarked by words. The pastor would have to temporarily suspend the sense that his reputation had a big, blotchy, red stain on it. Suffice it to say, however, that his resolve to see Bria had only been strengthened. If people judged him when he'd done nothing wrong, what difference would it make if he really *did* mess up?

Rev. Jackson parked near the main entrance. "You sure about this?"

"I'm not sure what *this* is, but I'm sure I need to check on her. We almost died together," Mark tried to give an explanation, but he was sure Jackson couldn't comprehend the ineffable bond.

"Come on, then. Ride or die." Rev. Jackson exited the vehicle.

Mark matched his stride toward the building. "Man, how you go from darn near accusing me of cheating to standing by me?"

"I was gon' stand by you whether you cheated or not. I just wanted to know the truth so I could know *how* to stand for you—by your side, in the gap, whatever," Jackson spoke wisely.

"I guess you're all right then, old man." Mark slapped the reverend on the shoulder. "Ride or die."

They had to stop at the information desk to find out Bria's room number. "I'm sorry, but due to the press's attempts to get in, we're only allowing family to see Bria at this time," the long-hair, hippie throwback receptionist apprised them.

"We're her church family," Rev. Jackson offered. "And this gentleman here was actually in the accident with her."

Mark raised his arm slightly.

The lady bunched her lips and twisted them to one side. "Okay. But if you two are lying, may you burn in hell forever."

Mark and Rev. Jackson both looked at each other, then back at the woman.

"Do you know what you're saying?" Mark asked.

"Yeah. Liars won't go to heaven. Isn't that what y'all believe?"

Mark ignored her cynical air, careful to stay in her good graces so she'd give them the room number. "We believe that even a liar can be changed through Christ because He has already decided to forgive every lie we might ever tell."

She redirected her attention to the computer screen. "You're definitely not the press. Room four ten."

They took the elevators to the fourth floor which, Mark

166

gladly noted from wall signs, was the step-down unit from ICU. In all those hours he'd spent at home bored out of his mind, he'd searched high and low to find out if anyone had posted any kind of update on her status. No one had written anything except to say that she was almost dead. Mark thanked God that Bria's condition had improved.

He couldn't speak for Rev. Jackson, but when the elevator doors opened, Mark was almost afraid of what might transpire when he saw Bria again. Would she be angry? Would she remember? What if she looked terrible? In his years as a pastor, Mark had been called to many bedsides and seen people's bodies deteriorate to the point where they were unrecognizable. Of course, he always manned up for the family's sake. But he knew there was no way he could have endured what he'd seen were it not for the grace of God.

"Here it is," Rev. Jackson sighed as they stood in front of Bria's door.

They both nearly jumped when the door came swinging open and they came face-to-face with a woman wearing a top that, unfortunately, left nothing to the imagination and skin-tight jeans that traced every pothole in her thighs. Her fire-red braids swung to stand-still, settling against her arms.

She looked Mark up and down, disgust written across her mouth. "Whatchu doin' here?"

"I came to check on Bria."

"Momma, who is it?" a groggy voice sputtered. The beep-beep-beep of a machine competed with her volume.

Mark stepped to his right, trying to look past the woman who'd made herself a barricade between him and Jackson on one side and Bria on the other.

The woman glanced back over her shoulder. "Nobody.

Just some more nosy reporters."

Bria's mother put her hands on Marks and Rev. Jackson's chest and pushed them both back into the hallway. "You got a lot of nerve coming here."

"Mrs...Ma'am," Mark spoke in his most respectful tone, "I don't mean any harm. I just came to check on her as her pastor and as someone who survived that accident with her. How is she?"

The woman crossed her arms which, Mark noticed, squished her chest up a few inches higher and exposed the muffin top above her pants. Really, he wasn't trying to look at her body—but it looked at him.

"She's doing fine for somebody who got shot and whose head got smashed into a windshield and right leg got crushed, thanks to you."

"How is it my fault?" Mark wanted to know. Rev. Jackson put an arm on Mark's shoulder.

"'Cause you was the one driving, fool! You didn't have no business with my daughter in your car, your wife chasin' y'all down the street like she crazy," she said.

"My wife has nothing to do with this," Mark disagreed.

"You gon' wish she didn't after we finish suin' y'all and that big ol' church you got. My daughter gon' be a handicap for life. And she ain't gon' never look the same. Never get married, never find a man—least not a good-lookin' one. He gon' be ugly."

She glanced at Mark's arm. "And what you walk out the hospital with—a five dollar arm sling and some Tylenol?"

He couldn't answer the question because he was still stuck on 'suin' y'all and that big ol' church'. "I don't know where you're getting your information, but the person chasing us was not my wife. It was a man, and Bria knew

168

him."

"You tryin' to say my daughter was a slut? That she was sleeping with somebody other than you?" The woman got in Mark's face.

Rev. Jackson stepped up. "Whoa, now. We didn't come here for all of this. Why don't we all just let the police do their job and the pastor and Bria can go on about the business of getting healed. It was nice to meet you, ma'am. Please let Bria know that her church family cares about her, alright?"

He stepped back, and Mark followed suit.

"The last thing Bria needs is a bunch of church folk comin' around here. I'm her family. We look out for her, and we look out for each other. I suggest you and your wife look out, too."

The threat in her tone caught Mark off guard. "Excuse me?"

"You heard me. And you and your wife betta stop comin' up to this hospital. Don't, next time, I'll have somethin' waitin' on you." She flipped her braids and ducked back into Bria's room.

Chapter 24

Sharla had pretended like she didn't want Mark to go with Rev. Jackson, but the timing couldn't have been better. She and Danny Hernandez, the family attorney, planned to meet up with Rozanno and squash his foolish theory before it gained any momentum.

Danny had warned Sharla that sometimes once a detective has made up in his heart or mind that a suspect was guilty, he or she would proceed with the investigation in a biased manner.

"But that's not fair," Sharla had complained, even though she realized she sounded naive.

"It's human nature," Danny said. "No one wants to be proven wrong."

"The thing is, I haven't done anything wrong," Sharla reiterated. Didn't it matter that she was actually innocent?

"That may be, but you still have to defend yourself against allegations. You can't imagine the number of people sitting behind bars right now because they thought being innocent was enough," he said.

As much as Sharla wanted to think that Danny was just trying to make himself seem extremely valuable so he could bill her for as many hours as possible, a part of her couldn't deny what he was saying.

Her Uncle Jimmy had spent twelve years in prison for an armed robbery that he swore on his deathbed he didn't commit. Her grandmother vouched for Jimmy's whereabouts on the day of the robbery, but she couldn't prove that Jimmy had been in bed asleep because...well, how do you prove that someone was asleep? There's no record, no evidence of someone *not* being somewhere.

Largely based on the eyewitness testimony of a person who was two aisles over in the mom-and-pop convenience store, Uncle Jimmy spent the first part of his adult life rooming with murderers, rapists, and drug dealers. If he wasn't a hardened criminal before he went in, he sure was one when he got out. He admitted to doing wrong the second time he went to prison, but Grandmother always said it was the system that had turned Uncle Jimmy into a criminal.

That same system was pointing fingers at Sharla. She thanked God they had the money to afford a good lawyer. Even if they didn't, she'd have sold everything to retain Danny because without him, she'd probably end up broke anyway.

Danny met her outside the police station ten minutes before their appointment. They sat on a bench as he prepped her before going inside. "We'll sit side by side, just like we are now. Look at me before you answer a question. I'll nod and tell you to go ahead or I'll answer for you. Got it?"

"Got it." Sharla gave a child-like nod.

After the lecture he'd given her when she called to tell him about what happened with Rozanno, Sharla wasn't about to deviate from the plan.

"You follow my lead and this interview will be over before you know it," Danny assured her.

"Interview? I thought it was an interrogation."

"He said 'interrogation' to intimidate you. But when I set it up, he called it an interview, which is exactly what it is, legally. I know his type."

Rozanno was visibly upset with Danny's presence in the interrogation room. The attorney was taller than Rozanno by at least four inches, with a nose that had clearly been broken at least once, and intense eyes. Sharla smiled inside.

Rozanno would get the chance to know what it felt like to be intimidated.

As soon as all the equipment was prepped and the same identifying questions were asked, Rozanno started, "Mrs. Carter, did you know that your husband was having an affair with Bria Logan?"

Danny popped in, "An *alleged* affair. You're trying to get at a motive; I'm advising my client not to answer this question based on the fact there's no proof an affair was taking place. She won't subject herself to supposition."

Rozanno's skin flushed a shade. He stretched his neck. "Well, let's go to something we can prove. Lisa Logan said that you were at the hospital waiting in the ICU to see Bria. Is this true?"

Again, Danny jumped in, "What proof do you have that my client was at the hospital?"

"It's not hard to run the tape," Rozanno laughed uneasily.

"But have you done it?" Danny pinned him.

"Not yet."

"Until you do, this is all heresay. Next question." Danny sighed as though Rozanno was wasting everyone's time.

While a part of Sharla wanted to cheer for Danny, she was still afraid. What if Danny's flagrant attitude made Rozanno even angrier? Wasn't the fact that she wasn't answering questions making her look guilty, like she was hiding behind her lawyer?

Rozanno clicked his cheek, "All right, wise guy, where was your client the night of the accident?"

Danny nodded at Sharla.

"I was at home watching television in my bedroom while my son and his friend played video games."

"They were upstairs and you were downstairs," the

172

detective stressed.

She knew he already knew the answer. For the record, Sharla confirmed, "Yes."

"Mrs. Carter, how many square feet is your home?"

Her lawyer intercepted, "We can provide you with the builder's estimate, provided you let us know why."

"If she was downstairs and the teens were upstairs, there is always the possibility they weren't aware she left," Rozanno exposed himself. "She has no way of proving that she never left the house."

"And you have no way of proving that she did," he turned the tables. "There must have been witnesses to the accident. Have you interviewed them?"

"Of course we did."

"Did any of them indicate seeing my client's car?"

"I-I-don't know," Rozanno said. "We haven't had opportunity to compare the descriptions with Mrs. Carter's vehicle."

"Do you know what kind of vehicle my client drives?"

"No," Rozanno said.

"She drives a bright red Mercedes, detective. If a bright red Mercedes were chasing a big white Escalade down a busy street, that detail wouldn't have escaped you. If there are no more questions, shall we conclude that my client is no longer a person of interest?"

"Not until we run forensics on her car."

My car? Sharla's eyes darted to Danny.

He remained as calm as he'd been the entire meeting. "And once it's clear?"

"*If* it's clear, then…" Rozanno shrugged.

"Then she's clear."

"Unless something else comes up." Rozanno rolled his

lips between his teeth.

"Let me ask you something, if I may," Danny snooped, "do you have other suspects in this case? How about— what's his name?" Danny turned to Sharla.

"Boomie."

"Yes. Boomie," Danny suggested.

Rozanno's redness deepened again. "I don't need you two to tell me how to conduct my investigation."

"Fine. She'll leave her car voluntarily. Sharla, give him your key."

She wrestled with the ring for a second, then handed Rozanno her fob. I'm in the east parking lot."

Danny asked, "What time can she pick it up tomorrow?"

"Not sure. She can call the station and ask for—"

"No. We're not playing that game. She'll be back at noon tomorrow. If you're not finished with it by then, you'll need a subpoena." Danny turned to Sharla. "If your car isn't ready tomorrow at twelve, give me a call."

"Good day, detective." Danny gave the officer a quick handshake and escorted Sharla past the secure doors and out to a public sitting area.

"Thank you," she said, though she wasn't quite sure if they'd done the right thing.

"Look, Rozanno's got some other agenda going on here. My hunch is that it has nothing to do with you, which means it doesn't concern us. So long as you get off the bad list, my job is done."

Danny checked his watch. "Aye! I gotta go. Can you call someone for a ride?"

"What?" Sharla flexed her arms like she was carrying two platters. "I thought you were going to take me home?"

"I'm so sorry. I can't, I've got to get to my daughter's

birthday party at the daycare. They should be waking up from naptime now."

His excuse melted Sharla's heart. If only Mark had been there to witness that moment. "Go ahead. I'll get a ride."

She couldn't help but think that if Mark had been at home, where every grown and married man with children ought to be after he left work at a decent hour, maybe they wouldn't have been in that predicament.

Why was he so overly-dedicated to New Vision? Wasn't there something in the Bible about taking care of home first?

Mark was the last person Sharla wanted to call to come pick her up. He'd probably grill her worse than Rozanno. She could hear him already: Why'd you leave your car? Why did you go see the detective without me? How many hours have you racked up on our tab with Hernandez?

She really didn't want to hear all that. She called the one person who could be trusted with that sensitive request. Unfortunately, Candace didn't pick up the phone.

Next on the list was another long-time First Lady, Jasmine. Sharla was sure that Jasmine would share the incident with the other first ladies, but it would go no further than that. "Hi, Jasmine, this is Sharla. I was wondering, can you could pick me up from the police station?"

"The police?" she squealed, "What are you doing there?"

"Well, you know all the stuff that's been happening with Mark. They wanted to ask me some questions. And they're scouring my car."

"Wow," Jasmine said. "That's really, really sad, Sharla. Terrible."

"I know. So can you pick me up?"

"Definitely."

Sharla gave the address and took a seat on the bench

175

outside next to a mother and her infant daughter. The baby had a headful of curly black locks, and skin the color of black coffee. Beautiful. She was totally preoccupied with the toys dangling overhead in her car seat. "How old is she?"

"Ten months going on fifteen years," the young mother laughed. "She's got way too much energy for me."

"She's gorgeous."

"Thank you."

Sharla admired how well the young mother had dressed her baby. Pink and purple from head to toe, with little studs in her ears. The mother's wedding ring hadn't skipped Sharla's notice. It was a platinum band, lightly dusted with diamonds. Sharla didn't feel the tinge of jealousy. The woman *deserved* to have a baby, unlike all the other women who'd simply laid down with a man and pushed out a baby nine months later.

But even though she wasn't jealous, Sharla had to wonder: What made her better than me? What was it about her that made God say, "*That* woman should give birth to a baby, but Sharla shouldn't?"

Jasmine blew, taking Sharla's attention from the silent appraisal.

"Have a good day," Sharla dismissed herself.

"You, too."

Sharla hadn't even had a chance to fasten her seatbelt before Jasmine sped off. "Where's the fire?"

"Girl, I got to watch my back," Jasmine said, eyeing every mirror and checking every inch of her view. "You know you're the most talked about woman in town right now; there's got to be somebody watching you."

"Watching me?"

"Mmm hmm."

176

When Jasmine lowered the brim of her sunhat, Sharla knew exactly what she meant. "You have been watching too many television shows."

"We got to keep low profiles, sis." Her vibrant makeup and sequin-top maxi dress wouldn't have allowed her to be inconspicuous anywhere. "My husband really didn't want me to come pick you up, but I told him if we didn't help the needy, what good were we?"

I'm needy? "Thank you."

"You got it, girl. Now what possessed you to get dropped off at the police station instead of driving your own car?"

Sharla hinted at the situation without giving up too much information. She owed Jasmine some kind of clarification, but not her life.

"You know cops are people, too. You got your good ones and your bad ones," Jasmine summarized. "Just like pastors."

"Yep," Sharla agreed.

"Now, what are you going to do about this other woman?"

Sharla gasped, "My husband was *not* seeing that woman."

"Mmm," Jasmine groaned, giving Sharla the girl-please eye.

"I'm serious."

Jasmine was silent, turning on the major thoroughfare that would lead them back to the Carter residence. After hitting a long stretch, she sighed, "Look, now I know I'm not supposed to be gossiping and I know it is not my place to tell another woman that her husband might be lying, but as first ladies, we've got to have each other's backs."

Sharla put up the time-out signal. "If this is a bunch of

177

he-said-she-said, I don't want to hear it."

"No…well, yes it is what someone else said, but it's someone I trust."

"Who?" Sharla pecked.

"Montel. My hair dresser. He used to date the other…the woman who was in the car with your husband. Apparently, she's a real good-lookin' girl, looks much younger than she is. Montel said she's been using men to pay her bills for years. Matter of fact, that's why he broke up with her," Jasmine advised.

"What's that got to do with Mark and me?"

"I'm just saying. If Mark *did* get caught up with her, I don't want you to do anything drastic. At least not right away. Get some counseling first because evidently this woman is a seasoned home-wrecker. This ain't her first rodeo. The enemy bombards men of God with temptation, you know?"

Jasmine went off on a tangent about the spirit of Jezebel and Delilah. She re-told the story of David with a slant toward painting Bathsheba as a seductress. Really, she could have made a tape and sold a CD of it at a pastor's wives conference.

"Why is everybody so quick to believe the worst?" Sharla blurted out.

"I didn't say I believe the worst," Jasmine yapped back.

"But you're sitting here telling me how to reframe the picture of my husband cheating when I don't even own that picture!"

"You honestly don't believe he's cheating?" Jasmine fished.

"No! That woman wasn't his mistress—she's Amani's mother, okay?"

178

"Oh my gosh!" Jasmine put a hand over her mouth. "Now I see! I knew people were saying he'd been in the wreck with his baby Momma, but I didn't believe it because I knew that you and Mark had adopted Amani. Girl, I was starting to wonder if the girl was a surrogate mother – if y'all had done a Sarah and Hagar thing."

Sharla couldn't take it anymore. She warned calmly, "Jasmine, shut up."

"Oh, I know you didn't." Jasmine made a quick right into a driveway about half a mile from Sharla's house. "You not gon' sit in *my* car and tell *me* to shut up, not when I'm doin' *you* a favor. You can get out right now."

"Gladly." Sharla reached for the door's handle.

"You need to quit," Jasmine fussed. "You know I ain't about to put you out over this. I'm not tryin' to be funny; I just don't want to see you get hurt."

"Too late. I'm already hurt. I'm tired, I'm upset, I feel like I've been to hell's waiting room and back," Sharla admitted.

"I've been there, too. The good thing is, you came back."

Jasmine had a point. Sharla was still there, still madly in love with her husband, still dedicated to her family despite all the chaos. "I'm sorry I told you to shut up."

"Well, sometimes I probably should shut up," Jasmine had to agree. She backed out of the stranger's property and proceeded down the street. "It takes a real friend to tell me when I need to shut my trap. You alright with me, sis."

Jasmine had been the best choice for a ride home after all. Candace probably would have listened, shared a few thoughts, and then prayed. As wrong as Jasmine was for sharing the latest beauty shop gossip, Sharla did appreciate the fact that she wasn't trying to make everything all...holy.

Well, except for that little mini-sermon.

As she walked into her house, Sharla could only laugh.

That laugh quickly faded when she found Mark sitting on their bed with his veins standing out in livid ridges. "Why in the world did you go to the hospital to see Bria?"

Chapter 25

Her slumped shoulders told Mark she was guilty before her mouth admitted it. "I wanted to see for myself, I guess."

"See what?" Mark searched for a reasonable response.

Sharla shrugged. "I don't know. I wanted to see if she was going to live, why she was in the car with you. If she looked like Amani."

"Why would any of that matter?"

"It doesn't, okay," she agreed, "that's why I left before I went into her room. I realized it was stupid and I left. But Bria's mother saw me before I could get out."

Well, at least they saw eye-to-eye about the fact that she shouldn't have been at the hospital.

"How did *you* know I was at the hospital?" Sharla flipped the table.

Mark had every intention of telling Sharla that he'd gone to the hospital. Later. Alas, the suspicious line darkening the corners of her mouth demanded an immediate answer. "I went there, too."

Sharla threw her hands in the air. "How you gon' get mad at *me* for going? What did *you* go for?

"Because I'm her pastor. I went to see her the same way I visit every other sick member if I can," he tried his best to minimize.

"No, no, no." Sharla wasn't going down so easily. "You and Rev. Jackson told me you were going for a ride."

"We were."

"How did y'all end up at Ben Taub?"

Mark really didn't have a good explanation. To say 'it just happened' wouldn't suffice, even though it was the truth. He couldn't think of a good excuse for why he'd done

181

the same thing his wife had done. The whole thing was silly. "I don't know, Sharla."

"Now you know exactly how I feel." She sat down at the foot of the bed. "This whole thing has got me going crazy. Between the TV reports, taking care of you, not resting well...it's amazing I've still got my head on straight."

Mark scooted toward her and gave her a hug. "I feel you, Mamasita. But everything's gonna be alright."

"I got something else to tell you."

Mark waited for her to spill it.

"My car has been...retained for the investigation until tomorrow."

"What?"

"Yeah. Danny Hernandez made a deal for me to leave the car until noon. When it turns up clean, I'll be eliminated as a suspect."

It was all news to Mark. "A *suspect*?"

"Oh. Yeah. I forgot to tell you that."

Mark looked down his nose at her. "Seriously?"

She gave the baseball "safe" signal with her hands. "I just want you to worry about getting well, that's all. The sooner we get all this investigation out of the way, the sooner the insurance will go through and life can get back to normal."

For the first time, Mark realized how exhausted his wife must have been, both mentally and physically. She'd been carrying so much stress already; he couldn't possibly add the news that Bria's family was considering a civil suit.

"Don't worry about me, Sharla."

"How can I not? Every day that the insurance doesn't come through is another day without therapy. I want you to start rehab soon so your arm won't heal all crooked."

As serious as Sharla's intent was, her word choice injected humor into the otherwise somber situation. They both collapsed into each other, laughing.

Mark stood and twisted his left arm against his side. "You still gon' love me if I look like this?" He then added a limp leg and contorted his face.

Sharla fell over on the bed. "You'd better stop before you end up like that for real."

It felt good to make his wife laugh.

"That's not funny," she giggled.

Instantly Mark thought about Bria. He wondered if she would end up disfigured. Lame. "You're right, babe. It could have been me." He sat down next to her again.

"But it wasn't, thank God."

"Yeah." His mind replayed the one part of the accident that still didn't make sense: the pressing on his chest that kept him stable during the impact. It was in him and on him at the same time.

He rubbed his bare feet against Sharla's ankle.

"Stop! I don't want your big, hairy feet on me!"

Amani appeared at their doorway. "Y'all alright in here?"

"Come on in," Mark invited.

"I heard y'all arguing," he said. "Is everything okay?"

"We weren't arguing," Mark reassured him. "We were just talking. And laughing."

"Cool."

"Did you make up your bed yet? And there better not be any food in your room," Sharla started in on him.

"Dang, baby, it's summertime. School's out. Give the boy a break," Mark stepped into Sharla's territory.

She gave him the butt-out glance. "Ants and roaches don't care if school's out."

Amani seized the chance to be an advocate for himself. He grabbed Sharla's brush off the dresser and used it as a microphone. "Ladies and gentlemen, children, dudes and dudettes gathered here today, I'm here to say that everyone deserves a break now and then, especially teenagers like myself who work hard all year. We go to school for eight hours. We go to extracurricular practice for another hour. Then we come home and do homework for another ten minutes...ahem, ahem...two hours afterward, and—"

"When do *moms* get their break?" Sharla cut the impromptu speech short.

Amani gave her the hand. "Ma'am, you're going to have to wait until we have a press conference—"

"Give me that microphone!" She snatched the brush from her son.

"Security!" Amani yelled, beckoning toward the doorway.

Mark doubled over laughing at his wife and son. The boy was hilarious, a regular stand-up comedian. He'd heard a few of Amani's humorous comments here and there, but now Mark saw that his son could be as witty as he was temperamental. He'd make a great actor. Maybe a sitcom writer or even a savvy politician. He definitely had a charisma about himself that would attract people and bring them together, given the right opportunities. Given the wrong outlet, his gift could be abused.

Sharla wrestled the "microphone" from Amani and attempted to convince the "audience" that she needed a break, too. "I cook, I make sure you all have everything you need, and I support you especially, Amani, in all your extra stuff."

Amani raised his hand. Sharla acknowledged him with a nod.

"Ma'am if you get your son a car when he turns sixteen, you won't have to be his taxi cab anymore."

"Uh, no!" she replied sharply. "He can't even keep his room clean. How can I trust him with a car?"

"Booo! Hiss!" Amani yelled, giving two thumbs down.

Sharla playfully lunged at Amani, trying to bop him on the head with the brush. He covered his head, calling for security again.

Mark couldn't remember the last time they'd had that much fun together as a family. If they spent more time together, maybe Sharla would get off his back. Plus, he could make sure Amani learned to use his graces for good, not evil.

Wait a minute. Isn't that what Sharla has been trying to tell me? Maybe, but the way she said it didn't sound quite so positive. Sounded more like punishment. If I can have fun spending time with my family, that would make all the difference.

"I've got an idea," Mark announced as Sharla set the brush back in its place. "Let's go on a family vacation."

Sharla and Amani looked at Mark like he was under the influence of medication.

"A vacation?" Sharla squeaked. "We can't go anywhere with you still on so many pills and those pins still in your arm. What kind of excursions could you do?"

She had a point.

"I can't go on a vacation with *y'all?*" Amani exaggerated.

185

The parents stared at their son.

Amani shook his head. "No offense, but I don't want to be in no hotel room with you two."

"Ever heard of a suite—with a closing door? You two are acting like we've never gone anywhere together." Mark counted off previous destinations on his fingers. "We've done Disneyworld, two cruises, Branson, skiing in Santa Fe."

"Yeah, but that was back when I didn't know it wasn't cool to hang with your parents," Amani protested. "Let me stick to my youth group retreats—or let me invite a friend."

"No," Sharla shot the idea down. "I'm not takin' no more musty boys with me nowhere. One is enough."

Amani sniffed his armpits. "Who says I'm musty?"

"You would be if I didn't stay on you about it," Sharla busted him.

"I'm hurt."

Mark's brain was churning past both Sharla's and Amani's objections to a family vacation. Plus, being in June already, prices for flights and hotels would border on extortion.

"Wait a second." Mark dug his phone out of his pocket and managed to open and search through his email messages. He was getting good at tackling routine tasks with one hand. "How about not a vacation but a short getaway to…drum roll, please…Peasner, Texas!"

"Pee *who*?" Amani choked.

"Peasner, Texas. My cousin, Son, send me an evite. His mother, we all call her Mama B, is getting married. They're having her engagement party—" Mark scrolled to the bottom of the message, "—this weekend!"

"You're not serious," Sharla chided. "When people send those evites, they don't really expect you to come. They just want you to send a gift."

"I'm calling Son right now."

Amani mouthed to Sharla, *Peasner?*

With his family watching in horror, waving their hands as though trying to flag down a car, Mark made the call and mashed the button to put the conversation on speaker despite his family's gyrations. "Hey, Son!"

"Tugga! Boy, how you doin'?"

"I'm good. Got my family right here on speaker. You remember Sharla and 'Mani?"

"Yeah! Hey Sharla and 'Mani."

They singsonged in unison while giving Mark the evil-eye, "Hi. How are you?"

"I can't complain," Son said. "Your momma told my momma you were gonna make it after that car accident. I'm glad you're all right."

"God is good, that's all I can say. Look, uh, I got the invitation to Mama B's engagement party this weekend. Is it too late to RSVP?"

"Naw, you know Mama. She'll be glad to have you there. But go ahead and give her a call so she can add you to the count."

"Will do, will do. Look forward to seeing you again, Son."

"Same here. I'll talk to you later."

"Later."

Mark ended the call as protests gushed from his wife and son. "We can't go this weekend!"

"Why not?" he asked them both.

"Because it's too soon! I won't have time to pack properly," Sharla fussed. "And I don't have time to get my hair tightened."

"And I haven't even told my friends," Amani said.

"Please," Mark dismissed their objections with a wave. "Sharla, we're going to Peasner. No one there has seen any of your clothes. They'll be brand new to them. And it's okay to wear your real hair. Did you know that?"

Sharla gave him a bratty grin.

"And 'Mani, your friends can live without you for one weekend."

"No, they can't. I run the videogame tournaments."

"Boy, for a minute there, I thought you had a full-time job," Mark laughed as he re-opened the email invitation and sent a call to Mama B.

He silenced the room once more with the speaker. "Mama B!"

"Who is this?"

He could hear the smile in her voice. "This is Mark, Mama B."

"Hey, Tugga! So good to hear from you! How's your wife and your son?"

"Sharla and 'Mani are right here."

Again, the reluctant vacationers paid respect by saying hello.

"My goodness, did that deep voice belong to that handsome son of yours?"

Amani grinned.

"Yes, ma'am. That's him. He's thirteen now."

"Won't be long before he's a man," Mama B laughed.

Amani thumped his chest.

Sharla pinched her son's ear, whispering "Traitor."

188

"Mama B, we're gonna take you up on the invitation to come to your engagement party this weekend. We'll get in Friday afternoon. What's the closest hotel?"

"Mark Wayne Carter the third, if you don't stop teasin' me about stayin' in a hotel, I'm gonna reach through this phone and pinch your ear," she threatened with a giggle. "I got two extra bedrooms. Got plenty room here so long as Amani don't mind sharing a room with his cousin, Cameron."

"Now, we don't want to impose on you—we're perfectly fine with staying in a hotel."

"Well, I ain't," she insisted. "No family of mine's gon' be stayin' in a hotel when I got two bedrooms to share. I'm not gon' let you block my blessin', you hear?"

"Yes, ma'am. We'll see you Friday."

Chapter 26

Amani grew as restless as a 5-year-old sitting in the back seat on the way to Peasner. "How far is this place?"

"Two hundred and sixty loooooong miles," Sharla answered. She'd propped her elbow on the side panel and set her fist against her temple about a hundred miles ago.

Mark ignored their unpleasant comments. Once they got a taste of something or another from Mama B's oven, they'd thank him later. Growing up, he had spent anywhere from a few weeks to a whole month in Peasner with his cousins Son, Debra Kay, Cassandra, and Otha.

There were always a bunch of kids at Mama B's in the summer, so many that Mama B would have to sit them all down and explain how they were related to one another. Mark's grandmother and Mama B's mother were sisters. Mark and Otha always had a hard time wrapping their minds around the fact that, although they were nearly the same age, they were in two different generations.

Seeing everyone that weekend would be a welcome break from the stress of things in Houston. By then, some of them had probably heard about the wanna-be scandal, but they were the people who had scraped knees and run from dogs with him; they'd been through a few things together. If anyone asked, he'd tell them the truth and they (or at least Mama B) would say a prayer, then Otha would probably crack a few jokes about it and take another piece of pie.

Finally, they approached the exit to Peasner. "Thank God," Sharla sighed.

"Ditto," Amani grumbled.

"Alright, enough," Mark declared. "We're here now. Let's get rid of these bad attitudes and have a good time with our family this weekend, okay?"

There were three cars filling Mama B's driveway already, so Sharla had to park next to the curb. "My car better not get any scratches on it," she fussed at Mark.

"Just be thankful you have *possession* of your car right now," he spoke over Amani's head.

Mark could hardly wait to get into the house. He grabbed the heaviest bag with his left arm and told Amani to get the other ones. Together, they walked toward Mama B's door.

"Hey, y'all! It's Tugga!"

Like a pack of bees, several cousins swarmed to the wooden porch. Someone announced that a preacher was in the house, and instantly a foot-stomping, hand-clapping gospel beat ensued. "Can't nobody," Son started. The impromptu congregation said, "Preach like Tugga, can't nobody do you like him, can't nobody preach like Tugga, he's my friend!"

Mark couldn't contain his laughter. Nothing had changed. They always teased him about being a preacher. He knew it was their way of showing him they were proud to have a preacher in the family.

Once on the porch, he was surrounded by hugs and pats on the back. His family pounced on Sharla and Amani as well, remarking on how well they looked.

"Where's Mama B?"

"She in there cooking up a storm, as usual," Debra Kay said, pursing her lips. "We can't get her to sit down for anything."

"She's just nervous," Cassandra defended.

"Who's this man she's marrying?" Mark asked.

191

Son relayed, "He's alright. Good people. A doctor."

"Mama B done got her a doctor, eh? Watch out there now!" Mark slipped into the dialect he always picked up when he spent a little time in Peasner.

Sharla and Amani looked at each other as though they didn't know that country man.

"Come on in, Tugga," Otha guided them inside.

A mixture of complementing aromas swirled up Mark's nostrils. "Now that's what I'm talkin' about."

He noticed Sharla's slight grin. She had to be hungry, too, since they—well, *she*—had driven four hours from Houston non-stop. "It does smell good."

Amani gave in, "If she asks me if I'm hungry, I'm going to break the rules, Mom, and tell her that I am."

Otha assured Amani, "You don't have to be all proper here. You're with family now. If you're hungry, just say the word."

"The word," Amani joked.

"Boy, you're about as goofy as your Daddy," Otha snickered, punching Amani's shoulder. "Y'all go on in and say hi to everybody. I'll take your suitcases to the back rooms."

Mark, Sharla, and Amani stopped to greet other family members strewn across the couches, mostly people who had married into the clan, from what Mark could tell. One asked about his arm. Mark simply replied, "I was in a car accident."

"Aw, man. You gon' be all right?" Cassandra's husband wanted to know.

"I'm still standing!"

"Amen to that," from Son's wife, Wanda.

192

In the kitchen, Mama B was on the phone, but she immediately dismissed herself from the conversation when Mark and his family entered the kitchen. "Tugga! Oh my goodness! I can't believe you made it! Come here, all of you!"

Mama B pulled them all into a hug, planting a kiss on all six of their cheeks. "My goodness! Is this Amani?"

Sharla beamed. "Yes, ma'am. Thirteen years old."

"My Lawd! He 'bout to pass you up, Tugga. And so handsome!" Mama B gushed. Then she looked at him above the rim of her glasses. "Now, you listen here. Don't you let no little girls get you in trouble, you hear?"

"Yes, ma'am," Amani smirked.

"You hungry?"

"A little," Amani said.

"Nonsense. You a growin' boy, you starvin'. Y'all always are. Look up in that cabinet and get you plate," she pointed to her right. "We got plenty in the oven and in the refrigerator. Help yourself. And you can go on out back with the other teenagers."

She didn't have to tell him twice to fix his plate.

Two little boys who couldn't have been more than six or seven years old ran into the kitchen and attempted to reach for the cookie platter on the table.

"Na-ah! Wash your hands first," Mama B stopped them. The taller one reached up and turned on the faucet. They splashed around for a second, wiped their hands on their shirts. By that time, Mama B had already separated four of the smallest cookies from the stash. She handed them two each. "Now, don't try to eat no more until you finish supper tonight."

They nodded. "Thank you," one of them minded his manners. Then they both took off toward the loud chatter in the living room.

Mama B, turned to Mark. "Tugga, you betta be teachin' him right; don't, this good-lookin' boy gon' break a lot of hearts," she warned Mark.

"Aw, he just turned thirteen."

"The enemy don't care nothin' 'bout him bein' thirteen. He take 'em at ten if you let him. Don't fool yourself, this boy need you every step of the way," she lectured. "You betta come out from around that pulpit sometime so you can keep up with him. He's a good boy. Special to the Lord."

Really? Did I come all the way from Houston to hear the same song? He avoided eye contact with his wife.

Sharla hugged the elderly woman again. "Ooh, Mama B, I am *soooooo* glad we came to see you. And you look so good! Haven't changed a bit since the last time I saw you."

"Thank you, sweetheart. I tell you what, though, I done picked up a few extra gray hairs plannin' this weddin'. They done added so much stuff—seem like you spend more time plannin' on stuff to thank people for comin' than the actual weddin' itself! My goodness!"

"Well, if there's anything I can do to help, you just let me know," Sharla volunteered.

"As a matter of fact, we got to finish decoratin' the church tonight. That's where we havin' the party tomorrow," Mama B took Sharla up on the offer.

"Be glad to."

Somehow in less than five minutes, Mama B had managed to win both his son and his wife, while giving Mark a good tongue lashin' by revelation of the Spirit— there was no way she could have otherwise known the particulars of his household. Leave it to somebody in tune with the Lord to read him like a book, in love.

Sharla made a plate for herself and Mark. They joined the cousins out on the front porch again. Mama B's flowers added a pleasant fragrance to the early evening air. The citronella candles worked overtime to keep the mosquitos away, emitting a light stream of repelling smoke from buckets.

Though they were all sitting within ten feet of each other in a circle of chairs and swings, the volume level escalated with each speaker, each new recollection of the good-ole-days when they used to go fishing and when Otha caused them all to get a whippin' because he wouldn't admit to swinging the stick at the rock that broke the back windshield of Uncle Albert's Monte Carlo.

"Hey, I hit the rock, but we were all outside hitting rocks with sticks! It could have happened to any one of us!" he deflected.

"But it was *you*!" Mark hollered.

"It was just a matter of time before *somebody* did it!" Otha screamed back.

"You know that's how Otha was. He didn't take the blame for anything he did wrong," Debra Kay blasted, laughing. "That's why I didn't feel bad when I used to lie on him and he got in trouble. It was just payback."

"Oooh! I'mma tell Momma! You just admitted it!" Otha yelled.

"You tell her and I'll deny it."

"Naw, I got a neutral witness," Otha said, pointing at Sharla. "You heard her, right?"

Sharla stuffed her mouth with a spoonful of potato salad. The entire porch erupted in laughter.

"Aw, naw! We kinfolk, Sharla! We kinfolk!" Otha tried to persuade her, to no avail.

Later, Mama B led Mark and Sharla to their room. They transferred Amani's suitcase into the third room. "Cameron will be over here later on to keep Amani company. Sounds like some of the other kids are gonna stay over tonight, too. Probably playing video games 'til the wee hours of the morning."

"Oh, that's right up Amani's alley," Sharla said.

Mama B left them alone to get settled a bit, saying she'd need help at the church in another hour or so.

As soon as she left the room, Mark asked Sharla, "When was the last time you said 'up somebody's alley'? You 'bout country as they come!"

Sharla muffled a smile and denied, "That's not country. It's just old school."

"Yeah, right," Mark teased. He grabbed her from behind, interrupting her as she attempted to hang their garment bag in the small closet.

"Mark! We just got here."

"We've got an hour until she needs us," he propositioned, wearing a mischievous grin.

Sharla gawked, "Are you serious? There's, like, a million people in this house."

"A million people who are all preoccupied with each other," he said. He walked back to the door, locked it. "You feel better now?"

"A little," she smirked.

"Well, I want you to feel *a lot* better."

"I sho' reckon that's alright with me," Sharla said in her most countrified twang.

Chapter 27

Things had been awkward with that arm sling, but he and Sharla worked around it, thank the good Lord.

Then it was time to join the relatives trekking to and from the church like ants carting food to the anthill. Sharla had gotten herself involved with the particulars in the kitchen with the women, while the men ran back and forth.

"Dad, we're having a party at a church, and the church is right behind her house?" Amani mused, carrying a big platter of croissants as they walked across Mama B's back yard toward the sanctuary.

"Yep. This is what you call a close-knit community. You don't know nothin' 'bout that. I apologize for not introducing you to the other side of the world, son."

"The *dark* side of the world," he croaked in a witchy voice.

"Nothin' dark about Peasner, Mama B, or Mount Zion Baptist."

Mark wasn't much use. The most consistent thing he could do was hold open doors since he only had one arm available. Actually, since his rendezvous with Sharla, he'd begun to feel a pinching sensation toward the wrist. Those pain pills would come in handy, but he'd go as long as possible before taking one. He didn't want to miss one moment of fun with his extended family.

As they approached the church the next time, Mark saw the backside of a car in the front parking lot. He held the door for Amani to enter the fellowship hall, then said, "You keep on. I'm gonna go around to the front and see who this is."

"Cool."

Upon closer inspection, he saw that the car was an old, but well-kept Pontiac Bonneville. When the door opened, he recognized its driver immediately. "Pastor Phillips!"

"Ha-ha!" the elderly man bellowed. "Look what the cat done drug in!"

Mark gave his fellow clergyman a hearty hug. "So good to see you!"

"Right back atcha!"

He patted Mark on the back a little too hard, sending achy waves down his right side.

"Now you know Mama B's family so big, I can keep track of faces, but I'm not so good with names no more. Tell me who you are again?"

"I'm Mama B's nephew, Mark Carter. Everybody calls me Tugga."

"Yes! Tugga! You the one grew up to be a preacher, right?"

"Yes, sir."

"Yeah, I heard about your accident. God spared you for a reason."

"Amen."

Suddenly, the car's horn blew. Pastor Phillips flew to the passenger's side. "My word. I keep forgettin'. Gotta get back into the habit."

A full-figured seasoned woman with a baby-face unfolded herself from the seat as Pastor Phillips opened the door for her.

"I'm sorry, Ophelia."

She certainly wasn't the woman Mark recalled as the first lady of Mount Zion. As a matter of fact, he remembered Ophelia as one of Mama B's best friends—not Pastor

Phillips' wife. He'd have to ask Son about all that later. "Hello, Miss Ophelia."

"Tugga! Mama B told me you'd be here. She's so glad y'all made the effort to come celebrate her wedding." Ophelia plopped a kiss on his cheek and he returned the gesture. "Look like you puttin' on a little weight there."

Old folk sure had a way of pointing out the obvious. Mark sucked in his gut. "Yes, ma'am. Working long hours at the church."

"Well, you need to get home at a decent hour so you won't have to eat so late. Once you hit forty, you got to cut back; don't, you'll be big as a house before you know it."

Was this a conspiracy? "Yes, ma'am." Mark was grateful Sharla hadn't overheard his second reprimand. He was starting to get the feeling that maybe Sharla wasn't simply nagging him. She cared about him and couldn't turn off the God-given nurturing instinct. Like Jackson said, it was part of their makeup. She couldn't have turned it off if she wanted to. Maybe she could tone it down, but it wouldn't go away so long as she was his helpmate.

"Can I help you with anything, Pastor Phillips? Afraid I'm not much help with this sling."

"I'm sure I can put you to work," he laughed.

Ophelia marched on over to the house while Mark followed Pastor Phillips into the church building. They bypassed the hustle and bustle in the fellowship hall and journeyed on toward the pastor's office. The room had to be a fourth the size of Mark's office. Two walls were covered with plaques and certificates memorializing his service to the members of Mount Zion and the community at large. The pastor had tacked a number of phone numbers and reminders on the surface behind the telephone. The last wall, a built-in bookshelf, boasted a gold mine of books. Mark read as many spines as he could, recognizing the names of well-known scholars and commentators in the collection.

"Pastor, this is amazing," Mark gasped. He had books on his bookshelf, of course, but not the classics. Not the kind where you had to cross-reference with a dictionary and two or three different translations of the Bible. Basically, Mark read the Cliff-notes versions and stuck to the texts written in the twentieth and twenty-first centuries. "I wish I had time to read so many books."

Pastor Phillips cautiously lowered himself into his worn leather seat. "You got to remember, I been pastoring almost forty years."

Mark parked himself across from the pastor in a hard wooden chair. "Yeah, but you've got some *serious* books in here. How do you find the time?"

"Well, now, nobody can't *find* time or *make* time. You got to *section off* time to study the word, you see."

Mark admired the pastor's easy demeanor. "I hope that when I get to be in my sixties or seventies, I'll be able to slow down and enjoy good books, too. But right now, my church is bursting at the seams. Well, once I get us past this little mess we're in right now. I think I've lost some of my members. But we'll be all right as long as we follow the plan."

The senior pastor raised an eyebrow. "You think it's up to *you* to keep the church on track?"

"I have to. I mean, right now my other ministers are filling in until the media finds someone else to rag on. Plus I gotta get this arm back on track. If I don't eventually take the reins back, my church will...I guess, collapse."

Mark figured he must have amused the pastor, by the way he laughed. Pastor Phillips rested an elbow on the arm of his chair and pushed up the wrinkles at his temple with his forefinger. He stared at Mark for a second. "You think the entire church rests on you?"

"Of course it does. I founded it—after God told me to, I mean," Mark corrected himself.

"You threw that last part on there like you didn't want to sound prideful, but you really *do* think you founded *your* church and those men are *your* ministers and the people are *your* members. You in dangerous territory."

Mark couldn't refute that those words had come out of his mouth only seconds earlier.

"Who's your mentor?" Pastor Phillips demanded.

"Dr. Kevin McMurray."

"Yes, Dr. McMurray. I'm familiar with his ministry. Powerful. You been sittin' down with him lately?"

Mark shook his head, feeling somewhat ashamed. "No, sir. I've been so busy, you know, running the church. He's called me, has set up appointments. I had to cancel the last two. I know I need to talk to him more. We're both pretty busy."

The pastor nodded, seemingly ignoring Mark's excuses. "Well, first things first: you got no business running around like a loose cannon. How old are you?"

"Thirty-eight."

"You still a lad, far as I'm concerned. Numbers don't mean nothin' to God, we all know, but there's a reason Elisha had Elijah and Timothy had Paul. So I'mma tell you like *my* pastor told me. Son, you got to recognize that the church you've been appointed to shepherd is not *your* church—it's *Christ's* church. The *real* church ain't in these

201

walls no way." He motioned toward the ceiling. "The real church is the body of Christ. Some folk in the building ain't in the body of Christ—they just come to give the believers a hard time. But that ain't your business. Most time, them kind of folk don't stay around long no way. They can't stand to be around a whole bunch of love. They either get drawn in or find their own way out. God said He'd separate the wheat from the tares in the end, anyway."

Theoretically, Mark understood the pastor's roundabout way of telling him not to put himself in God's place. Yet, there was still the issue of his calling to preach and minister to people, to bring them into the fold. "But Pastor, people's souls are hanging in the balance. If I don't get up there and find some kind of way to...keep them engaged and active in the church, they might end up in hell, and I don't want that on my record."

Pastor Phillips reached over to the bookshelf wall and grasped a large Bible from the lower shelf. He threw it toward Mark. "John chapter 10, verses fourteen through sixteen. Read it out loud."

Mark observed the version on the spine – The Amplified Version. He flipped to the scriptures. "I am the Good Shepherd; and I know *and* recognize My own, and My own know *and* recognize Me—even as [truly as] the Father knows Me and I also know the Father—and I am giving My [very own] life *and* laying it down on behalf of the sheep. And I have other sheep [beside these] that are not of this fold. I must bring *and* impel those also; and they will listen to My voice *and* heed My call, and so there will be [they will become] one flock under one Shepherd."

"Who's the Shepherd?" Pastor quizzed him.

"Jesus."

"Who gives the sheep the desire to come in?"

"Jesus."

"You doin' pretty good so far." The old man smiled.

Mark was beside himself with joy. Though Mark had, no doubt, read the passage before, it took on new meaning that day in his heart.

"Now skip down to verse twenty-six and read to about thirty."

Mark obeyed, reading again, "But you do not believe *and* trust *and* rely on Me because you do not belong to My fold [you are no sheep of Mine]. The sheep that are My own hear *and* are listening to My voice; and I know them, and they follow Me. And I give them eternal life, and they shall never lose it *or* perish throughout the ages. [To all eternity they shall never by any means be destroyed.] And no one is able to snatch them out of My hand. My Father, Who has given them to Me, is greater *and* mightier than all [else]; and no one is able to snatch [them] out of the Father's hand. I and the Father are One."

"What does that tell you?" Pastor Phillips reviewed.

"It means that those who belong to Christ will always belong to Him," Mark managed to speak.

"Son, your job—every believer's job—is to follow the leading of the Holy Spirit within. You should read books, listen to counsel, and heed advice from your mentors, but at the end of the day, you got to know it's a reason God chose *you* to be the pastor at the church where he's allowing you to serve. You do what He says do, you preach what He says preach. Period. If every person in your church gets up and walks out, so be it. He'll bring in some more who are thirsty for what thus sayeth the Lord. But you got to answer to God for what you believe He told you to do!"

203

With lowered eyes, nodding slightly, Mark replied, "Yes, sir." He couldn't help but think that if he'd obeyed God's directions in the first place, the predicament waiting for him in Houston might not even be there.

"Of course, you can't rightly hear what He's telling you to do if you ain't talkin' to Him. You got to get in His face, hole yourself up with the word, section off time with Him— don't let nobody intrude on it," he continued passionately, his jowls shaking with conviction. "I guarantee you, you spend time with God, you teach the church to look to the head, Jesus, in everything, and He will draw men unto Him. Not *you*, Him."

"Yes, sir."

"Now, Mark, I'm gon' pray over you," Pastor Phillips said as he stood and circled around to stand behind Mark. He put his hands on Mark's shoulders. Mark kept his head bowed. "Father, we thank You for the calling to preach, to share Your word with a dying world. God, I thank You for filling this young man with Your holy boldness and for bringing us together today. I ask a blessing on him and the ministry You have given to him and his wife. Let him rest in Your strength and Your power. Let him turn the reins over to You. Cover him with humility as he steps down from trying to assume *Your* position so that Your power can rest all the more upon Him for Your glory. In Jesus' name we pray. Amen."

And with that prayer, the weight of the church lifted off Mark's shoulders, over to Christ's, where he now realized it had always rightfully belonged.

Chapter 28

While Mark, Amani, and the rest of his cousins went bowling, Sharla hung behind with Mama B and Debra Kay to rest. They'd finished decorating the church—which included blowing up fifty balloons with their very own lips, a feat that nearly wiped Sharla out.

Now that the house was silent and empty, except for the cutest little 3-year-old girl who was far too sleepy to go bowling, the women had a chance to sit down in the kitchen and chat.

In addition to tomorrow's engagement dinner, Debra Kay and Mama B still had quite a list of tasks to accomplish before the actual wedding in three weeks.

"I can't do but one thing at a time, Debra Kay," her mother fussed as she wiped the countertops clean again.

"Momma, come sit down."

Mama B closed her eyes and sighed. "Okay, okay."

Sharla pulled a chair for the tired woman to utilize.

"Thank you, sweetheart."

"You gotta take it easy some time, that's what I'm always trying to tell Mark."

"Well, you know how men are. They feel like it's their job to fix the world," Mama B advised.

Sharla chuckled softly. "So it's not just my husband?"

"Please," Debra Kay said. "It's in their blood. Especially a decent man. Tugga's always been the kind to try to help people, unless he's not on your team. You ever played Monopoly with him?"

Sharla squinted her eyes, trying to remember. "I don't think so."

Mama B gave a high-pitched hoot. "Don't ever play with him and Son. Chile, them two was about to tear my house down playing Monopoly. Mark didn't back down 'cause Son was older. Them two so competitive, I had to stop the game 'til they could get all that testosterone under control."

"And you remember, Momma, they found the game and set it up again after you and Daddy went to sleep? And they got busted for arguing so loud!"

Sharla had no trouble believing that story. Mark and Amani talked so much trash when they played video games together, she wondered if it was actually productive father-and-son time. "I just want Mark to slow down, stop being so wound up and busy with work."

"Shoot, I wish mine would *keep* a job!" Debra Kay exploded. "Don't get me started on the other end of the spectrum."

"You right, don't get started, hear?" Mama B warned her.

Debra Kay stood, rolling her eyes. "I'mma go check on the baby. Y'all call me back in once y'all start talking about something other than husbands because I have nothing nice to say right now."

"You doin' the right thing, 'cause you know I'm not gon' sit up and listen to no woman bad-mouth her husband in front of me," her mother agreed. Then she turned her attention back to Sharla.

"Sounds like you and me in the same boat," Mama B surmised. "I'm marryin' a doctor. He got his office hours and such, but he cares about his patients. If one of 'em takes a turn for the worse in the middle of the night, I know good and well he's gonna run up to the hospital."

Sharla hung her neck out. "So…are you gonna be *okay* with that?"

"Yes, I think so. Long as he don't turn on a whole bunch of lights and wake me up," she giggled.

Sharla couldn't imagine any woman being okay with her husband being gone from home so much, even if it was for something urgent. "What about *you*? I mean, his job is going to take him away from *you*. Doesn't that…upset you at least a little?"

Mama B bit her bottom lip. "I can't say it won't concern me a teensy bit, but you got to remember I been widowed for eight years. I'm perfectly content bein' by myself. I wouldn't be marryin' Frank if I didn't believe he would add joy to my life. I sure ain't signin' up for no extra headaches and drama in this last quarter of my life."

"You know? I might actually be okay with Mark being gone so much if I knew that he was being called away to life-or-death situations," Sharla guessed.

"I think what Tugga does is more important than being a doctor. I mean, eventually, all of Frank's patients die—we all gon' die. But a preacher's work never dies, goes on into eternity. Can't be nothin' more important than that," she explained.

Sharla looked down at her hands. "I never thought of it like that."

Mama B lifted Sharla's chin with a finger. "Sweetheart, what's on your mind?"

Tears brimmed Sharla's eyes as she poured out the truth. "Mark could have died in the accident, and I would have been a single mom left to raise a boy all by myself. All for *the church*. And this same church has turned against him right now. Why can't he see that he doesn't mean as much to them as they do to him? Why would he put them before us?"

She collapsed into Mama B's arms, crying like a baby.

The woman's chest vibrated as she asked, "Honey, the church isn't the enemy. The *enemy* is the enemy. Are you standing beside your husband in the battle?"

Sharla rose up, wiping her nose. "No. I mean, at first I thought I was, but it's like the expectations kept getting higher and higher because I was a first lady. I couldn't talk to anyone, couldn't tell anyone how I felt because I didn't want it to make Mark look bad. And now, I can't even ask anyone else to mentor Amani because that would make Mark look like he's not being a good father. It's like, I'm always on stage in this play. I don't want to be a first lady, I'm not…all *deep* and…I'm just not *there* yet."

"Where is *there*?" Mama B asked.

"*There* is…" Sharla paused, then pointed, "like *you*. You probably pray every day, read your Bible all the time. And you don't let people gossip around you. Like just now, I wanted to hear what Debra Kay had to say about her husband. Even though I know it's wrong to talk about people, I like it. Like, I love juicy gossip and people arguing and drama on reality television shows. It makes me feel good. But Mark says it's a sign that I'm a baby in Christ. If I have to stop watching my TV shows, I don't think I'll ever be a mature Christian."

Mama B patted Sharla's hand and groaned, "Mmm, bless your heart."

"Anyway, that's just one example of *there*, which is where I'm *not*."

"Honey, you got a whole bunch of stuff poppin' off inside of you. You worryin' about Tugga slowin' down when you the one need to cast all your cares on the Lord before you have yourself a nervous breakdown."

Sharla had heard that one before. From Mark himself. "I know. I do need to stop worrying so much."

"You need to stop worryin' *at all*. Stop worryin' 'bout what folks think about you as the first lady, stop worryin' 'bout if you there yet in Jesus, and stop worryin' 'bout Amani and Mark. Turn both of 'em over to the Lord."

"But what am I supposed to—"

"Mmm-mmm," Mama B stopped her sharply. "I know you ain't asked for my advice, so I'm just gon' tell you one thing. Mark is a full-grown man. You can't make no full-grown man do nothin', even if what you tellin' him is right. The best thing you got in your corner is the Holy Ghost. He can tell your husband stuff in five minutes you been tryin' to tell him for five years.

"Chile, I don't sit up prayin' and studyin' the word every day 'cause I don't have other stuff to do up through the day. I pray and study the word 'cause after walkin' with Him fifty years, I know everything work out better *His* way."

Sharla swiped her eyes. "But what about the TV shows?"

Mama B waved her hand. "Don't you worry 'bout that. God said He'd write His words on your heart. He got a plan for everybody. Might be He gon' work on something else in you first, heal up a hurt or restore your joy. You seek His face. When and if y'all get to the point where He get ready for you to stop watching those shows, He'll take the taste for 'em right out your mouth. Let Him do it however He want to, and don't get confused 'cause I guarantee you, ain't nobody *there* until we get out this physical body, according to the word. All you got to do is give Him a blank check with your life.

"But how? It's not that easy," Sharla whined. "All my life, people have said, 'Turn it over to Jesus, stop worryin'' but that doesn't work."

"Have you ever actually *tried* it?"

Sharla thought about the question. The last time she tried to leave her most precious possession in God's hands, He hadn't come through for her. She'd lost the baby. And then, when she tried to adopt Amani, God almost let Bria's mother get custody. She answered honestly, "Yes, I *did* trust God about something. But He didn't do anything, so I had to handle it myself."

"And what did that get you?"

She answered matter-of-factly, "It got me what I wanted."

"And doing it your own way didn't cost you anything?"

Without warning, the pieces of this situation came together in Sharla's mind like a puzzle. What she'd done all those years ago, when she took matters into her own hands to ensure that she got to keep Amani, was at the root of all their current troubles. Her preoccupation with making sure that Amani lived up to the risk she took, her insecurities as a mother, even the whole situation with Bria could be traced back to the underhanded way she'd resolved her own problem.

"You're right. It has cost me something."

Mama B nodded. "Don't get caught up on it, though, Sharla. We all done wrong. We keep God plenty busy fixin' our mistakes. Even now, you can ask Him to come in and make it right."

Sharla threw her arms around Mama B's neck. "Thank you, thank you, thank you."

"Chile, thank God."

Chapter 29

Mark had to readjust his brain for a moment because it was odd seeing Mama B sitting next to Frank, but they made a handsome couple seated at the head table. The room bustled with chatter, laughter, and fellowship as members of both sides of the family and respective church members filled the hall.

Sharla's signature decorating skills could be seen in the purple and green centerpieces and tiebacks on the chairs. "Baby, you did a wonderful job." He pecked her lips.

"Thank you."

Had Amani been sitting next to them, he probably would have gagged. However, Amani had found a place with three other teenage cousins and never looked back once he got to Peasner.

Pastor Phillips stood and opened the party with prayer, followed by a speech, thanking Mama B for her service to Mount Zion since its inception. There was hardly a dry eye left in the building. When his voice began to crack, even Mark got a little misty. Those people loved Mama B. Not because she was on the roll or because she'd donated the land for the church or even because she served so faithfully. They loved *her*, period.

Next, Frank stood. "I have to admit, I feel kind of bad stealing Mama B away from Mount Zion."

A good-humored rumble filled the room. "But we'll be back. Pastor Phillips is a gem. Over these past months, he's almost become a second father to me. As you all know, I'm a father. I know what it's like to marry your daughter off, so I wouldn't dream of not visiting Mount Zion often."

Pastor Phillips led the applause.

211

"B and I have decided that, before we eat, we would like to share the sacraments with those closest to us. More than anything, our union is centered around Christ. It's because of His sacrifice that we have a picture of perfect love. We do this in remembrance of Him."

Pastor Phillips called for all clergy in the house to come forward and officiate communion. Members of Mount Zion, presumably ushers, distributed miniature juice cups and broken cracker pieces. Then, Pastor Phillips read from Luke 22, reminding everyone of communion's significance.

Mark looked out in the audience. There couldn't have been more than sixty people there. So much smaller than what he was used to at New Vision. Yet somehow, the solemnity of the moment seemed magnified.

His eyes met with Sharla's. *What?* He focused harder to confirm his suspicion. *Yes, she is crying.* Alarm bells went off inside him. *Why is she crying? What have I done wrong now?*

Though he was in no hurry to be belittled, he couldn't be comfortable with Sharla crying. As soon as communion concluded, two ladies approached the podium to sing a song, freeing the clergymen of their duties.

Mark rushed back to his seat. "What's wrong?"

She dabbed at her eyes. "That was beautiful."

Relief swept through him. "Yes, it was."

Whatever diet Mark might have thought about following would have to wait until he got out of Peasner, TX, because the food could not be refused. Even the simple salad, obviously made with garden-fresh lettuce, tomatoes, and onions, tasted amazing.

"Baby, you got to get some of these recipes," he told Sharla.

"I'll try," she said, keeping her eyes on the plate, "But some of this stuff just won't taste the same. You've got to make it with country *water*, country *eggs*, and country *vegetables* from country *soil*. All I know is, we've got to come back here again."

"Mamasita, you ain't said nothin' but a word."

Between dinner and dessert, Pastor Phillips allowed well-wishers to come up and give their two-minute congratulatory remarks to Frank and Mama B. People told funny stories, gave sage advice, and stuck to the time limit, for the most part.

That was until one tall, elderly woman with a wide-brim hat on took the podium. A younger woman, her spitting image, stood beside her, holding the microphone.

"I can hold my own microphone," the older woman barked.

"Okay, Momma, but I'm *right here*," the daughter mumbled as several people giggled.

"Most of y'all know me. I'm Henrietta. Me and B been friends for a long time."

"Amen," from the room.

"And even though we don't always get along, I just thank her for being nice today."

The daughter cued the audience to begin clapping, and they all followed her directive, clapping so long that Miss Henrietta must have finally decided she might as well step down and go back to her seat.

Mark and Sharla shared a sideways glanced and laughed. "There's one at every church," he whispered.

Dessert was served, which took Mark to a whole new level of understanding that only a few people on the planet at any given time have received a special gifting and anointing to make German chocolate cake. One of those chosen, called people resided in Peasner, TX.

Mixed with a dollop of Blue Bell ice cream—he remembered that Mama B always served ice cream with her cake—Mark had to wonder if there was any chance he could talk Sharla into moving to the country.

The white-haired gentlemen across from Mark and Sharla proclaimed, "I don't know why Jesus is taking so long to come back. He's missing out on this cake and ice cream."

Irreverent, maybe, but Mark had to laugh because that cake *had* to be on the menu at the great feast in heaven.

Several more guests wished Mama B and Frank a wonderful union. Mount Zion presented a desktop grandfather clock to them, engraved with 1 Corinthians 13:4-7, God's definition of love.

Mark grabbed his wife's hand under the table. She squeezed his back.

Since they couldn't all agree on a movie, the family settled on watching the kids play Wii later that night back at Mama B's house.

There was plenty of food left over from the party, which meant they could stay up all night snacking if they wanted to.

Amani challenged his older cousin, Nikki, in *Dance Dance Revolution*. She beat him the first time around, which sent Amani on a mission to beat her at least twice. The funny thing was, Amani couldn't dance, which sent the entire family into laughing fits that could only be topped when Mama B tried her feet at the routines.

Twice, Mark nearly choked while watching Mama B and Amani fumble through moves that were meant for people twice his talent and a third Mama B's age.

"I'm calling it a night," Mama B announced. "I'm pooped. Last one up, make sure all the food is put away."

Sharla rose from her spot on the couch. "I'm out, too."

"Aw, baby, you can stay up a while longer, can't you?"

"No can do. *Some of us* have been getting ready for the party since yesterday," she smacked.

"Amen," Debra Kay co-signed.

"Hey, we can't help it if Mark's incapacitated," Otha defended the men.

Mark eyed his cousin. "Man, I did my part. I held open the doors."

"Cuz, don't add to the problem," Otha said.

Nikki took Sharla's place on the couch as the games continued. Amani against Son's grandson, Cameron.

As entertaining as they were to watch, Mark couldn't take his mind off Sharla. From the yellow dress she'd worn to the party to the denim jeans and white top she'd donned afterward, she was beautiful. Sexy. Everything he'd ever wanted his wife to look like, plus she was fun to be around. Somehow, he'd forgotten all that between juggling the church and its responsibilities.

He loved her. And he realized, now, that it was never God's intent for him to pastor New Vision at the expense of his household. Though, historically, every pastor's family sacrificed to some extent, Mark couldn't imagine any pastor being called to abandon the shepherding of his own home.

God, I repent.

He found Sharla already in bed, but was glad when she turned to face him. "I knew you were tired, too," she badgered him.

"Not really. I just wanted to be near you."

"Awwww," she cooed, "that's so nice."

Mark hoped she wouldn't ruin the moment by getting all sappy on him. Mark struggled to unbutton his shirt. Sharla readily assisted him with getting undressed the rest of the way. *Man, I love this woman.* "You're on my side of the bed," he flirted.

"This is not our bed. You don't have a side," she argued in a lively tone.

"I want to sleep on the same side as last night. I don't want my right arm in the middle."

"But that'll put me by the vent," Sharla said. "It got pretty cold in here last night."

"Let's turn, then, and sleep at the foot."

Quickly, they threw the pillows at the other end and switched positions.

"Thanks, babe," Sharla said, snuggling under the covers once again.

"No problem."

He listened to his wife's breathing for a while, thankful that God had allowed everything to work out up until that point. Yet, the fact that they were returning to Houston after service the next day burdened him. Real life awaited them. Real problems, real issues that they couldn't dodge. Their real world might tear them apart again.

"The party was so nice," Sharla caroled.

"Sure was."

"And the way they are, Mama B and Frank. The communion, the love they share…"

Mark caressed the side of his wife's face. He fingered her hair, something he could never do with the weaves and wigs.

She raved, "There was just something about it that was so…*sweet.*"

"It's Jesus," Mark said.

He heard her head rub against the pillow as she turned to him.

"Is it really?" Her soft breath landed on his lips.

"Yes."

"If that's what He is, that's what I want for me. And us," Sharla professed. "I want Jesus."

Mark fought his way up onto an elbow. Accidentally, he poked her with his pinky finger.

"Ouch!"

"Sorry." Once settled, he spoke to his wife in the darkness. "Baby, Jesus is all I've ever wanted for us, too. I mean, I wanted to please God and do everything I could for Him. But I guess I forgot that life in Jesus *is* what pleases God. I'm sorry for putting pressure on you to be what I wanted you to be, what I thought New Vision needed from me and its first lady. I was wrong."

"My goodness, can you say that again for the record?" Sharla ragged.

Mark felt her lean forward. He found her lips for a slight kiss. They both lay on their backs again, breathing in the fragrance of their new relationship, where Christ mingled between them, in them, through them.

He heard her swallow.

"There's something I need to tell you. About Amani."

"Yeah?"

She exhaled until, seemingly, she had no more air to expel. Then she inhaled and rattled off, "Remember when we were, like, months and months into the adoption proceedings, and we were almost ready to adopt Amani, and at the last minute, that social worker, Demetria, told us that someone from Amani's family wanted to take him in?"

Mark's heart sped up, but he tried to keep his voice even. "Uh huh."

"Well, that person was Lisa Logan, Bria's mother. And, according to Demetria, the only reason Lisa wanted Amani was because, somehow, she found out that the state would pay her to keep Amani. It wasn't much, maybe a hundred and twenty-five dollars a month or so, but that was the only reason she wanted him. Plus, that would still give Bria a chance to seek full custody later on."

"Okaaaay. So what do you want to tell me?" Mark attempted to move the story along.

Sharla's body shook the bed. She sniffed and blurted out, "I bribed her. I paid her five thousand dollars to drop her custody suit and convince Bria to give up all rights to Amani."

Mark risked his right arm to embrace his wife. "*What*? I mean, *why*? I mean, over the years, a hundred twenty-five dollars a month would be worth more than five thousand."

"I know that and you know that, but people like Lisa have never had five thousand dollars at once. It might as well have been a hundred thousand to her greedy behind," Sharla cried.

"But Sharla, I don't think the state would have ever given Bria's family custody of Amani."

"You think, but I wasn't willing to risk it. Demetria said she'd seen worse things happen in the system. I just...I

218

loved him so much, and he was a part of me by then," she wailed. "If we had lost Amani, I would have lost my mind—especially since we'd just had the miscarriage. I couldn't! I couldn't lose him!"

Mark pressed her forehead into his neck. "Shhhh, it's okay, baby. It's okay." Her hot tears spilled onto his shoulders.

"No, it's not. Maybe Bria found out. Maybe she's going to turn me in for bribery," Sharla huffed.

"Baby, if she turns you in, she'll have to turn her mother in, too."

"I know, but," Sharla sniffed, "evil people stick together. They could come up with some crazy story and turn against me. And send me to jail. And get Amani ba-a-ack," she huffed. "I think that's why the detective has been giving me such a hard time. He knows more than he's saying—even Hernandez said so. He's building his case against me."

Mark kissed his wife's forehead as she continued to bounce with every sob. "Shhhh, it's going to be okay."

He wanted to believe his own words, but how could he? If Sharla's bribe came to light, which was highly possible, given Lisa's state of mind, his wife might actually end up with a conviction on her record, or serving time. Or even losing Amani, as absurd as that might be after all this time.

Now Mark's heart ached doubly. How could Sharla have done such a thing? What if they lost Amani on top of whatever punishment Sharla might face? It had gone from a civil case, which he hadn't even told Sharla about, to something with even more grave possibilities. He could only fathom one way through. "Baby, let's pray."

Chapter 30

Amani's long face in the rearview mirror pained Mark the whole way back to Houston. Obviously, the boy had done a lot more than enjoy himself. He'd experienced the sense of family that he'd been longing for, only to be ripped from it after a few days.

If Mama B weren't getting married, he'd ask her to let Amani come up for a few weeks when some of the cousins were there. But he wouldn't dare impose now. She needed some time to get settled with her new husband. Plus, from what Mark gathered, Mama B was moving into Frank's house. She was going to rent her place out after a while, probably. It wouldn't be the same.

Amani deserved the opportunity to know his biological family. The boy was wired for connecting with people, no wonder he was miserable. Even if the Logans turned out to be every bit as crazy as Sharla believed—as crazy as Bria had been before she met Christ—they were still his blood. Somehow, sooner or later, he'd have to persuade Sharla to put her pride aside and let Amani meet his people, for his sake.

"You tired yet?" Sharla asked. She was at it again already—nagging.

"Nope." He was in perfect control behind the wheel for the first time in almost two weeks. Once they hit the highway, it was a straight shot, no sudden turns, nothing he couldn't handle.

But Mark didn't want to waste energy getting annoyed. He had bigger fish to fry once he got back home.

He didn't know how big those fish were until after they unpacked their bags and got comfortable Sunday evening. "I'm gonna go next door to the Moor's and get the mail," Sharla said.

When she returned, Mark took one look at her shock-ridden face and braced for trouble. "What?"

Sharla stood with one paper in hand, a wad of envelopes tucked under her armpit. "Oh. My. Word. Mark, this is just the facility fee from the hospital. It's almost eleven thousand dollars!"

"Let me see that." Mark bolted from the couch and grabbed the paper from her. Sure enough, there it was in black and white: $10,846.92. "Okay. We got this, Sharla. We got eleven thousand dollars."

"Yeah, eleven thousand dollars that we've been saving up to move into our dream house!" she yelled.

"Well, God knew this was coming up. Maybe that's why He had us saving our money. He knew we'd need it—"

Amani came jumbling down the stairs, cutting Mark short.

"What the matter?"

"Nothing. Go back upstairs," Sharla ordered.

"Doesn't sound like nothing." Amani shot toward the window. "Is the press here again?"

"No. The press is not here. Hopefully, they'll never be here again," Mark redirected Amani's thoughts.

Amani continued to survey the yard through the slats. "Well, y'all are arguing about something."

"Go on back upstairs."

This time, Amani obeyed.

Mark clutched Sharla's wrist and led her to their bedroom. He closed the door behind them. "Sharla, I know this isn't what you'd planned on spending this money on. And it's very possible that we'll get it back after the dust clears with the insurance."

"But what if it doesn't?" She slammed the bill on the dresser. "Mark, this is just the *beginning* of the bills. We've still got doctors, surgeons, labwork, X-rays... You haven't even started rehab, and the doctors said you'd need at least one more surgery. We'll be lucky to keep *this* house, let alone move into the dream house."

"Hey," he stopped her. "We don't do *luck*, alright? I need you to quit gettin' all dramatic on me, acting like we don't have a God."

Sharla bit her bottom lip hard, gazing out the window. "I just...I don't see how."

Mark could almost see the wheels churning in Sharla's head. She was trying to formulate a solution.

"We need to start moving money overseas, getting stuff transferred to somebody else's name just in case we're getting ready to lose everything."

"Listen to yourself," Mark interrupted her think-aloud.

"What?"

"This is the problem—this is exactly why we're both in our messes, trying to solve our own problems instead of leaning of God."

She bugged out her eyes. "I'm just trying to be *practical* here."

"Baby, this is *it*! This is *it*! This is where we...where we stop playing the *role* of believers and actually *believe*. Together. Didn't we just invite Him into this marriage last night?"

She shrugged. "Yes."

"And didn't we both decide that we are going to trust Him with everything. *Everything?*" he pumped her up.

"Yes." Sharla shifted her weight nervously.

"Then what better time to start than right now? No more Ishmael's, baby. It's me and you, ride or die with Christ. You in?"

With quivering lips, Sharla sucked in a breath. She wiped a tear from her eye. "I'm in."

Mark had preached a similar message to the congregation a hundred times before. And he'd believed every word of it because the Bible said so. But as he exhorted his own wife in his own household, he realized that actually stepping out on faith—him first, with Sharla right behind—was about to, as he told her, *"take this here thing to a whole new level"*.

The first order of business Monday morning was personal prayer time at six, followed by family devotions and communion—a solemn practice both he and Sharla wanted to engage in intimately, thanks to their experience in Peasner, TX.

Amani fussed, of course, because Mark had all but yanked him out of bed at eight-thirty on a summer morning. "Why do we have to pray so early? God will still be up at around, like, twelve or one, right?"

"You can talk to Him again at that time if you'd like. But your Momma and I have some family business to handle today at ten. So, we're praying now. Not that I even *owe* you an explanation," Mark cautioned. "When I was your age, I was up at seven during the summertime so I could mow the grass before it got hot. Matter of fact, tomorrow morning, we're getting up early so I can teach you how to mow."

"What?" Amani objected a little too loudly.

Mark raised an eyebrow.

Amani slumped. "Yes, sir."

They gathered in the dining room, with Mark and his Bible sitting at the head of the table. He read from Hebrews chapter 11, teaching his wife and son about faith. Both Sharla and Amani had questions. Mark had to hide his disappointment because they were asking him things he thought they should have already known by that time. After all, everyone sitting at the table had grown up in the church.

But he had to admit to himself, he'd grown up in the church, too, and yet had very little revelation because he rarely cracked open a Bible between Sundays until he was in his mid-twenties. Aside from all that, he could only blame the man in the mirror. If he sat up week after week preaching to hundreds of people, but failed to take the lead in his own household, that was on *him*.

Lord, I repent.

Sharla had crushed a graham cracker and poured a small amount of fruit juice into three Dixie cups they would normally use for mouthwash. As soon as Mark closed the devotions in prayer, she brought the elements to the table on a plate, handing them to her family.

Amani looked at the crackers and juice and snarled his face. "But...wait a minute...this is a *graham* cracker and this is *not* grape juice. Should we be doing this?"

Mark fought his urge to snigger. Poor Amani had grown up around so much tradition, he didn't realize the power was in his faith. "What matters is that we remember Christ's sacrifice. He blesses what we bless."

Amani surrendered, "If y'all say so."

"We do," Mark ratified.

Mark had insisted that Danny Hernandez accompany him and Sharla to what would, hopefully and prayerfully, be a last meeting with Rozanno. After listening to Sharla explain in great detail what happened during the "interview", Mark had decided that crazy detective wasn't going to keep messing with his wife about shooting into the car. And whatever other suspicions Rozanno had, he needed to put them on the table so Hernandez could adequately prepare a defense.

Granted, Mark was no attorney. But the more he prayed and meditated about the situation, the more he felt led to get in Rozanno's face.

From what Mark could tell, Rozanno didn't appear to be quite the big man Sharla had described him to be. Yet, he probably came across forcefully when he was sitting alone with a woman. He had that air about him—like he'd buck up to a woman, but put his tail between his legs with another man.

Hernandez was a little late, which gave Mark an opportunity to sit in the chair across from Rozanno and just stare at him. Study him. Ask God for insight into him.

"Can I get you some coffee?" the detective offered with a pinch of nervousness in his tone.

"No, thank you," Mark declined, eyes dead set on Rozanno.

"Sorry I'm late," Hernandez breezed into the room, sitting on the other side of Sharla. He looked at Mark. "We haven't started here, have we?"

225

"Nope," Mark answered.

"Good." He homed in on Rozanno. "We're ready to officially clear my client's name so she can move forward with her life, right?"

"Not so fast. The results from the car sweep were inconclusive."

"What the—"

"Hold your horses, counsel," the detective challenged. "I think we can, however, exclude her on the basis of other eyewitness testimony. As I understand it, Bria Logan is fully conscious. If she corroborates Mr. Carter's testimony, that will suffice."

Hernandez laughed cynically, "We don't want to leave this technicality lingering. It'll give the insurance companies enough of a loophole to keep her in court for months. I don't understand how the car sweep was inconclusive; we're not talking DNA, here. Either you found gunpowder residue, tire irregularities, or whatever the heck you were looking for, or you didn't. Which one is it?"

"I don't tell you how to do your job. Don't tell me how to do mine. You got that?" Rozanno shot back.

"Look," Mark tried, "I was in the car. I know my wife wasn't shooting at us."

"What color was the car that chased you?"

"I don't know," Mark admitted.

"Was it a male or female who shot into the vehicle?"

"I...I can't be sure. It all happened so fast."

"Then you're not a reliable witness," the detective concluded. "Plus, you've got a motive to clear your own wife, just like she had motive to kill you."

"That's not true!" Sharla interjected.

Mark went in again, "What about Boomie? My wife told you that Bria's family said someone named Boomie was the shooter who also forced me to have the accident."

Angry lines crossed Rozanno's forehead. "That lead never panned out."

"Was it ever *in* the pan?" Danny questioned.

"I'm not at liberty to discuss another person of interest with you at this time," he avoided the question.

Mark smelled a rat.

Hernandez must have smelled it, too. He slurred, "I seeeee. So, if my client is no longer a suspect and you find no other leads, the investigation stalls. Everything's just accidental, and that's the end of it. Leave the *real aggressor* on the streets."

Rozanno shrugged. "Maybe. They *are* still looking for the *real killer* in California, you know."

Finally, Mark received discernment. The "real killer" was an allusion to the Nicole Brown Simpson case. As far as law enforcement was concerned, the guilty man had gotten away with murder.

Sharla wasn't guilty, of course, and this was no murder. But it was clear to Mark that Rozanno wasn't going after Boomie, regardless. For all Rozanno cared, Boomie might come back to finish Bria off.

Mark decided to test his theory. "I'd like to offer a reward for the capture of this Boomie character."

Just as Mark thought, the blood left the detective's face.

"Great idea!" Hernandez roused. "We could involve the press, the church. It would be great!"

"Wait!" the nearly ghost-white man yelled. "Listen, I can promise you a report that pretty much exonerates your client. Isn't that what you want, Hernandez?"

"Yes." The attorney stood and shook Rozanno's hand. "We'll expect it by week's end." He looked down at his clients. "Let's go."

Quickly, Danny led Mark and Sharla out of the building. They stopped at his car. "Get in."

Mark got in the back; Sharla took the passenger's side.

"What was that all about?" Sharla panted.

"There's something about Boomie that they don't want to mess with," Danny inferred.

"You think Rozanno's on his payroll or something?" Mark guessed.

"I don't know. Could be." Danny cracked his knuckles. "Or he might be state's evidence, they might be building a bigger case against him—drugs, prostitution. Bringing him in now might blow something they've already put millions into. I don't know."

"But what about Bria?" Mark pleaded.

Sharla shot a dagger at him with her eyes.

Mark ignored the jab. "This guy is dangerous. He wanted her dead—me, too, probably."

Sharla's eyes softened with the implication.

"I don't know what to tell you about that. All I can do as your attorney is advise you to take the report clearing Sharla and run. We're not gonna get Boomie off the streets with this particular case."

Maybe Hernandez could rest well knowing he'd cleared Sharla's name, but that wasn't enough for Mark.

Chapter 31

Thanks to Jonathan's texts, Mark was able to keep up with New Vision business to some extent. The numbers were still declining, though not as sharply. Local news had begun to devour its next victim: a teacher who'd been caught sleeping with her students. Like Jackson had said, they'd followed fresh blood.

The bloggers who'd trashed him had new headlines; the commenters posted their latest negativity. Within a matter of a few weeks, Mark's name had been dragged through the mud and left to dry.

Fortunately, he didn't have as much time to spend on the internet. Between preparing for and leading family devotions, teaching Amani how to do things that didn't involve screens, reconnecting with Sharla, and struggling through physical therapy, Mark couldn't have followed up on all of his Google hits if he'd wanted to. Besides, if something really important came up, Jackson or Jonathan would let him know.

This Friday was one of those times. "Pastor, I've got a few things I need to run by you before our next meeting. I know you're not officially back until next week, but could you come by the office a little early Friday?" Jonathan requested.

By that time, Mark had come to respect Jonathan's judgment as much as he could with someone who still looked like he'd have to show an ID to get a drink. "Sure thing."

Parking at the church lot again that early in the morning, got Mark's juices flowing. He'd already been in prayer for an hour at home before coming to the church—something

229

Pastor Phillips advised him to do when he'd called earlier in the week to check on Mark.

"Tell you like this, sin and pride and selfishness is like yeast – they rises overnight. That's why His grace and mercy got to be new and fresh every time the sun gets up. You got no business conducting God's business without dyin' to yourself fresh every mornin'."

Climbing in and out of Sharla's small car was getting old. He couldn't wait for his appointment with the insurance representative, an acquaintance from his days at StateWay. They could finally move forward with the claim now that all criminal implication had vanished with Rozanno's report. The day he got a taller cab—whether an SUV or a truck—couldn't come fast enough.

A pleasant sense of familiarity coursed through his veins as he unlocked the side door of the church and walked toward his office. The smell of plaster and carpet still lingered, welcoming him back to that place he now recognized wasn't actually *his*.

He unlocked the suite.

"Hello, Pastor!" Jonathan greeted him warmly from across the desk.

"Same to you."

"You look good, sir. Can't wait to have you back."

"Isn't this coming Sunday your turn to preach?" Mark guessed.

"Yes, it is."

"I look forward to it," Mark encouraged him.

He hoped Jonathan's message would be a nice addition to Jackson's personal testimony, shared the previous week. Jackson wasn't really a preacher so much as a storyteller, and a good one at that. He'd shared how Christ changed his life from that of a lyin', womanizin', juke-joint piano-playin' rascal to a clean man with one woman on his mind. He'd said he wasn't perfect, a statement Mrs. Jackson had "amened" loudly, but that God was faithful. And he trusted God to keep working on him.

"What's your topic for Sunday?" Mark asked.

Jonathan tapped a few keys on the computer and read from the screen. "To the Utmost. Coming from Hebrews chapter 7."

"Wonderful," Mark cheered. "I'm teaching my family from Hebrews this week. I'll share my notes with you, if you'd like."

"That would be great," Jonathan sparked. "I like this."

"What?"

"You know, the chance to collaborate with God, then you."

"So long as you keep it in that order, I think you'll be fine," Mark advised. "What did you want to see me about?"

"Oh, you may want to sit."

Mark blew out air. "Alrighty, then. Let me put my stuff in the office." Mark left the attaché behind his desk and rejoined Jonathan. "What's up?"

"Miss Bria has been trying to reach you. She's left messages." He handed Mark several pink slips of paper.

The pastor thumbed through them. She'd called six times over the last three days. All of them the same: "Call me."

"I wouldn't give her your number," he said, "but I promised that I'd let you know she called. What do you want me to do about her?"

Mark raised both eyebrows. "I'm going to call her back."

"Oh? I mean, after all the trouble she's caused, I just didn't think, you know, you'd want anything to do with her."

The confusion in Jonathan's face required an answer. In fact, he'd been so unquestionably faithful throughout that whole ordeal, Mark owed Jonathan a thorough explanation.

"Bria is Amani's birth mother. We adopted him out of the foster care system. I think, originally, she was trying to seduce me so that she could somehow get back into Amani's life. But in her efforts to get close to me, Christ got close to her. Next thing I knew, she apologized to me, and she was trying to tell me the truth at my car when some guy comes up shooting at us. We hopped into my car to get away, and that's what led to the wreck."

Jonathan's mouth hung open. "Wow. That's how it happened, huh?"

"Yep. Now you know."

"Thank you, Pastor, for telling me. You wouldn't believe how hard it was to fight back the press, the tabloids, the members...it was crazy." Jonathan shook his head and pressed palms against his ears.

"Thanks, Jonathan, for having my back. A lesser person might have caved under the pressure. You're alright with me."

"'Preciate it."

Mark checked his watch. "Guess I'll give Bria a call before the meeting."

He slipped into his office and closed the door for privacy.

Since the operator didn't give him any flack about transferring the call, Mark guessed the media had laid off Bria, too, thank God.

"Hello," a dim voice creaked.

"Bria. It's Pastor Carter."

"Hi, Pastor. I'm so glad you called."

Mark had to listen carefully to make out her words. "I'm so glad you're doing better," he replied cheerfully.

"How's your arm?"

Mark smiled. Given her injuries, his arm wasn't worth discussing. "Getting better every day. You?"

"Me, too. My swelling has gone down. And I can sit up pretty good."

Somehow, Mark knew what was coming next.

"I'm ready to see Amani, now that I don't look like a monster anymore."

A mixture of emotions flooded Mark's body. She had no idea how much Amani wanted to meet her, too. Nor how much Sharla dreaded their reunion. There was also the question of how it might go with Lisa in the room. Was it a set-up?

"Hello?" Bria sputtered.

"Yes. Um…yes. I'll bring him to you. I'll call you first, okay?"

"Okay. Thank you."

"You're welcome."

Chapter 32

Kit was early that time. Had his good church suit on with his briefcase and presentation folders ready to roll. As soon as Jackson turned the agenda over to him, he eagerly distributed them to Mark, Marshall, Jackson, and Jonathan.

"Before anyone says anything, hear me out. Straight?"

Though he'd asked for everyone's agreement, Mark knew Kit's request was aimed at him. "Okay."

"Theta Phi Mu is Houston's most active African American fraternity. Take a look at their numbers on page two."

Mark flipped through the manila folder and skimmed the numbers. Over twenty thousand likes on their Houston area Facebook page. Five alumni chapters throughout the metroplex consisting of almost four thousand active members.

"Granted, a city like ours has many organizations with active members," Kit adlibbed, "but they're not just four thousand men. They're four thousand *college-educated* men, which equates to better-than-average jobs, higher-than-average salaries, greater-than-average influence in the community. Plus their wives, who tend to have those same qualities. These are the kinds of connections we need for New Vision, the kinds of members we need to attract if we plan to get back on our feet and fly."

Marshall nodded. "Looks like you've done your homework, Kit."

"Thank you." He smiled. "What I'm proposing is actually on page six. A networking symposium hosted by New Vision and Theta Phi Mu fraternity here at the church. We'll have workshops and roundtables for established and

234

potential business owners. We'd have booth spaces available for rent so vendors could showcase their products, too. It's a win-win for everybody involved."

Presented in the "community effort" vein, it sounded harmless enough. But Mark had a few questions for Kit. "How will this further the cause of Christ? What makes it any different than if the fraternity had partnered with a recreation center or the chamber of commerce?"

"Well..." Kit stalled, "since the fraternity is not a religious non-profit organization, they really can't, you know, say anything in a way that makes it sound like they're proselytizing. But many of them, I'd say most of them, are Christians."

Marshall dove into the conversation, "Not everyone's a preacher, Pastor. In the real world, people have to be careful of what they say. Separation of church and state."

"I get that," Mark readily acknowledged. "But if it's taking place *at the church*, the separation is forfeited."

"Okay, we'll open and close with prayer," Kit conceded. "They still do it at graduations, so I'm sure we can get away with it."

Get away with prayer at church? Mark kept that one to himself and moved on to his main concern. "What about the fraternity itself? Will they hang banners and advertise themselves at the event?"

A crooked grin punctured Kit's face. "Pastor, I'm sure they'll say or do something to bring honor and recognition to the fraternity."

Mark couldn't have said it better himself. "That's precisely where the problem lies, Kit. No fraternity, no sorority, no worship of Greek letters and gods and secret societies should take place in the house of God. What people

235

do outside of church is on them. But I won't bring that inside *these* walls."

"Are you serious?" Kit laughed.

"As serious as I've always been about this issue, Kit. Don't act brand new," Mark laughed as well. Even before he'd made the decision to make Christ the vision for New Vision, he'd come to that conclusion and made his entire staff aware of his stance. Why Kit wanted to push it now was anybody's guess.

Mark felt the tension multiplying. He sensed that Kit and Marshall were on the same page. Jackson and Jonathan hadn't uttered one word. At that point, the only thing coming from their side of the room was the ticking of the wall clock.

Not that he could be persuaded otherwise, but Mark decided to ask them for their input. "Jackson?"

"I don't know enough about Greek groups to know what's what. I gave my granddaughter four hundred dollars so she could pledge in college. Other than that, I got nothin'."

"Then, obviously, you saw nothing wrong with it," Marshall deduced.

"I saw nothing at all," Jackson spoke for himself. "She'd been watching a whole bunch of old episodes of *A Different World*; next thing I knew she wanted to attend a black college and pledge a sorority. She got a job, worked for some of the money during the summer, I gave her the rest. If your granddaughter's in college, doin' good, not pregnant, when she asks for something, you give it to her."

His humorous anecdote loosened the stiffness in the room.

"Amen to that," Marshall concurred.

"Jonathan," Mark asked, "what's your position?"

All eyes focused on the youngest man in the room. Jonathan shook his head. "No, I don't know a whole lot about them, either. I have a friend who was going to pledge, but decided not to after…you know…it all started."

"Too weak, huh?" Kit leered.

"No, actually *she* read through the Rho's books of rituals and chants and hymns they gave her and decided she couldn't do it."

"Wait a minute – my granddaughter is a Rho. What kinds of rituals?" Jackson urged Jonathan to spill the beans.

"I don't know. It's all secret stuff," Jonathan said.

"Naww. Young folk ain't got no better sense than to put everything online these days." Jackson sat up in his chair. "Go on the internet and pull up a ritual book for the Rhos. I'll bet we can find something. Shoot, I paid four hundred dollars. I got a right to know what my money went toward."

Jonathan flipped open his iPad and tapped the screen. Seconds later he announced, "Got it. Let me print it off. I'll be right back."

Jonathan darted from the room, toward the main office.

"The Rhos are *not* Theta Phi Mu," Kit objected in the meanwhile.

"True, but my point is—it's important for everyone in this room to understand where I'm coming from."

Kit puffed up his chest, then expelled a huge gust of air.

"I want to know *exactly* what the words are," Jackson fussed, caught up in his own drama.

Jonathan returned, laying a copy of the sorority's lyrics in front of each man.

Rho National Hymn
Rho, dear Rho,
Our faith we pledge

237

For the love and grace
Bestowed by thee.
With faith in God and Mind and Heart
To serve thee is our aim.
Carrying out the great commands
Of heaven and earth.
That the praise of Rho
May be sung.
Always.
Rho, dear, our own.

Rho, dear Rho.
The bond of sisterhood
That we live to be.
We cherish thy teachings.
Your light shines
Across the world.
That thy glory, thy honor,
and praises be sung
Always.
Rho, dear, our own.

And when this life is over,
Rapture our souls to thee.
We'll forever be,
Faithfully,
Rho, dears, your own.

Jackson exclaimed, "What in the world is this mess she done pledged to?"

"Hmmm…" Marshall muttered, "it does sound questionable."

"Like I said, Theta Phi Mu aren't the Rhos."

"Let's pull up *their* song," Marshall suggested.

"That's disrespectful," Kit argued.

"Fine. Can one of them let us know what song they're singing every time they meet?" Mark asked.

"If you look on page two, you can see that they're based on Christian principles," Kit spewed.

"That's just like saying everyone who wears a cross on their necklace is a believer. Based on Christian *principles* doesn't mean based on *Christ*," Mark maintained.

Kit threw his hands toward the sky. "You're impossible. I can't deal with this old-school, backwards thinking anymore." He snatched his folder from the table.

Mark couldn't believe his eyes. Kit, a man who'd been with New Vision since its inception, was preparing to walk away. "Kit, why are you doing this? I've always taken this stance."

"That's the problem! You won't embrace the *new* thing Christ is doing in the church!" Kit exploded passionately.

Mark stood, his blood pumping wildly. "But the gospel isn't new. The gospel of Christ is timeless!"

"Everything in the church isn't about Christ!"

Mark paused, hoping that the irony of Kit's statement would hit him. "Kit, come on, let's pray about this. The Lord will bring us to an understanding."

Kit stood on the other side of the table, sweat forming on his distressed forehead, nostrils flaring. "No."

And then Mark noticed the torturous gleam forming in Kit's eyes.

Kit blinked twice. "I'm out."

Mark's heart ripped down the center as he watched a man he'd once considered a good friend walk away from the

239

ministry they had built together. It was Kit who had been there to negotiate the loans with banks, review contracts, and research the best resources and grants. Granted, Kit was a bit money-hungry, but his obsession with the bottom line had been part of the reason the church was able to operate so smoothly, with little waste.

More than anything, Kit had once believed in Mark.

But he was gone.

Jonathan, Marshall, and Jackson looked up at Mark in shock.

"You gonna go talk to him?" from Jackson.

Mark gave a short-term answer, "Not now", but he feared that the long-term answer wouldn't be much different. As much as he wanted to bring Kit back on board, he couldn't do so without compromising his own personal convictions. If other pastors wanted to preach motivational speeches and join forces with fraternities, so be it. But as for him and *this* church, they wouldn't be mixing the two.

"Guess since that was the last item on the agenda, we can dismiss," Jackson ventured.

"Before we do, I just want to state for the record that New Vision is returning to its first love—Christ. Anybody else who doesn't feel led to stay with this mission is welcome to leave in peace now," Mark affirmed to himself as much as the men still sitting around the table.

"I'm in." Jackson led the declaration.

"I'm in."

"I'm in."

Mark waited until after twelve noon, which was the soonest he could call Pastor Phillips, because before then, the older man would be in his prayer closet.

At 12:01 he typed his newfound mentor's number. "Hi, Pastor Phillips, it's Mark Carter. Tugga."

"Hello, son! Good to hear from you!"

And like a father might listen to his son, Pastor Phillips listened as Mark recounted the state of affairs at New Vision.

"Well, people—even Christians full of the Holy Spirit—don't always agree. The important thing is to remove all the malice from your heart, stay prayerful, and keep doing the work of the Lord as you believe you are led. If everybody you know go a diff'rent way, don't you mind them."

"But what if, hypothetically speaking, I'm wrong?" Mark voiced. "What if God doesn't care one way or the other about the fraternity?"

"For the record, I agree with you. But you got to remember what Paul said in Romans. We free in Christ to do whatso'never we wanna do, only everything ain't beneficial. You got to get to a place in God where you hear Him clear as a bell. And don't let nobody talk you out of what you believe God told you to do. Even if you a little off, He'll honor your faith in Him and teach you a lesson anyway. Didn't we just have this conversation?"

"Yes, sir." His words reminded Mark of the many times he had to reiterate things to Amani. Sometimes it seemed like words barely skimmed his ears.

"I want you to look in Acts chapter fifteen. See where Paul and Barnabas, both of 'em filled with the Spirit of God, had a sharp disagreement. They went their separate ways, but they both kept on doing the work of the Lord."

241

Mark jotted down the scripture reference and thanked Pastor Phillips for his time before hanging up.

For as much as his heart weighed, Mark was yet lifted by the Word.

Chapter 33

The clank of metal on metal behind him raked Mark's nerves. Nothing like a long-forgotten sound to remind him that though time had passed, little had changed between him and his father. Mark Wayne Carter, II was yet again behind bars, and Mark Wayne Carter, III was yet speaking to his father through a thick glass window.

Mark sat in the hard orange chair, studying his father's features for a moment before picking up the blue phone receiver. If Sharla were there, she would have wiped both ends and the handle with a Clorox wipe. Thankfully, she wasn't. And he wasn't about to tell her that he'd gone to visit his father for help.

As far as Sharla was concerned, Mark Wayne Carter, II had done nothing but cause trouble. Every time they tried to get something financed or register to volunteer, there was always the question of Mark's criminal record, which belonged to his father. It had gotten to the point where Sharla offered the information up front to avoid the embarrassment or, worse, flat denial that would come otherwise.

His father had lost weight. Twenty pounds or so. And despite the fact that he hadn't even turned sixty yet, he looked like he'd lived a long, hard life already. Scars on his forehead and cheeks, a missing tooth, deep lines beneath his eyes.

"Hey, son."

"Hi."

"Glad you made it," his father teased.

"Me, too." Mark wasn't exactly glad about the meeting, but he was glad to have the connection. "Dad, I've got a situation."

"Yeah. I heard it on TV," he said. "Thought you might end up in here with me for a minute."

"No," Mark shook his head, "I don't think so."

"You never know," his father said with a hint of optimism, "Father and son together again."

Rather than look at his father like he'd lost his mind, Mark ignored the off-track comment. "Well, since you already know what happened, I'll just tell you why I'm here. The man who was chasing the young lady and me, I think he's either paying someone off or they're scared to look for him, but *I* need him off the streets."

"Hmmm," the senior said, rubbing his stubbly chin. "You got a name?"

"Boomie."

His father's eyes sparked with recognition. "Yeah, I heard the name. He's crazy. Likes to shoot people. They don't call him Boomie for nothin'."

"That's what I'm afraid of. He might want to finish off the girl, and me, too," Mark explained.

"Well, you've come to the right place." His father surveyed the room, then leaned in toward the glass, whispering, "Don't worry. I'll handle it." He resumed an upright position.

Mark mimicked his father's movements, settling his back against the chair. His father might have been a drug dealer and a money launderer, but he'd never been a liar. If he said he was going to get Mark a 10-speed bike for Christmas, he got it. If he said he was coming to the birthday party, he came. Mark just had to worry about *how* his father would fulfill his promise. "Dad, I don't want him...you know..."

"What you don't know won't hurt you," he kicked Mark out of the particulars. "I might be an old cat, but I still got my connections. And you still my son. Nothin' I wouldn't do to protect you. Some of the guys in here started clownin' when they saw you on TV. I told 'em straight up, you ain't one of them hustlin' preachers. You ain't all about the money, 'cause I always told you, you could make *far* more money sellin' crack."

Mark thought to himself, "Now, how many Dads have told their sons *that?*" Still, he had to be grateful for whatever help his father had to offer.

"Thanks."

"Yeah, I told 'em you ain't no average fakin' and shakin', jack-legged preacher," his father bragged. "You the *real thang*, son."

His father's words hit him hard in the chest. Confirmation, even from a man behind bars, couldn't be denied. "I appreciate you sharing that with me."

"Hey – I ain't done much for you except give you good looks, you know. So now, when I save your life from Boomie, that'll count for something, right?"

"Umm...yeah, that'll count."

"Good. How's Sharla and Amani?"

"They're fine," Mark answered.

"How's your Momma?"

"Good."

"She still married to the midget?"

Mark had to laugh at his father's ongoing joke about his mother's vertically challenged second husband. "Yes, they're still together."

"Well, long as she's happy with him. Tell everybody I said hi."

Everybody, of course, included his brother and sister. As far as Mark knew, they hadn't gone to Huntsville to see their father. He was out of sight and out of mind, which was usually best, Mark had to admit. If he sat around thinking about his father's life of crime, he might start to question the blood running through his veins.

"I'll see you later, Dad."

"See ya."

Chapter 34

Mark got up extra early so he could spend half an hour in prayer before he talked to Sharla about Bria's request. He could have almost kicked himself for not running it by Pastor Phillips when they spoke the day before. Maybe the man could have given him some guidance.

But even as he mentioned his negligence to God in prayer, the Father reminded Mark that He knew more than Pastor Phillips. In fact, He was the source of the more seasoned minister's wisdom.

"Thank You, Lord," Mark heard himself whisper into the cup of his hands. Though it seemed almost trite, Mark revisited the story of the two harlots who came to Solomon complaining that the other had stolen her baby. The real mother was discovered by her love for her child; she would rather give him up than split him in two.

Perhaps I should share this story with Sharla. Or not, seeing as his wife had bribed Amani's grandmother. At first, Mark couldn't believe Sharla had done it. But the more he thought about it, the more he realized that Sharla would have done anything to keep Amani. Back then she was working full-time and probably spent every spare dime on Amani. He was the best-dressed baby, the best cared-for toddler, perhaps even the most worried-over child.

He recalled one night in particular when Sharla asked him if he would be willing to relocate to Mexico if the judge didn't award them Amani.

"Relocate? You mean run away?" he had asked her as they lay in bed together.

"Whatever you want to call it."

He'd looked down into Sharla's face to gauge the level of intent behind her words. Her somber expression said she was dead serious.

"I'm gonna pray for you 'cause you're taking this too far. Demetria told us not to get attached to the baby until the ink dried—*if* it dried," he ran the warning by her again.

"It's too late. I love him. I *can't* let him go back, knowing he'll be in the hands of a wild party-girl and her mother who raised her to be a wild party-girl. If I turn on the television in fifteen years and see my sweet Amani's face on a mug shot, I'll blame myself forever."

He'd sent up a couple of half-hearted prayers, but not nearly the kind of intercession his wife must have needed. Once again, he'd left things at home unattended and made room for his wife to fend for herself. She was a grown woman with a will of her own, but maybe if he'd paid more attention to what was happening at home, she might not have been able to get so desperately attached, let alone pilfer $5,000 from their accounts without notice.

He should have done better.

Now that he knew the whole truth about how Amani had come to be their son, Sharla's insecurities made sense. She tried to keep him close, never wanted him to latch on to his teachers, and she worried excessively about whether or not she was being a good mother. No wonder her moods could change at the drop of a hat.

It had resulted in her nagging Amani non-stop about all that she expected of him, because any failure on his part meant failure on her part.

But it had to come to a stop. Even if it meant Sharla might have to endure legal consequences; she couldn't go through life on pins and needles. Mark loved her too much to see her suffer that way.

Sharla was already up and making breakfast by the time Mark exited from his prayer time. Still in his nightclothes, he joined her in the kitchen. "Waffles?"

"Blueberry. They're Amani's favorite." She smiled contently.

Mark stole a piece of bacon from the platter before Sharla could swipe his hand away. "Go on, Mark. Wait until we've called Amani down and we're all gathered for devotions."

Somehow, devotions seemed to go better when they broke bread together first.

"Baby, I need to talk to you before Amani gets down here."

"Okay." Sharla rinsed her hands in the sink and wiped them on her dishtowel. "Go."

"It's about Bria. She wants to see Amani."

Sharla rubbed her hands against her white apron. "Oh."

Mark watched as his wife tried to hide the fear that must have been creeping up her body, inch by inch.

She caught hold of the island countertop. "And how do you know this?"

"She called the church and left a message. I called her back."

"What did she say?"

Though Mark figured he'd already given his wife that information, he repeated himself, "She wants to see Amani."

"What *else* does she want?"

"That's it."

"Does she want to be in his life?" Sharla squeaked. The tears were forming already.

"She is his birth mother. I can't imagine why she wouldn't...if he wanted to be in her life, too."

"I do," Amani's voice broke into their conversation.

Sharla and Mark turned abruptly to find their son standing at the foot of the staircase.

"Amani, honey," Sharla said nervously, "um...I made blueberry waffles..."

"I know, Mom. The smell woke me up. But that's not what you guys were talking about."

Mark gritted his teeth, then relaxed them. "You're right. Come on, 'Mani. Have a seat. Let's pray, then we can talk while we eat."

Mark wasn't sure how the conversation would go, but a part of him was glad Amani would be included. His presence all but insured that Sharla wouldn't go flying off the handle.

Sharla served the plates full of food to Mark and Amani first, then she joined them at the table. Mark said grace, asking God for wisdom and understanding as they ate and talked.

"The lady I was in the wreck with is named Bria Logan. She's your birth mother," Mark started carefully.

"Yeah, I figured. I *can* Google and read, you know?" He crammed a gob of waffle into his mouth.

For once, Sharla didn't point out that he'd put too much into his mouth. She nibbled aimlessly at a corner of a piece of bacon.

"Here's the thing, 'Mani. We don't know Miss Bria's family—your family. We don't know anything about them, anything about their beliefs, their lifestyle. Like I told you before, God has a reason for giving us the privilege to raise you. We want you to get to know your blood relatives. But we don't want you to be confused about who you are and what God wants to do in your life."

Amani swallowed his food hard. "Thanks, Dad. I mean, sometimes, when I'm chillin' with the twins or at somebody's house and they start arguing with their brothers and sisters and cousins, I feel jealous because all our family is, like, not here. When we went to Mama B's, I felt like I belonged."

"You *do* belong. Here. With *us*," Sharla finally spoke.

"Yeah, but you guys are, like, *old*. And *boring*. No offense. And y'all hardly let me go anywhere, so it's like, maybe if I had some family members, y'all would loosen up, like when we were in Peasner," he explained. "I need peeps."

Sharla dove into her waffle. Mark wondered why on earth his wife was taking this so personally. Amani was growing up. He needed more than his Mommy and Daddy.

"I hear you, 'Mani." Cutting the waffle with his right hand slowed the process and sent shockwaves through his arm, but Mark followed his therapist's orders. Patience.

"What about your church friends? You've known them for more than half your life now," Sharla groped.

"They're cool."

Mark stared at the side of Sharla's face, but she didn't look at him. He felt he owed it to both Amani and Bria to orchestrate a reunion; he wasn't so sure he wanted Sharla there. Amani seemed to be handling the situation gracefully, but Sharla wasn't ready.

Mark transitioned them into devotions by reading from Ephesians 4. He prayed for them all to find their truest sense of family in the body of Christ. Then he announced, "I told

251

Miss Bria we'd come by the hospital this morning. You ready to meet her?"

"Cool."

Sharla's fork tinked loudly on her plate. *"Today?"*

"Yes. Today," Mark said.

She wiped her mouth with her paper towel. "May I see you in private?" She didn't wait for his answer, but stormed off to their bedroom.

"Put these dishes in the dishwasher and go ahead and get dressed," Mark told his son. "We'll be leaving in a little while."

"Dad, go easy on her," Amani pleaded for his mother. "She still thinks I'm, like, a baby."

"Gotcha."

Mark couldn't have said it better. He was glad to know that Amani had some sense of how hard this must be on Sharla. Of course, he didn't know about the bribery. Maybe it was best that he never knew about what shady lengths Sharla had gone to, to adopt him.

Unsure of exactly what Sharla would say, Mark asked God for the wisdom to interpret her heart, no matter what words came spilling out of her mouth. He closed the door behind him, then leaned his backside on the dresser.

Sharla sat on the bed, arms folded. "Why do we have to go today?"

"What's wrong with today?"

"I need more time to…to process," she pouted.

"Process what?"

"Everything! What if…what if she wants to visit him regularly? What if she wants to blackmail us? What if Amani…" Sharla slapped her forehead. "What if it's already been planted in Amani's heart to love her more? Why

252

wouldn't God let me have kids, too? What if *God* loves her more, too?"

And now Mark was hearing something he hadn't heard in nearly a decade: this business about having babies. Mark had wanted a blood-related son as much as the next man, but given his relationship with his father, Mark knew there was no magic to having a natural kinship. Growing up, he'd had more of a relationship with the men at the barbershop than his own father. He had hated the fact that he was named after a man everyone in the neighborhood talked about negatively—for good reason, too.

God hadn't given him a son by birth, but He had allowed them to raise Amani, and he'd given Mark a peace about the situation. To hear her rip the scab off that old wound angered him slightly. Until he got the answer to the prayer he'd prayed before entering the bedroom.

Rather than give Sharla a lecture about how it wasn't about her, how she was going on forty years old and needed to get over the fact that she wouldn't or couldn't give birth and be thankful that they'd been able to adopt, seeing as so many people couldn't even do that much, Mark listened.

He walked over to his wife and kneeled down, cupping her hands into his. "Baby, there is no way anyone can question your love for Amani. You've been a great mother to him and he knows it. It was wrong of you to bribe Bria's mom. It was also wrong of Amani's grandmother to accept money in lieu of her grandson. The whole deal was bad on both sides. Maybe her family will want to blackmail us. Maybe Bria will go to the authorities. I don't know. But we can't keep hiding behind our faults to protect ourselves. This isn't about me or you or even Bria. It's about Amani and what's best for him."

253

Her warm, wet tears dripped onto his hands as he looked up into her face. The makeup she'd so delicately applied ruined in the wake of emotions. "But how do we know that meeting Bria is what's best for Amani?"

"How do we know it's not? This whole saga started with her trying to reach out to him. After all that's happened, all *she's* been through, all *we've* been through, it would seem ridiculous not to let her meet him."

Sharla dried her eyes with the back of her hand. "If you say so."

"I say so. You trust me?"

She sniffed. "Yes."

"You trust God?"

"Yes."

"Let's do this."

Chapter 35

The thought of seeing Bria again after so many years seemed to split Sharla's personality right down the middle. On one hand, she wanted to take Amani and run as far away from the female who'd been so busy partying that she put her precious son in danger. On the other, Amani was so obviously obsessed with meeting his birth family that denying him the opportunity could leave him hurt and embittered to the point where Sharla would probably end up losing him emotionally forever.

She'd told Mark that she trusted both him and God. She trusted them both, alright, especially since Mark had been teaching her things in God's word that she'd never even considered before their family devotions time. But still…Amani was her baby. If he decided to make Bria his "real" mom, where would that leave Sharla?

Mark forged ahead, knocking on Bria's hospital room door. "Hello?"

Sharla held her breath as her husband entered first, then Amani, then herself, relatively far behind. The room was filled with flowers and cards. Obviously, a lot of people cared about Bria. Where had they all been when it was time to adopt Amani? Were these new acquaintances? Co-workers who'd sent things to be politically correct? Attorneys who wanted to represent her?

Despite her pale skin, the darkness under her eyes, and scars crisscrossing her face, Bria exuded an optimistic air. Someone had also recently braided her hair in cornrows.

Stop it, Sharla. She knew better. For Amani's sake, it was a good thing that people loved his birth mother. Maybe she'd gotten herself together and become a better person.

"Pastor?" a woman's weak voice creaked.

"Yes, it's me. And I brought someone to meet you."

Startled at the sound of the hospital bed's movement, Sharla grabbed the cross charm on her necklace. She zipped the charm across the silver links a few times, calming herself with the familiar rhythm.

Mark and Amani stepped to the side of Bria's bed, within view. Sharla stayed several feet away from the foot. Amani inched closer to Bria's head.

She reached for him, ran her hand down the length of his arm. "Hello, Amani."

"Hi...um..." Amani stuttered.

The three laughed together. Watching them standing there—her husband and son with that woman—was almost like watching her family with someone else.

"Just call me Bria." She laughed slightly. "I'm not much older than you."

Amani gave an awkward grin and waved. "Hi, Bria."

Mark stepped away, joining Sharla's side. The quick squeeze around her shoulders reminded her to breathe.

Now that Amani and Bria were standing side by side, Sharla saw their close resemblance. With all the publicity Mark got because of the church and the remnants of Amani's tell-tale port wine stain, it was only a matter of time before she found him.

Even from that distance, Sharla could see tears trickling down Bria's face. Her insides melted as she witnessed the tenderness of Bria's gaze into Amani's eyes, how her fingertips gently outlined Amani's strong features. For what it was worth, Sharla could appreciate what it must have felt like to finally meet the son she'd been thinking about all those years. There was no denying the love for Amani branded on Bria's heart. Sharla could do nothing except respect it.

Maybe someday Sharla would meet the children she'd lost before they were ever born. If it were possible, she hoped their meeting would be that sweet.

"It's so nice to see you again," Bria whispered. "You're so handsome."

"Well, you know, uh, what can I say?" Amani joked in classic J.J. Evans mode.

Bria laughed herself into a coughing spell.

Mark rushed back to her side. "Are you okay? You need some water?"

"No," she sputtered to a calm, "I'm fine. And he's quite a character."

"Definitely," Mark agreed. "His sense of humor sometimes gives my wife a headache."

What? Why on earth had Mark insisted on dragging her into the conversation? She was just fine being a fly on the wall.

"Yes. Sharla, I'm so glad you're here." Bria motioned for Sharla to come closer.

What do I say? What if she hates me? Does she know about the money? She fought the instinct to flee with every step toward the other side of Bria's bed. "Hi."

"Hello."

Grasping Amani's hand on the left and Sharla's on the right, Bria breathed deeply. She looked up at the son she'd given birth to. "I'm so happy right now. I can see that your mom—" she squeezed Sharla's hand,"—has done such a good job of raising you. I'm thankful. There's no way I could have done better."

Sharla squeezed back, letting the dam of her soul break. "Thank *you*. He's a great son." There was no doubt in Sharla's mind—Bria had become a better person. Maybe the best person.

Mark moseyed up to Sharla's side. "I'd like to think I had a little something to do with this, too."

They all shared a laugh, which loosened the last of the tightness in Sharla's chest. Until the room's door swung open again.

"I know you didn't come back here! And got the nerve to bring your wife with her triflin' behind up in here!" Lisa raged.

The fury in her face reignited Sharla's fears. Mark grabbed his wife's free hand.

"Mama, stop it," Bria intervened with a sharpness Sharla was surprised to hear coming from such a frail-looking body.

"I don't think so." Lisa marched herself right up to Sharla's face.

Mark, of course, made himself a shield. "Let's not do anything crazy."

The alcohol on Lisa's breath had already made its way around the room. "You got a lot of nerve, after what you did."

"All she *did* was raise Amani. And raised him well, at that," Bria said.

Lisa stopped cold, looking past the adults to Amani. "Oh my gooooooodness! My grandson!" Lisa flew around the hospital bed and swallowed Amani in a bear hug. "I've been looking for you all your life!" She wagged him back and forth, kissing his face with a ferocity that could only be explained by her apparent inebriation.

"Hello, ma'am," Amani choked out, bewilderment written on his features.

"Mama, that's enough, you're cutting off his circulation," Bria ordered.

"I ain't got to let him go. This my grandson! They took him from us!" she spat back at Bria.

"That's not true," Bria argued.

"Oh, yes they did. Paid a pretty penny, too," Lisa hinted.

The hair on Sharla's arm stood on end. Was this woman about to air all their dirty laundry in front of Amani?

"Wonder who they paid it *to*?" Bria threatened.

Amani managed to respectfully free himself from Lisa's grip. He rushed to stand by Sharla and Mark.

Lisa drew in closer to Bria. "Honey, you can't side with these people. We suin' them, remember?"

"There was never a *we*. Only *you* tryin' to sue. But you won't win. I'll testify against you."

Lisa gawked in disbelief. "But what about—"

"If I'd raised Amani, he'd have been on the streets, under the jail, or probably somewhere slingin' with Boomie right now, wherever his crazy behind is. I hope they catch him, too."

"They will," Mark interjected.

Lisa looked him up and down and snarled, "You betta hope they do 'cause he don't appreciate you ridin' around in the car with his girlfriend."

"*Ex*-girlfriend," from Bria. "And we weren't riding around, I told you. I was asking about Amani."

"Is that what this was all about?" Amani asked. "Me?"

"Yeah," Mark said, slapping Amani on the back. "Everybody in this room cares about you."

All except one, Sharla thought to herself.

"Cool."

Once Lisa reluctantly sat her happy behind down, Mark, Sharla, and Amani were able to talk with Bria for a few more minutes before a nurse came in and said that visitors needed to leave the room.

"Certainly," Mark answered for them all.

"Sorry," Bria apologized. "Gotta go to the restroom. In a weird way."

"No need to apologize," Sharla offered. She couldn't imagine what Bria was still going through. Of all the things she'd hated most when she went to visit her grandmother, before they put her in the nursing home, the worst was helping her go to the restroom, a humiliating experience for everyone involved.

"We're going to let you rest," Mark said. "We'll be back to visit again."

"Wonderful," Bria gushed. "I should be moved to rehab soon."

"Great. Wherever you are, we'll find you," Mark assured her.

"Good-bye, Miss Bria," Amani said, still standing by his parents.

Bria smiled. "Such a respectful young man. Good-bye, Amani. It was good to meet you."

"Same here."

"Come give your grandmomma another hug," Lisa demanded.

Though Sharla felt tempted to tell him he didn't have to, Amani complied.

"We love you. You hear?" Lisa proclaimed.

"Yes, ma'am. Thank you."

Sarcasm bubbled in Sharla's throat. *You didn't love him more than you loved my five thousand dollars.* Still, she bit her tongue.

Amani had to stop off at the restroom on the way out of the hospital. When he ducked into the passageway, Sharla sank into Mark's arms.

"That was so hard," she spoke into his shirt.

He kissed her forehead and said with a country twang, "You done good, Mamasita. Real good."

As she sopped up the last seconds in Mark's arms before Amani emerged from the restroom, Sharla reveled in this new, more attentive husband she'd encountered after the accident. Though she didn't think God had *caused* the wreck, it was clear that He had *used* the wreck to bring them closer to each other. Closer to Him.

For quite some time, she'd been asking God to restore what they used to have—that giddy, wild-and-crazy kind of love they'd had when they first got married. Then she realized that the situation had deepened their love. Matured it. Whatever God was doing in Mark, she'd definitely been the beneficiary. She was even ready to be a part of it. Even if "being a part of it" meant supporting him more at New Vision. She would do it so long as this new Mark continued to take care of home first.

Oh, she could definitely be a first lady under those circumstances.

Chapter 36

Mark, Sharla, and Amani sat on the first pew of New Vision. Thus far, the service had been a refreshing display of God's gifts and callings on the lives of the young people at New Vision. Well, the ones who were left. A quick glance at the audience yielded roughly half the number of people who'd attended before the accident.

And yet, miraculously, they were in no worse shape financially. With Kit gone and many of the programs cut from the budget that Mark never really was keen about supporting anyway, New Vision had managed to stay in the black, despite the distraction.

Mark and his remaining advisors could only credit God for balancing their books. Even Marshall had remarked in their last meeting, "I've heard people testify that they lost jobs, lost income, but somehow their bills never missed a beat. Now I know what they mean. On paper, looking at the charts and graphs, the trends, I don't know how He did it. I just know He did."

As Jonathan took the pulpit for the first time to deliver the Sunday sermon, he recounted to the church how faithful God had been to the congregation. He thanked them all for their continued support. "But," he noted, "it's not me you're supporting. It's not Pastor Carter you're supporting. It's the work of the Lord, the work Jesus commanded us to continue—feed His sheep. Make disciples of men. Love one another. *This* is what you support."

Mark nudged Sharla. "That's what I'm talkin' 'bout."

Sharla smiled and nudged him back.

He leaned over and whispered in her ear. "Are you flirting with me in church?"

She licked her lips slightly, rolled her eyes at him and returned her gaze to the pulpit.

Yes. She definitely was flirting with him, something she'd been doing a whole lot more lately, thanks be unto God.

"Before I begin, however, I would like to thank Pastor Carter for being an example of a man of God before me. Um...I'm pretty young."

The congregation chuckled.

"But I've had an opportunity to work with several men of the cloth. I can say beyond the shadow of a doubt that Pastor Carter's integrity, his convictions, and his heart for Jesus has impacted me in a way that he may never know. Pastor, thank you for your example. I've never been more honored to serve anyone," Jonathan commended. "He's not just a preacher, he's a pastor. A shepherd under the Great Shepherd. We love you, Pastor Carter. I'd like to officially say welcome back."

A thunderous roar of applause rippled through the building, followed by a standing ovation. Mark was flooded with emotion as he turned around to witness the outpouring of love from the remaining members of New Vision. In that moment, he realized that the people who'd left needed to leave. Maybe God had another place for them to serve. Maybe they'd been there for the wrong reason to begin with. Whatever the case, *those* people, *those* members were the ones God still wanted him to serve. And he would, for the cause of Christ.

He felt Sharla's squeeze and quickly beheld her expression. Love. Pure love shone in her eyes. "This is soooo who you are. And I am sooo behind you."

"Thanks, Mamasita."

263

On the other side of Sharla, Amani leaned into Mark's line of vision. He gave a thumbs up and mouthed, "Cool."

Epilogue

Two months later

Mark's father made good on his promise. The particulars weren't disclosed on the newscast. All Mark and Sharla knew was that one night they were snuggled up on the couch watching the news when the ugliest mug shot on record flashed across the screen announcing the capture of Dedrick Wilson, also known as "Boomie," after a two-hour stand-off with police. They also mentioned his connection with the shooting that caused Mark's accident.

"My gosh! They caught him!" Sharla sat up, shrieking.

"Amen and amen," Mark praised.

"Babe, that's the last of it! No more delays from the insurance companies!"

As soon as Sharla settled back into the warm place underneath his neck, he said, "I told you God would work it out."

"You sure did," she cooed.

"And you was all tryin' to send stuff overseas."

She slapped his stomach. "I was scared. And that was a long time ago. I'm better now."

She told the truth. Since they'd been having family devotions, both Sharla and Amani had begun taking turns studying to share insight during their sacred gathering time. Sharla liked the Psalms best, elaborating on God's protection and love for His people. Mark had noticed a difference in her ability to let go of the small things.

But as great as it was to have his wife growing in her faith, Mark had to admit to himself that he was even more godly proud to see Amani rightly dividing the word, too. No

265

doubt, God had placed Amani under Mark's roof to be trained for the call to preach. He didn't want to scare his son with that revelation, but even the new youth minister who'd replaced Kit, made mention of Amani's insight when they discussed the Bible.

"He's a chip off the old block," Mark was told. To which he smiled like a man who'd just watched his son score the winning touchdown at the Super Bowl.

Once school had resumed, the family devotions had to be moved to the evenings, three times a week. Amani's gift, however great, was not fully functional at six forty-five in the morning.

With the Carter devotions set in stone at eight-thirty on Mondays, Tuesdays, and Thursdays, Mark had good reason to be out of the office and home at a decent hour. He kept the Wednesday and Sunday sermons divvied up between the other preachers on staff, which kept him free to spend time with God alone and shepherd at home, as well as edify the other men who took the pulpit. Building on one another's sermons was proving to be one of the most beneficial outcomes to sharing the load. Even though it meant neither of them could expect the church to grow at exponential rates as it had when Mark was the only one bringing the word, the message of Christ, the meat they doled out to the maturing body of Christ at New Vision, and the move of the Spirit in the congregation was unmistakably powerful.

Sharla would just have to wait on that dream house. Patiently. She wasn't quite where Mark wanted her to be yet, but he realized he had to be patient with her, too. As the Lord softened her heart, she'd been a better sport about Amani casually getting to know Bria. They'd visited her in

266

rehab twice, and on both occasions, Sharla handled the delicate situation well.

With his house back in order, Mark could say, in retrospect, that God had kept His promise in Romans 8:28 to work all things, whether good or bad, together for the good of them who love the Lord. Stepping down had been the worst thing and the best thing that could have ever happened to hone the vision God had given him. Christ be forever glorified!

The End

Want More?
Get to know Mama B better
in her series of award-winning novellas.

Book 1, Mama B: A Time to Speak - The good folks at Mt. Zion Baptist are doing their best to keep the church flowing smoothly while Pastor Phillips takes time off to be with his wife in her final days. Beatrice "Mama B" Jackson even opens her home so that the women's groups can continue to meet faithfully after some "rascal" stole the copper from the church's air conditioning unit. With her semi-estranged granddaughter and great-grandson staying in the guest room, Mama B soon has a full house.

When the interim preacher and his wife start touting messages that don't line up with the Bible, Mama B can only take so much of this foolishness. Soon enough, she realize that there is much more at stake than she or anyone else at Mt. Zion ever imagined. It's time to speak.

Book 2, Mama B: A Time to Dance - Mama B thought her life would return to normal, but when her nephew, Derrick, comes knocking on her door, she has to reconsider. Though she's not known for housing marital fugitives, she realizes Derrick is looking for more than a place to stay; he needs help finding his way back to God.

Of course, help is almost Mama B's middle name until Henrietta crosses the line with her accusations about Mama B's intentions with the recently widowed pastor. Mama B isn't looking for romance with either the pastor or her suitor, Dr. Wilson—but will love come looking for her?

Book 3, Mama B: A Time to Love - Mama B was supposed to be helping people at the community food pantry, but Eunice needs more than just a bag full of canned goods. Though Eunice has plenty money, she can't seem to manage what matters most in life. Maybe if she stopped all the "cigarette-ment" (as Henrietta says) she might turn out all right.

Dr. Wilson's not letting up on his pursuit of Mama B. Will he come on too strong and scare her away, or will Mama B throw caution to the wind and fall in love at age 72?

Catch up with Mama B again in the small town of Peasner, TX. She's still servin' wisdom and humor as only she can.

Mama B books are available online now!

About the Author

Michelle Stimpson's works include the highly acclaimed *Boaz Brown*, *Divas of Damascus Road* (National Bestseller), and *Falling Into Grace,* which has been optioned for a movie of the week. She has published several short stories for high school students through her educational publishing company at WeGottaRead.com.

Michelle serves in women's ministry at her home church, Oak Cliff Bible Fellowship. She also ministers to women and writers through her blog. She regularly speaks at special events and writing workshops sponsored churches, schools, book clubs, and educational organizations.

The Stimpsons are proud parents of two young adults and one crazy dog.

A Note from the Author

If you have yet to start your journey in Christ, let me encourage you to seek Him. Seek Him in all of his glory, all of His love, and His wisdom. If you feel the tug in your heart, Thank Him for His goodness, ask Him for forgiveness, and invite Him to live in you. He stands knocking on the door of your heart and is more than pleased to come in and be your Lord (Rev. 3:20).

Other Books by Michelle Stimpson

Fiction

A Forgotten Love (Novella – Book 1 in the "A Few Good Men" Series)

A Shoulda Woulda Christmas (Novella)

Boaz Brown

Divas of Damascus Road

Falling into Grace

I Met Him in the Ladies' Room (Novella)

I Met Him in the Ladies' Room Again (Novella)

Last Temptation (Starring "Peaches" from *Boaz Brown*)

Mama B: A Time to Speak (Book 1 - Novella)

Mama B: A Time to Dance (Book 2 - Novella)

Mama B: A Time to Love (Book 3 - Novella)

Mama B: A Time to Mend (Book 4 - Novella)

Someone to Watch Over Me

Stepping Down

The Good Stuff

Trouble In My Way (Young Adult)

What About Momma's House? (Book 1 - Novella with April Barker)

What About Love? (Book 2 - Novella with April Barker)

What About Tomorrow? (Book 3 – Novella with April Barker)

Non-Fiction

500+ Ways to Say Said

Did I Marry the Wrong Guy? And other silent ponderings of a fairly normal Christian wife

The 21-Day Publishing Plan

Uncommon Sense: 30 Truths to Radically Renew Your Mind in Christ

Visit Michelle online:
www.MichelleStimpson.com
www.Facebook.com/michelle.stimpson2